Triple Play

Also By Ally Wiegand

Chicago Heartbreakers Series:

1. *First Base*
2. *Going for Two*
3. *Triple Play*

Triple Play

ALLY WIEGAND

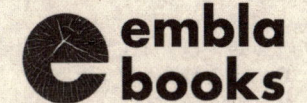

embla books

First published in the UK in 2025 by

embla books

An imprint of Bonnier Books UK
5th Floor, HYLO, 105 Bunhill Row,
London, EC1Y 8LZ

Copyright © Ally Wiegand, 2025

All rights reserved.
No part of this publication may be reproduced, stored or transmitted in any form or by any means, electronic, mechanical, photocopying or otherwise, without the prior written permission of the publisher.

The right of Ally Wiegand to be identified as Author of this work has been asserted by them in accordance with the Copyright, Designs and Patents Act, 1988.

This is a work of fiction. Names, places, events and incidents are either the products of the author's imagination or used fictitiously. Any resemblance to actual persons, living or dead, or actual events is purely coincidental.

A CIP catalogue record for this book is available from the British Library.

ISBN: 9781471417023

Also available as an ebook and an audiobook

1

Typeset by IDSUK (Data Connection) Ltd
Printed and bound in Great Britain by Clays Ltd, Elcograf S.p.A.

MIX
Paper | Supporting responsible forestry
FSC® C018072

The authorised representative in the EEA is Bonnier Books
UK (Ireland) Limited.
Registered office address: Floor 3, Block 3, Miesian Plaza,
Dublin 2, D02 Y754, Ireland
compliance@bonnierbooks.ie
www.bonnierbooks.co.uk

For the women who have worked in male-dominated fields and been told to play by their rules.
Screw that. Play by your own.

Chapter 1

Harper

"Nelsons don't quit."

My mother's voice echoed in my head as my finger hovered over the send button, centimeters away from firing off the resignation letter I'd had typed up for months.

That's because you've never experienced failure, I wanted to say back to her.

Tonight, Nick O'Connor's face took up the entire television screen hanging above the bar like some sick cosmic joke as he conversed with the hosts of our network's most prestigious show about the games he had been covering for spring training. He'd spent only a few days in Arizona, but they sent me to Florida for the whole spring training season without so much as a "thank you."

I tossed my phone down on the bar with a sigh and signaled to the bartender for another rum and soda. Not only would my parents endlessly nag me if I quit without a backup plan, but pressing that send button would waste all my hard work. I would confirm that I wasn't cut out for this reporting job, proving my parents and all my worst critics right.

Truthfully, I'd known when I first wanted to go into this industry that it was a boys' club, and I would have to work ten times as hard as my male counterparts. You not only had to play your cards right, but you had to have connections to get the leg up you needed—which I did not have.

Nick was going on about the interview he had with the top pitching prospect for the Denver Diamonds. His megawatt smile was nearly blinding and not a single hair was out of place on his perfectly styled head. He was exactly what the network was looking for—charismatic, charming, and knowledgeable.

My eye twitched.

Over the past four years, I'd worked myself to the bone to prove my worth as a field reporter, and last year, Nick O'Connor, the son of a long-time executive, waltzed in and received the best stories to cover. Getting passed over was becoming all too familiar.

People like Nick ruined my five-year plan. Shredded the goals I had. Unforeseen circumstances out of my control. What made it even more unbearable was that I was *good*. I deserved a promotion just as much—maybe even more—than any of my coworkers that got it instead of me. But they always overlooked me. Something along the lines of always the bridesmaid and never the bride.

The last thing I wanted was to stare at Nick's face on the late-night slot I had been dreaming about since my first day on the job, so I opened my mouth to ask the bartender to change the television.

"Can we change the channel? Anything but baseball, please." It took me a moment to realize I wasn't the one who had spoken as a figure was sliding into the open seat next to me, a hat drawn low over his eyes.

He glanced over at me for only a second as the bartender changed the channel from Nick O'Connor's face to a comedy show. But that was all I needed to realize I was sitting next to Jamil Edman, the home run season record holder and starting centerfielder for the reigning World Series champions, the Chicago Cougars.

Jamil had been thrust into stardom last season after the success he and his team had, which earned him a new contract that came with an eye-popping salary and brands lining up for a chance to work with him. He was featured in commercials, his face was on billboards, clothing brands were rushing to make him his own line. Everywhere you turned you were met with Jamil's crooked smile. He was no longer just an athlete. He was quickly becoming part of our pop culture.

But the Jamil Edman sitting next to me was missing those well-known qualities. The corners of his mouth were turned down and his shoulders drooped with defeat. There was no trace of the happy-go-lucky centerfielder that had made a name for himself in the league for his upbeat personality and silly pranks he loved to pull on his teammates during games. This man looked like he was carrying the weight of the world on his shoulders and all he wanted was to go unnoticed for one single night.

When the bartender slid a beer over to him, he wrapped his hands around the glass like it was a lifeline. A good reporter would have tried to get to the bottom of Jamil's melancholy, but tonight I didn't want to be a reporter. I just wanted to be a girl at a bar who desperately needed an escape from her world, and it looked like Jamil wanted the very same thing.

"Thank you," I told him, motioning toward the television. "I was just about to ask him to change the channel."

Jamil studied me from under the brim of his Chicago Bobcats hat, sizing me up to see if I was going to be a threat to the peaceful night he was hoping for.

"Not a fan of baseball?" The rich timbre of his voice rumbled in his chest. I noticed the smallest twinkle in his hazel eyes as he waited for my answer. The smile lines around his eyes made a quick appearance as his lips barely turned upward. It was a shame that smile wasn't on display all the time.

"More like I need a break from it."

"Drinking your sorrows away?"

I nodded. He lifted his glass.

"To chasing happiness at the bottom of this glass," he offered, extending his toward mine. He smiled at me, all good looks and easy charm—like he'd sat down next to a woman alone at a bar a hundred times before, looking to strike up a conversation, and maybe something more. He probably had.

"Are you from Florida?" Jamil asked. From the way he had hunched over the bar when he first sat down it seemed like all he wanted was to drink his beer in silence, but maybe what he really wanted was to have an interaction that reminded him what normal felt like.

I shook my head. "Washington DC."

"Politics?"

A harsh laugh escaped me. "My mother would prefer it if I was."

Maria Nelson had tried to groom me from a young age to follow in her footsteps. She was a well-loved congresswoman who had paved a way for herself on Capitol Hill. Many even speculated she could make a run for president. She was a straight shooter who missed nothing. Her dedication to her job was admirable. But I had grown up watching the way she had always prioritized her job over her family—how the country had always come before her daughter.

I snuck a glance at Jamil. A bit of stubble had started to grow on his face, but sharp cheekbones and the angular line of his jaw were still visible. His lashes were long enough to brush against his cheeks when he blinked. Even the wrinkles he'd begun to collect accented his best features. My stomach clenched as a laugh burst from his mouth. I would have classified it as one of the best sounds I'd ever heard if it weren't for the snort that shortly followed.

His eyes widened before he looked over at me to see if I had noticed, a hint of red coloring his cheeks.

How was it fair that someone could be so beautiful?

My shoulders shook, a laugh daring to break free. His brows pulled down into angry lines as he crossed his arms over his chest. "Are you laughing at me?"

One of my hands shot up to cover the evidence as I failed to hold it in. "Not at all."

Then that crooked smile I saw next to an advertisement about a new energy drink nearly every day was right there in three-dimensions. I busied myself with the straw in my cup, if only to keep from staring at him any more than I already had.

When Jamil turned to his phone, checking notifications, I could feel our conversation ending. The two of us becoming strangers once more. I had the sudden urge to be reckless. I'd been working myself to the bone, never turning down any work that came my way. Only to be left feeling unappreciated and unfulfilled.

Would it hurt if I let myself indulge for just one night?

But before I could strike the conversation back up, I was staring down at an outstretched hand. "I'm Jamil."

I know, almost slipped out. But I bit it back. There was a chance if either of us was reminded of who we were out in the real world, this perfect moment would be broken.

And did I really know Jamil Edman? I knew the version of him he showed to the world. But I didn't know this conflicted person sitting next to me, laughing over stand-up comedy, trying to forget everything that happened beyond the door of this bar. He was a paradox, a puzzle I wanted to unravel to take my mind off my own problems.

I slipped my hand into his and watched the way his fingers engulfed mine. Time came to a screeching halt, the world narrowed to a pair of hazel eyes. "Harper."

"That's a beautiful name." My hand was still in his. Someone holding my hand should *never* feel this good.

I swallowed the lump forming in my throat before dropping my hand back to my lap. Not missing the way his stayed on the bar top, still in the shape of mine. His fingers flexed before he flipped it over.

"My dad is a really big Paul Newman fan. *Harper* was one of his favorite films. I guess not many people get to say they're named after a fictional private eye."

There was that crooked smile with his lips pulling up slightly higher on the right side. "Well, it's nice to meet you, Harper, whose father is a really big fan of Paul Newman."

Now it was my turn to blush. "It's nice to meet you, too."

"I would ask what a beautiful girl is doing alone at a bar, but I feel like you're the type that would roll her eyes at such a question." His teeth were a bright white as he flashed me a smile. The words had slipped out of his mouth like second nature. As if he never really had to try very hard to pick a girl up.

I raised an eyebrow at him. "Does that normally work for you?"

He winced. "Something of the sort normally does."

"You clearly haven't been giving yourself much of a challenge." I stirred the straw in my drink around in circles as I gazed at him.

Jamil threw his head back and laughed, the sound doing something strange to my insides. "I like a challenge."

My stomach twirled the second his eyes met mine again.

I lifted a finger off my glass and pointed toward another woman sitting by herself at the end of the bar opposite us. "She looks like a challenge." She was older by a few decades, but her ring finger was bare. She looked like the kind of woman hoping for an escape, just like me.

His eyes cut to who I was pointing at before he brought a hand to his chest. "You wound me. Am I not good company?"

I lifted one shoulder. "You're suitable company, I suppose."

That was the understatement of the century. This conversation was the most interesting one I'd had since I came down to Florida. But I wasn't above making him work for it.

He turned in his seat to give me more of his attention, his knee bumping against mine, and I sunk my teeth into my bottom lip, my body tingling at the contact. I leaned into him until my legs were between his, our bodies fully turned to face each other now. Jamil's playful energy was more intoxicating than the alcohol in my hand. The exact remedy my day needed.

It had been far too long since I'd flirted or even been touched by someone of the opposite sex and the racing of my heart could be chalked up to that very reason. Or it could be because of the man with a crooked smile, dimple in his right cheek, and eyes the color of starlight. But I highly doubted it.

"Do you like tacos?" Jamil asked as he drained the remainder of his beer.

My eyes fell to his throat as I watched his Adam's apple bob up and then back down. Suddenly thirsty for more than just a cocktail.

"Tacos?" I heard myself ask as I lingered on the gold chain peeking out from beneath his shirt.

"This may be a little forward, but I know a great food truck a few blocks away. It's one of my favorites from when I used to live here." A hint of red colored Jamil's cheeks for the second time tonight as he rambled on. "Maybe I read you wrong, but it feels like you could use a night of distraction as much as I can, and I always find food can be the perfect way to take your mind off of things—"

"Tacos sound great."

Before I could fish my card out to pay for my drink, Jamil threw a few bills down on the bar to cover our drinks and a hefty tip.

"Do you mind walking?" He let me lead the way out of the bar. My body was painfully aware of how close his tall, broad frame was to me as we walked past the patrons wearing tropical button downs and sandals before heading out the front door of the small dive bar together.

"After the day I had, walking is exactly what I need," I told him.

Jamil reached around me to hold the door open. His chest brushed my shoulder, and I caught a whiff of his cologne. Either those two drinks had made me tipsier than I thought, or the cologne was the reason my foot caught on the crack in the sidewalk.

My body careened forward, the ground rushing toward me.

"Woah, there!" A strong arm wrapped around my waist, stopping me before my face met asphalt. "Are you sure you're okay to walk? I can give you a piggyback ride."

I quickly sidestepped out of his grasp, heat filling my cheeks and my stomach. Maybe I had more to drink than I thought. That was the only explanation for why I was considering his offer. My mind imagined what he'd feel like between my legs. "I'm fine but thank you for the offer."

He raised an eyebrow before making a pointed look at the crack in the sidewalk that had almost been my demise.

"I promise." I reached over to squeeze his arm. Both of us glanced down at my hand before I dropped it back to my side. *God, how is this man tying me up in knots just by touching him?*

Jamil cleared his throat. "Right. The food truck is just around the corner." He motioned for us to cross the street and head in the direction of the bay before shoving his hands deep in his pockets.

Night had fully settled in Tampa and the sticky humidity of the day was giving way to a nice breeze that lifted my hair off my neck. It was a welcome change from DC, where the last bits of winter still clung on to the city.

I eyed Jamil as we continued down the street together, matching each other's steps. He looked more relaxed than when he first sat down at the bar. His shoulders were a little lighter and his face clear, as if the ocean breeze was slowly peeling away his burdens. His steps held a bounce that reminded me of the player I had watched on television, living out his dreams and soaking up every second of it.

"You grew up around here?"

He nodded his head and shoved his hands deep in the pockets of his shorts. "On the north side of Tampa."

"Do you still have family in the area?" We were both dancing around asking anything personal—and I respected that—but I tucked away any piece that he was willing to give me.

I wanted to know why the guy with the biggest smile in the room looked like he carried more weight than he could manage when he walked into that bar. I wanted to know why the guy that everyone assumed had the world at his fingertips and was *supposed* to be so happy, was clearly *not*.

Definitely because of the reporter's instinct in me and not because I cared.

"My mom, dad, and sisters still live here," Jamil told me. "My brother moved to Chicago with me."

A muscle jumped in his jaw at the mention of his brother, and I feared for a moment that I had walked into dangerous territory. "My oldest sister had her first baby a few months ago. I came down so I could meet my niece. Being around them makes me miss home."

"I'm sure they love having you around for a portion of the year."

The food truck came into view. We stopped to read the menu next to the window. "It's nice to feel normal again." My chest cracked in half at his admission. I wasn't sure he even realized he'd said it as he studied the menu. He'd gradually pulled himself away from everything outside of playing over the past few months.

Media couldn't pin him down for a comment or interview and fans really had no way to interact with him after he catapulted into stardom. The change had been instantaneous, with people showing up at his home or tracking his movements to try to get a photo.

"Anything in particular good here?" I asked, desperate to change the subject before we wandered past the point of no return. Jamil began naming off the different tacos that he suggested I try. As soon as he started on the margaritas he swore were the best ones on this side of the state, I stopped him. "Surprise me?"

His eyes widened before he rubbed his hands together in anticipation. "You won't be disappointed."

I'm sure I won't be, I thought, as I slid into a seat at one of the open tables nearby.

A few minutes later, Jamil walked over balancing two margaritas on top of two trays full of the most delicious-looking tacos I'd ever seen. He had his tongue stuck out the side of his mouth as he concentrated on not dropping anything. I was glued to the boyish look on his face, unburdened and free.

"Let me help with that," I told him as I sprung up from the table to take one of the trays and drinks from him.

"These are the only tacos I think I've ever gotten a 'foodgasm' from," Jamil said casually as he took a sip from his margarita.

Thankfully I hadn't taken a sip yet of my own or I would have spit it all over the table. "Did you just say 'foodgasm'?"

Jamil nodded. His face solemn before he took the first bite of his taco. He let out a moan that was borderline inappropriate to do in public but had me unable to take my eyes off him—a look of disbelief surely on my face.

A laugh slowly built inside of me until I was nearly doubled over in stitches. Tears leaked out the corners of my eyes. The second I had a hard time catching my breath, I knew what was about to happen. A snort ripped out of me.

Jamil's eyes widened with delight. "And *you* made fun of *me*!"

I reached for my margarita, still enthralled with the way Jamil's face lit up. The second the tequila and salt hit my tongue, I was in trouble.

Tequila was my kryptonite, and I wasn't sure if I could be held accountable for whatever happened next. Especially when he gave me a smile over the rim of his margarita that had me daring to ask if he wanted to get out of here.

Chapter 2

Jamil

She had a tattoo down the center of her spine.

I had already taken my time kissing my way along it. Twice. But what was one more time for good measure?

With every kiss that I whispered along her back, I watched her body wiggle beneath me. It happened after the very first kiss I placed along that tattoo, and I just couldn't stop myself from making it happen again and again and again.

"What does this mean?" I asked her as my fingers traced the unfamiliar letters.

"It's Greek for 'Take courage, my heart.' It's something my grandmother used to tell me when I was a child."

I placed one more kiss between her collarbones and relished in the gasp she released. "That's beautiful."

Her skin smelled like cinnamon.

My thumb brushed across the pulse pounding against the side of her neck, the rapid beat telling a different story from her calm exterior. I pushed aside the long, chocolate-brown hair covering her neck so I could place another kiss on her nape, letting my tongue swipe out to taste the saltiness from the layer of perspiration lining her skin.

She sucked in a breath.

If I wasn't already on fire, the sounds this woman emitted made me a blazing inferno.

My hands ran the length of her body, wanting to memorize every piece of her. Every piece of this night. I almost hadn't noticed that the familiar pain in my chest was gone or that I felt like I could breathe again, too caught up in the woman beneath me. Exactly the distraction I needed, but not the one I'd been expecting.

Harper flipped over. Her hands wove into my curls. Her lips bruised and swollen. Her skin flushed. She pressed her hips up into mine and swiveled them as she teased me. I leaned down and placed a kiss to her lips with a groan. Every move this woman made left my mind focused on one thing—the overwhelming need to absolutely devour her.

I hadn't felt this free in months. Being in this room with Harper was my own personal escape from it all. No one demanded to know which commercial I wanted to do next, or which brand I wanted to partner with. No one cared about my at-bats from the last game and if I was on track to beat my own record this season. All that mattered was figuring out every way I could make her scream and the utter joy that brought me when I did. The moment I sat down next to Harper at that bar, I felt a tug in my chest. As if we were meant to walk into each other's lives just when we needed it the most.

Harper lay limp as waves of pleasure swept through her. Her eyes were closed, and her face was peaceful.

The scowl I'd first noticed her wear when I slid onto the stool next to her was nowhere to be seen.

It was long after both of our breathing had returned to normal that she finally stirred. "I probably should get going," Harper whispered against my lips. I tried to ignore the way my chest ached in a completely unfamiliar way.

"Stay," I pleaded. I had never been one to feel desperate, but I *desperately* didn't want this moment with her to end. The only thing keeping the world at bay was her.

Every minute that we'd spent together was one more minute that I didn't think about the calls and texts from my brother asking me for more money. Or asking me to throw games so he could make a quick buck. There was a fissure in my heart that grew wider every time he used my success for his benefit. But tonight, with Harper in my arms, none of that mattered. None of that existed. Tonight, the world felt a little brighter.

Harper looked conflicted, like she knew she should leave—if only to spare us both from allowing whatever was happening from going any further.

"Just stay with me," I whispered as I smoothed the hair off her forehead and leaned down to place a kiss there. "The world can wait a little longer for us both."

I flattened a palm against her sternum and covered the tattoo she had between her breasts. Her resolve crumbled beneath my touch.

"And what about this one?" I asked.

"That is a waxing moon. It represents growth, manifestation, and creativity."

There were complexities to this woman I had yet to even fathom. Like the way she sucked my bottom lip between her teeth, which made me want to flip her back over and go for another round. But before I could do that, Harper grabbed the hand I had pressed against her and brought it up to her mouth to kiss each of my fingers. The function of breathing nearly slipped from my mind completely the second her lips touched my skin. But this time I welcomed it.

With our drinks from the bar still buzzing inside of us, Harper and I had a few more margaritas along with our tacos. During our second margarita she had slid onto the bench next to me, her long leg pressed into mine. As soon as both of our trays were empty, we were stumbling back toward my rental with our fingers intertwined.

We had barged through the front door and had barely made it to the bed, leaving a trail of clothes behind us. I was nearly positive we sent a lamp careening off one of the side tables in the living room on our way to the bedroom.

Now I gazed down at her tanned body, sun kissed from long days spent out in the Florida sun. Her eyes were a rich brown with flecks of gold depending on the way the light hit them. She lined her hand up with mine until our fingers were tangled together.

"The world can wait," she agreed.

With the taste of tequila and salt long gone, it wasn't alcohol that made me feel drunk. I'd remember the sound of her moans and the way she tasted long after the sun came up tomorrow. When she hooked her legs around my hips, I buried my nose in the waxing moon on her chest and felt her pulse beating rapidly. Goosebumps were left where my fingers touched.

"Another round?" she asked me with mischief in her eyes. She propped herself up on her elbows, bringing her face only centimeters from mine. Desire pooled within me as she brought my bottom lip between her teeth once more.

This woman was insatiable.

I pulled her onto my lap and the gasp that she let out made my stomach clench. All I did was *want* with her. I wanted to know what she felt like in my hands. I wanted to know what she tasted like. I wanted to know what kind of sounds she made when I was the one sending her over the edge. I wanted to know what she looked like when I woke up next to her in the morning. With every answer I got, a million other things were added to the list.

I was putty in her hands with every word she whispered into my ear.

Give me more.

You feel so good.

Yes!

And the word that had me nearly seeing stars the second she said it.

Jamil.

"You are perfect," I told her as I kissed along her jaw. I pulled the sheets up around both of our bodies as I rolled into the spot next to her. My fingers traced along the moon on her sternum. "You are like the moon shining in the dark for me tonight."

"Tonight was exactly what I needed," she rasped, her voice raw.

I turned on my side and propped my head up in my hands so I could see every inch of her. "You are the sole reason I can consider today one of the best days I've had in a long time."

Harper peeled her eyes open. She reached her hand out and placed it on my cheek. "You are more than what this world wants to beat you into. You should never let the expectations of others dim the way you experience everything around you."

Her words felt like I'd run myself straight into the outfield fence while chasing down a fly ball. Sudden and immediately painful. She was dangerously close to the truth of it all for not knowing what it was that weighed me down.

"That's easier said than done," I muttered, thinking about all the times I'd tried to push all the noise out of my mind. It always found a way to slip back in, no matter what I did.

"It always is. Life gives its toughest challenges to the ones it knows can handle them the best." Harper's voice had grown sleepy, and her eyes were heavy lidded.

As she closed her eyes and snuggled under the covers next to me, I wished for everything to be as easy as she made it out to be. Nobody prepared you for when you were thrust into the public eye. Nobody prepared you for when the people closest to you stopped looking at you for who you were and started looking at you as their source of wealth instead. That pain was nearly unbearable and kept me up most nights.

I fell asleep the quickest I had in months while smoothing my thumb back and forth over Harper's bare skin.

The early rays of morning sun shone through the blinds that I forgot to shut the night before in our hurry to the bed. I groaned as I threw an arm over my face to try to block it out. Birds chirped outside the window, and I burrowed further under the covers to soak up every second I could in bed. There was a spring training game later today and I wasn't expected to be at the complex until after lunch. Normally I stayed in bed until the very last minute, dreading the day to come.

I reached out in front of me, wanting to feel that warmth I fell asleep with in my arms last night. Only the other side of the bed was strangely cold. My hand swept even further, thinking that maybe she had moved away in the middle of the night, but I was still met with emptiness.

My eyes flew open.

Rumpled white sheets.

No sign of a girl with chocolate-brown hair, sun-kissed skin, and a moon on her chest.

Please tell me it wasn't a dream.

The hallway to the kitchen was silent. There were no sounds of someone milling about. I held out hope that when I turned the corner into the living room I'd see her leaning against the kitchen counters, drinking a cup of coffee.

But the kitchen was empty, like any other normal morning.

There was not a single trace anyone had been here. Even the lamp I was sure we'd knocked over the night before had been put back in its place.

The only proof that I hadn't imagined it all was the stray mark of red lipstick smeared just under my ear that I saw in the bathroom mirror. My fingers ghosted over the mark as if I could feel her lips kiss their way down my chest and then wrap themselves around me—knowing I'd never have a better view in my life again. Then maybe I could manifest last night into something more than just a memory.

But I'd woken up to an empty bed with only a first name and a location to identify her.

Long after I'd wiped the mark away in the shower and left for the complex, images of the delicate tattoo on her spine and the sounds she moaned in my ear lingered in my mind. I barely even registered the shouts from the media that lined the players' entrance, calling out for a comment from me on the game. It was also the first time this spring training that I didn't feel overwhelmed by the number of objects being thrust toward me from fans hanging over the wall as I walked onto the field from the outfield fence. I still didn't stop to give a comment or an autograph. The weight of the shouts only grazed me on my way to the locker room.

"You should never let the expectations of others dim the way you experience everything around you."

Instead of worrying if I lived up to every fan's expectation, I remembered why I played this game in the first place. I remembered the sacrifices my mother and father made to help me succeed because they realized I was better at this than the average kid. I could fully express every emotion I felt on this field, and it was the place I felt the most alive.

And up until last night, it had been the only place I'd ever been able to be my most authentic self.

Chapter 3

Jamil

Three weeks later

"Are you seriously still hung up on this girl?" Tommy asked me as we waited for our turn to take some swings on the field. It was opening week, and our first series of the season was away in Texas. Tommy had caught me back in the locker room, trying to find Harper for the tenth time over the past three weeks.

Unfortunately, there were thousands of people with that first name living in Washington DC. And not even one of them had dark brown hair or eyes that held the golden highlights of the sun within them.

"I just want to connect." Tommy saw right through my attempt to sound casual. And because he was my best friend and knew me far better than anyone else, he leveled me with a look to try harder next time.

"Don't you think she would have left you her number or any way to contact her if she wanted to *connect*?"

I didn't mention that I'd thought that very thing multiple times while up late at night.

Neither of us had been looking for anything more than a distraction. Hell, I hadn't even started the night thinking it would end up with a woman in my bed. I'd tried to move on, I really had. But it was the chemistry I felt that kept me coming back—the kind of tug and pull that had me on my toes. Or in Harper's words, a challenge. That single night had me floating on a high through the last few weeks in Florida. Who could possibly blame me for wanting to reach out?

Tommy placed a hand on my shoulder. "If it's meant to be, it will happen."

"Since when did you start giving sage advice?" I asked him. "You sound like Adam."

"Well, someone has to do it now that the old man's gone."

"Adam is rolling over in his metaphorical baseball grave for calling him old."

Tommy walked backward toward the plate. It was his turn for practice swings. "You call him old every other day in our group chat," he hollered back at me. He wasn't wrong. Any time Adam sent another picture of a project he completed on his house during his retirement from the Cougars, I couldn't help myself.

As soon as Tommy squared up to the plate, the sound of cameras capturing a shot flickered around the stadium. Tommy's shoulders stayed relaxed, and he never once glanced over at the group of media waiting to get the perfect picture of him to sell to different online sources. The only person with a camera that he bothered to look at was his girlfriend, Maggie Redford. She was one of the team's photographers, alongside her best friend, Olivia Thompson.

How he let all the attention slide off his shoulders, I wasn't sure. Maybe it was because he had already been through the dark side of the media during his partying days back when he played for San Diego, and he learned how to move through it. Maybe it was because he didn't care what anyone thought of him or wanted from him except for one person.

It must be nice always having someone as an anchor to keep you steady while the chaos of the world ensued around you. They were the only person to truly see *you* and without them, you risked drifting farther out to sea until you washed up on an island all by yourself.

I want that.

Hopefully Tommy was right and if it was meant to be, I'd run into Harper again.

"How are things with your brother?" Tommy asked me as we walked back to the locker room.

The question filled me with a deep exhaustion. "He's in rehab again, but I'm not sure for how long this time."

Tommy was one of the few people that knew the truth about my brother. I had never intended for anyone to find out, but he had been over at my house one night when my brother had shown up, desperate for cash to bail him out of a pinch with his bookie. Ever since then, Tommy had made sure to check on me. He'd never once offered advice or told me how to handle the situation, which I appreciated, but he'd always been there to make sure I was keeping my head above water.

"Will your family be at today's game?" Tommy had fallen in love with my niece, Kyla, and Maggie swore he had worse baby fever than most women. He'd even insisted they get her a little Cougars jersey to wear at the games. I put my foot down when I saw him trying to put his number on it.

"They will. They wanted to be at the season opener. I'll ask Janessa if you can take Kyla for a spin around the bases after the game." His eyes lit up. "What about your parents?"

Tommy had struggled with his relationship with his father after everything that had happened in San Diego. The two were still figuring out ways to have a healthier relationship that didn't center around baseball, but it was nice seeing him happy to have his family in the stands.

"They will be here, too. I think they are going to take a month off this season to follow us around. My mom is trying to sell it off to my dad as a way for them to explore different places for retirement."

"Is baby Kyla coming?" Olivia jumped out of the office she and Maggie were set up in just outside of our locker room as we passed. "Is she going to wear the jersey that Tommy got her? I *need* to get a picture of that for the socials."

Olivia and Maggie had become two of my closest friends after the three of us had all started with the team at the same time. Maggie, who I called Canon for her skill behind her camera, had been a kindred soul and was always there when I needed someone to talk to. While Olivia had matched my energy from the very first day I met her—the two of us were dangerous on the dance floor together.

"She is coming," I told Olivia. The two let out a shriek of excitement. To say my niece had become the star of the show in her short four months on this planet was an understatement.

"Cougar fans are going to go crazy over her!" Olivia exclaimed before she and Maggie ducked back into their office to prepare for the game.

"Jamil!" I turned around to see my agent, Nico, walking toward me. There was a wide smile on his face, and I could practically see dollar signs in his eyes whenever he looked at me.

This can't be good.

Tommy hooked a thumb over his shoulder. "I'll catch you in the locker room."

A pang settled in my stomach as I watched him disappear around the corner. Most athletes were excited whenever they met with their agent because that normally meant they were bringing good news. However, I'd grown to resent these kinds of meetings.

I knew the routine by this point.

Nico would tell me that another brand wanted to work with me or there was another appearance I needed to make that would bring in even more money. Which meant more signatures, more pictures I needed to pose for, more of myself I had to give everyone else.

When I first started playing, these were the moments I dreamed about. This was the kind of success and money that would change not only my life, but my family's. It was the only reason I hadn't turned anything away yet. I'd been able to put my family in good homes and because of that, the number of smiles or public appearances I would endure was infinite.

"Hey, Nico," I greeted.

My agent's smile grew impossibly bigger as he prepared for what he was about to tell me. "We've got a great opportunity. A few different streaming platforms are interested in doing a documentary on you. A sort of behind-the-scenes into your life. The dollar sign is a big one."

My stomach dropped.

The thought of the entire world getting an unfiltered look at my life terrified me. I'd spent the last few years trying to keep the pieces of my life out of the media—like my brother.

"I'm not sure that's something I'm interested in right now."

Nico narrowed his eyes. He was used to me being open to every opportunity that came our way. He cleared his throat and placed a gentle hand on my arm. "I'll let you sleep on this one. It's a big opportunity. I don't want you to regret letting it slip away. How about we circle back around to it this week? No rush."

Nearly every cell in my body was screaming at me to insist that I wouldn't be doing this one, but the reminder that I would be affecting more people than just myself with this decision had me nodding in agreement.

"Great!" Nico cuffed me on the shoulder enthusiastically. "Have a great game, bud. Give everybody the show they came for."

Right.

Triple Play

Because I was a product that needed to continue performing well for everyone to collect on their piece of the return.

No pressure.

When I finally stepped out onto the field, I put the outside noise behind me and remembered that it was just me and my teammates. No matter what kind of circus I had been thrown into before a game, I could always rely on how playing the game of baseball made me feel.

Every season felt a little different than the last. This year, Adam Steel wasn't taking the mound. The Cougars had a new pitcher from a trade deal that was taking his place. A few new players filled various positions, but I still had Tommy in front of me at shortstop. The familiarity of it all was what kept me grounded.

By the end of the game, nothing felt like it could bring my mood down. Not even the few reporters that asked for a comment on the three home runs I hit. Not even the fans asking for autographs on my way to the locker room.

"What a game!" my mother exclaimed when I met my family outside of the locker room. "Look at my baby go."

"Heck of a way to start the season, J." My father wrapped me up in a hug, pride shining in his eyes for me. "Your grandparents wish their congratulations as well."

"Where are they nowadays?" My grandparents stayed in Florida with my family part of the year. They spent the rest of their time traveling the country.

"I think they're at Niagara Falls. They're supposed to be in Maine by the end of the week."

Then I swooped my niece out of Janessa's arms. "I want kisses from my biggest fan."

Kyla let out a giggle as I peppered her cheeks with kisses.

"She's the only groupie that matters," my oldest sister, Janessa, joked.

Even my younger sister, Jayden, looked excited. She wasn't the biggest fan of sports and sat most of my games out, but that never lessened the support I felt from her. She thrust her phone in front of my face to show me a picture of baby Kyla in her Cougars jersey, rocking her little sunglasses and sun hat. "Olivia took some of the cutest pictures of Kyla that are quite popular on the Cougars' social media."

This was the reason that I shouldered it all. These people surrounding me made all this worth it.

There was only one person missing.

As if summoned from mere thought, my phone began to vibrate. "Oh, Jordan is video calling."

A mix of emotions reflected on my family's faces—excitement, trepidation, anger, sadness.

"Hey, champ," my older brother's voice boomed out of my phone's speakers. "What a way to start a season, am I right?"

"Thanks, man," I told him. Every time he called, I immediately scanned his background, hoping that he was still at the rehabilitation center and that he hadn't given up on it again. Thankfully, I recognized the light blue paint that was on the walls of his room at the facility. My shoulders relaxed.

Triple Play

"When are you coming to visit next?"

My father's mouth screwed to the side as he wrapped an arm around my mother. The two of them had done nearly everything to try and help Jordan, but nothing had ever stuck. When he had announced that he was moving to Chicago to be closer to me, no one thought it would be a good idea. He needed stability and the support of our family. That wasn't something I could fully give him with how busy I was throughout the year. But he had insisted, and his gambling addiction had only grown worse.

"I'll try to come see you when I get back from Texas," I told him, my smile strained.

Growing up, Jordan had been everything to me—my hero. But the light I had placed Jordan in had started to dim when he began asking for more and more money. He put me in a difficult position repeatedly when he took the one thing I considered a blessing for our family—my career—and used it to his advantage.

"Wish I was there with you all," Jordan told everyone.

"We wish you were here, too," my mother stepped into the view of the camera so she could see her oldest son. "We love you and are proud of you for working on yourself."

Jordan's lips pressed into a tight line as he gave our mother a short nod. I noticed the pink in his cheeks as he rubbed the back of his neck, so I stepped away from our mother and gave him a breather. Even though Jordan had put me through hell these past few years, I still loved him and would do nearly anything for him.

"I'll see you soon, J." For just a moment, it felt like I had my older brother back—the easy-going guy I had grown up with—and I relished in the moment long after I hung up the call, hoping that maybe this time would be different.

Chapter 4

Harper

"Want to grab a beer with us?" my cameraman, Neil, asked me as we all finished packing up after the game.

It had been a hellish broadcast. We were sent to cover the DC Capitols who had double-digit runs put up against them by the end of the game. The network had tasked me with being a field reporter for the team this season and to say my interviews after the game were lackluster would be an understatement. I packed my notes away, tabbed with all my ideas for today's game, color-coded by the player and listed the level of importance that ended up being useless. A beer was exactly what I needed.

But before I could say so, a voice called out for me. "Harper!"

My boss, Terry Wilson, was bounding down the steps of the stadium toward us.

"What is he doing here?" Neil asked.

Terry rarely made appearances out of the office if they didn't benefit him or the network in some way. To see him in his perfectly tailored suit walking down toward us could only mean one of two things—either

I was getting fired or I was about to get the promotion I'd been hoping for these past four years.

"I'll catch you guys some other time for that beer," I told my crew. Neil gave me a sympathetic look like this might be the last time he saw me and I had to fight the urge not to roll my eyes.

Thanks for the vote of support, Neil.

"What can I do for you, Mr. Wilson?"

Terry came into the company as a field reporter, much like I had. However, instead of staying in that position for four years, he had climbed the ranks to host a show for the network and then on to the c-suite. He was a shark in the industry, climbing the ranks through various shows of ESPN until he had the kind of power to shape careers. Eventually, they put him in charge of SC News, an ESPN subsidiary that specialized in regional news. I admired everything about him, but I also hated him. I hated him because he held my future in his hands, which had gone nowhere.

God, I want to be him.

"I was hoping to catch you before you left the field," Terry started. "I have something urgent to discuss with you."

Butterflies began to swarm inside of me.

Is it finally my time? Is there an opening on one of the shows in New York?

"We had a last-minute opening in an important position for the network and we wanted no one else to fill the position, but you."

Oh my gosh.

"The field reporter position in Chicago is open and we would like you to fly there as soon as you can. We were hoping you could be there to report for the games starting on Monday. This weekend should give you enough time to get your affairs in order. The network also found you an apartment, as we know this is quite sudden. We paid for half of the year's rent as a courtesy for this ask."

Every single butterfly dropped into a pit that opened in my stomach. The music still playing in the stadium faded into nothing as I stared at Terry, wondering if I had heard him wrong.

"We will send your normal crew out with you so you can hit the ground running and not have to rebuild any relationships. Obviously since the Chicago Cougars are the reigning World Series champions, we want our best person on this," Terry continued.

The disappointment was overwhelming. I barely registered Terry call me one of the network's best. If that were truly the case, would I still be hustling on the road nearly two-hundred days out of the year?

"Do you think you can make that happen?" Terry was now looking at me expectantly.

Do you think you can make that happen? Echoed in my brain before I remembered I needed to respond. Tears pricked at the corners of my eyes that I had to fight off as my mind raced through my choices.

Either I could accept the offer and continue working toward the same goal I'd had since I was hired here. The five-year plan that I had written out meticulously when

I'd first started on this path and the vision board at home would still mean something. Or I could walk away right now and hang up my dream.

You shouldn't be contemplating quitting something you love every other week, a voice whispered in my head.

Sometimes the most rewarding outcomes come with the rockiest paths.

"What a wonderful opportunity." I managed to keep my voice even as I addressed Terry. "I believe I can make that work, being in Chicago on Monday."

A wide smile spread across Terry's face, like he knew this moment would happen. He was a man that was used to getting his way and I was a woman that was used to not getting mine.

"I'll have my assistant send over your new contract. I made sure to give you a bit of a raise for this. We really are hoping for some inside information on the Cougars this season so we can provide the baseball fans with unique access." Terry took off back up the stairs, his phone already up to his ear. He turned around when he got to the top of the stairs. "I just knew you were the perfect person for the job!"

"Yeah, thanks," I mumbled under my breath as I watched my boss disappear. I'd sacrificed for this job. I'd gone wherever the network wanted to send me—a playoff football game for the Chicago Bobcats, to the lowest ranked baseball team in the league, or a mid-season hockey game. I did it all with no questions asked.

You just have to do it a little longer.

With a sigh, I hoisted my bag over my shoulder and wished that conversation would be the biggest disappointment of my night, but I still had dinner with my parents on my schedule. This was just a warmup for what was to come.

Maria and Robert Nelson were sure to have a few opinions over my new "promotion." I was going to need more than Neil's suggestion of a beer to get through this dinner.

Chapter 5

Harper

"You're moving to Chicago?"

Both of my parents stared at me, mouths hanging open, as if I had just suggested I was selling everything I owned and joining a cult.

"To cover the Chicago Cougars—last year's World Series champions," I repeated.

"How will you network there?" My mother asked. Because the most important thing to her was making sure I lived where I could make connections, climb social ladders, position myself in society with an abundance of opportunities.

"Do you at least have a place to stay? That's a quick turnaround," my father added, the more sensible one of the two.

"The network has an apartment set aside for me. They are going to pay for the first six months of rent. That should leave me with only a couple of months that I will have to pay before the season is over."

My father's eyebrows raised, clearly surprised that my job would go to such extremes to have me in Chicago. Neither of them were sports fans and they held the belief that there wasn't much money or benefits from the kind of career I was pursuing. They didn't have the same vision I did.

Reporters were in a unique position to provide and uncover the kinds of stories that could make a difference. I was the one that could highlight the good that people do in the world or the one to highlight the bad, especially when it was needed. I loved the thrill of being the first one to a big story or the satisfaction I got after a successful interview with an athlete. This job made my blood sing like nothing else.

I knew my parents loved me and I hoped they would come around. Eventually, I would prove to them that all these nights on the road would be worth it. Today was still not the day.

"What if this job goes away? What happens then? They're always sending you all over the country. How are you supposed to grow your expertise if you're covering all these different sports and teams?" My mother continued to press. I watched my father reach for her under the table, trying to tell her to back off. But once Maria Nelson got going, there was no stopping her. "You also said you'd help me campaign. How are you going to do that from Chicago?"

The waiter walked by during the inquisition I was receiving, and I signaled for him to refill my wine glass all the way to the top. His eyes were downcast, trying to look anywhere but at his patrons wrapped up in a verbal sparring match. Very few people ever stood up to my mother.

"Mom, sending me all over to cover different teams and sports is entirely the point. If I have any chance at being a host for one of the shows on the network, I have to have a vast knowledge of all sports. And I told you I would help if I had the time. That was the caveat. I don't have the time now." We stared at each other in a silent standoff.

My mother narrowed her eyes. "When are you going to settle down and stop traveling so much?"

This wine wasn't going to be strong enough to keep my patience long.

By the grace of some higher being, I managed to keep away any eye rolls. "When I get a host position with the network," I reminded her. We'd had this same conversation many times over the course of my tenure in this industry.

"Don't you think you would have been promoted into that position by now?" My hand clenched around the stem of my wine glass. If I shattered this glass, would the lecture I'd receive then be worse than the one I was receiving now? I bit my tongue to keep from spouting off something I would regret. "Honey, we can't keep stepping in to help you financially when you refuse to see the writing on the wall. Maybe it's time you came to work with me?"

"And do what?" I asked incredulously. "Smile and wave? Stand there and look pretty? What kind of life is that? I want to make a difference and journalism is where I think I can do that."

"Politics is more than smiling and waving, Harper. You know that. You make a difference in people's lives every day. I know there will be more certainty in it than there is in your current job."

My mother had worked her way up from being our town's mayor to a congresswoman for our nation over the course of her career. She'd never spent more than two terms in a position, always climbing to the next rung until she was at the top. In her eyes, if she faced opposition, whether that was an opponent in a race or stagnation, she would figure out a different way to achieve her goals. She viewed my hesitation to go elsewhere as weakness.

Showing that her point held any validity felt too close to admitting defeat and I refused to admit defeat. I glanced over at my father, hoping for some help in this argument, but he was too busy scrolling through his phone to bother defending his only child's dreams.

"I don't want to go on a campaign trail with you to be a pawn in your manufactured image. I don't want to work as an aid in your office and have to spend my whole life sucking up to people I hate when I could be covering a story about them instead."

The ominous look my mother leveled me with sent a chill down my spine. Whatever she was about to say next was going to be final. There was never any room for negotiation with her.

"After this season, if you aren't promoted and still scrounging for money from me and your father, then you will come to work for me." My jaw unhinged. Never had she forced my hand like this before.

"I have a feeling this could be *the* opportunity I've been waiting for. If I can impress the network with my coverage of the Cougars, I think a host seat could be mine." I hurried to defend myself, but any effort I made felt useless. My words were falling on closed ears.

The tension between my mother and I finally died when she realized that nothing was going to come from her efforts. But her disappointment remained evident in the deep frown set in her face and the purse of her lips.

My father nervously glanced between us before he flagged the waiter down. "We should get some cheesecake to celebrate then. We will send you off with some good luck."

One of my father's beliefs was that nobody could be angry over dessert. The three of us ate our cheesecake in silence to end one of our typical dinners together while I tried to figure out how I was going to pack up most of my life in a single weekend and move it all the way to Chicago by Monday.

Or how I was going to keep my dream career alive. The field reporter job was considered grunt work in the industry with all the travel, long hours, and minimal pay. I'd relied heavily on my parents to continue doing it this long. Without their support, I'd be forced to quit. The stakes felt much higher than they ever had before.

It wasn't until my third glass of wine that I remembered a very important detail that hadn't crossed my mind. There was a particular player with hazel eyes and strong hands that haunted my dreams every night and played for the Chicago Cougars.

That morning, three weeks prior, I had woken up to the sound of a rain shower tapping against Jamil's windows. We were both tangled up in his sheets, the comforter forgotten on the floor. Jamil was still fast asleep on his stomach with his hands tucked under his pillow. The muscular planes of his back were bunched up and my fingers itched to dip in and out of those valleys or sink back into his curls. But I had fisted them in the sheets instead. There wasn't a single version of our time together that ended with me staying that morning. That would only risk questions—about full names or if we wanted to get breakfast.

I didn't regret sneaking out in the early morning hours before the sun had even risen because I'd never thought I'd be around him again soon. It had been one perfect night of two strangers crossing paths at the perfect time. That was all it was ever supposed to be.

Serendipity.

Crossing paths again . . . now that was more than just coincidence. Maybe it was divine intervention. Maybe it was a disaster waiting to happen. Whatever it was, the universe was throwing a major wrench in my five-year plan, and it could fuck off.

Chapter 6

Jamil

It was a packed house for our first home series of the season. Even in the locker room we could feel the vibrations from the sheer amount of people inside the stadium. The anticipation that everyone shared for how this season would go—the fans, the team—was palpable. It was in the nervous bouncing my teammates were doing as we waited to take the field. It was in the way Tommy unlaced and relaced his shoes. It was in the way my heart felt like it would beat right out of my chest. But the moment I emerged from the dugout onto the field with Tommy by my side and heard the excitement from the crowd, the nerves fell away.

"God, I love that sound," I told Tommy as we stretched behind the foul line, taking in the size of the crowd.

"It never gets old."

"Want to play some catch?" I asked Tommy as I threw him his glove.

I took off toward centerfield to give us enough space to stretch out our arms. Centerfield was, in my biased opinion, the best seat in the house. If I could paint, the view of a full stadium from centerfield would be hanging in my home right now. The view of the perfectly manicured grass, the spotless infield, the white chalk lines, the fans in the stands. It was art.

Tommy lobbed the ball my way and I caught it with ease. As I drew my arm back to send the ball his way, I caught sight of chocolate-brown hair and a body that I'd been thinking about for weeks. It wouldn't be the first time I'd seen Harper in the people around me and every time before had been a figment of my imagination, like my brain was trying to conjure her. I couldn't see the woman's face, so I wasn't certain it was Harper, but this time felt different. Intuition was screaming at me that it was her. This woman was standing in front of a camera while holding a microphone—a field reporter.

I was fortunate to be surrounded by multiple medical professionals with the way my heart stopped beating in my chest. Was it really her? Or had I finally lost it? Maybe Tommy was right, and I needed to move on if I was starting to see Harper's curves in every woman around me.

"Jamil! Watch out!" I barely glanced up in time to see the ball come barreling toward my face. Only my reflexes managed to save me from a black eye. "Are you okay?"

I took off toward Tommy, ignoring his concern. "What are you doing?" he asked me once I was close enough. "You spaced out like you were stuck in a trance."

"Maybe I was."

Tommy's brows drew together.

The smile on my face probably made me look like a maniac. "I think the universe is on my side today, Tommy."

My best friend was looking at me like I'd somehow got concussed in the time I'd run out to centerfield and back. "What the fuck is wrong with you, J?"

"Do you see that woman?" I tried to point nonchalantly at potentially-Harper to avoid bringing any attention to us. Tommy turned his entire body to look, and I let out a hiss as I stepped in front of him, afraid we'd get caught looking.

"Do you *know* how to be discreet?" Tommy ignored me as he peered over my shoulder.

"What about her?"

Flashes of Harper's hair fanned out on the white pillow in my rental in Florida appeared in my mind. I could almost feel her skin against my lips as I kissed every inch of her body.

"I think she's my mystery girl." Tommy's eyebrows raised as he continued to stare at potentially-Harper. "Dude. Can you be any more obvious?"

He ignored me again as he continued to study the woman with narrowed eyes. "The one from Florida?"

"Yes," I hissed, as if we were close enough that she could hear me.

"What are you going to do about it?"

What was *I going to do about it?*

What if she didn't want to see me again?

I couldn't get her out of my thoughts. I was seeing her in people I passed every day. I had no idea why she lived in my head. Maybe it was because of the electricity that had jolted me awake for the first time in months, taking my mind away from the current condition my life was in. When I'd kissed her for the first time at the table outside the taco truck, I thought I was just looking for something to distract me—to take me away from my current reality. Now I wasn't so sure. Her leaving before I'd woken up without even saying goodbye was a clear message on what she wanted. So why was I even considering befriending her?

I must have waited too long to reply because Tommy squared his shoulders and told me, "I have an idea."

Panic seized my chest as Tommy tore off around me, heading straight for the woman with the microphone. There wasn't a single chance that whatever plan he had concocted in his head would turn out well.

"Tommy," I whispered at him as I followed close on his tail. "Stop."

"Just trust me." He came to a stop a few feet behind the reporter, but clearly within the frame of her shot. He inconspicuously waved me over.

Oh, so now he knows how to be subtle.

I shook my head and waved at him to come back over by me, but his stubbornness kept him standing awkwardly in the back of her frame, staring into the camera. This was bound to end up on the sports network shows later. Once I was next to him, I leaned over to whisper into his ear. "What was your plan now?"

Tommy shrugged and I had to fight the urge not to punch him on live television. "She'll notice eventually."

The world slowed down as the reporter began to turn around. First, I saw her side profile and then all at once I was looking at the woman I had held in my arms. Harper's eyes met mine and I saw them widen, just barely. But it was enough to know that she recognized me. Tommy was looking at me with concern as he watched me stare at her, frozen as a statue. Gone was any trace of my usual bravado or confidence. Harper's gaze left mine and focused on Tommy.

"Tommy Mikals. Hi, I'm Harper Nelson. I'm a reporter with SC News, part of ESPN. Do you have a few minutes for an interview before the game starts?"

Nelson. Her last name is Nelson. And she's a field reporter. For my team.

Harper must have known who I was in that bar when I sat down next to her, but she never mentioned it. She never even asked me a single personal question like I assumed a reporter would have. She enjoyed my presence the same way I enjoyed hers. My heart quivered.

Now my heart was clenching hard enough I was terrified I was having a heart attack on national television.

"Are you sure you don't want to interview Jamil? I think he's more a man of the people." I barely felt Tommy's arm wrap around my shoulder as I focused on Harper. She was doing an incredibly good job of avoiding any more eye contact.

The set of her shoulders was stiff and the grip she had on her microphone was turning her knuckles white. Her eyes darted back to me before looking away again—too nervous to hold eye contact. "I think he'd be great to interview after the game."

I deflated like a punctured balloon.

If only she would look at me for longer than a split second she'd maybe see that I wasn't upset that she left. I only hoped that we could continue our conversation from that night in Florida, because that was the first time, and the last time, all the stress I'd been carrying drifted away. That blissful feeling of peace was intoxicating, and I couldn't get it out of my mind.

"I'll catch you in the dugout," I told Tommy, my eyes still trained on Harper.

If she didn't want to talk to me, I wasn't going to push it.

From my spot in the dugout, I watched Harper interview Tommy. My best friend turned on his usual charm that he normally saved for interviews and managed to make Harper throw her head back with laughter by the end of it. Envy latched itself around my ribcage and squeezed. I wanted to be the one to make her laugh like that. I wanted to be close enough that I could hear the way it sounded.

The announcers began their pregame introductions and I only walked out of the dugout to join the team once Tommy was done with his interview.

"Why are you smiling?"

Tommy's grin only grew wider. "Because I could feel you trying to strangle me from the dugout."

"I barely know her." The words felt wrong leaving my mouth because while I didn't know who the world thought Harper Nelson was, I did know that after a few too many drinks she laughed hard enough to snort. I knew she could devour a basket of chips and salsa like she'd never have it again. I knew how the sensitive spot in the middle of her shoulder blades made her gasp. To me those were pieces of her that mattered more than what the world knew.

"You could cut the tension between you two with a butter knife," Tommy whispered as the announcers began to read off the starting lineup.

"I'm not talking about this right now."

Tommy leaned back over. "I like her. She's feisty."

A sigh pushed through my lips as I grabbed my glove and took off toward centerfield. I tried my best to push the woman standing near our dugout taking notes out of my mind. I had too much riding on my shoulders for a distraction like that. Questions about why she was here and what that meant floated through my mind. I wanted to swat at them angrily and banish them from my thoughts. But that would be an impossible task.

Harper was nowhere to be found when the game ended.

Chapter 7

Harper

I thought I could handle seeing Jamil again. I thought it might even be a good thing to see him again. Boy was I wrong.

I had spotted him well before he had realized who I was. He had run out of the dugout behind Tommy to the roars of a crowd thoroughly obsessed with him. A woman behind me even had a shirt that said she was his number one fan—I'd tried not to eye her more than once and failed.

Neil had given me a strange look during the second game of the series when I suggested that the pregame interview with Tommy was enough, and we could all go home after having such a long day. But bless that man's heart because he didn't question me as I tore out of the stadium like someone who'd seen a ghost.

That crooked smile reminded me of limbs tangled up. The feeling of ecstasy that had me slipping away from my own pathetic reality. A reality that I was now facing head on, starting with the mood board I'd hung in my apartment as the very first belonging I'd unpacked.

"What are you doing, Nelson?" I sighed as I poured myself a tall glass of wine and stared at the pictures I'd printed out of people I admired with jobs that I'd been chasing.

I'd spent the entire night cleaning my new apartment after I'd rushed back from the game, trying to wipe away those hazel eyes that looked at me with such yearning. Or the way my heart had pounded so hard in my chest, that I thought it would burst right out at my feet for everyone to see.

"You've been working for this for four years and you're going to let something as simple as feelings for someone get in the way? There's a reason you swore off men because you thought they would be a distraction for you and this job. Why change now?"

Nothing about the feelings swirling in my head feels simple.

Times like this I wished I had a friend I could call. The only people I talked to nowadays were Neil and my parents. None of those options felt like the right person to call up and spill my guts to about Jamil Edman. Neil never said more than a handful of words at a time. I'd have more luck talking to a wall. And my parents would only remind me of the ultimatum my mother had delivered to me before I left Washington DC. I was better off working through this myself.

My eyes drifted back to the mood board. I set my wine glass down on my coffee table and hurried to grab a dry-erase board I knew I had packed away in one of the boxes in my living room that had been dropped off while I was working.

"I know you're here somewhere," I whispered. "Gotcha!"

After nailing it to the wall next to my mood board, I uncapped one of my dry-erase markers and began listing out my plan to secure a spot on one of the network's daytime shows by the end of the season. I needed a sense of order back to my life after Jamil had tipped my world upside down and a plan was sure to do that.

1. *Secure interviews that will bring attention to the network.*
2. *Cover stories that are meaningful and display my style of reporting.*
3. *Convince Terry that I'm deserving of a promotion.*
4. *No distractions!!! (Jamil Edman)*

Satisfied with my work, I tossed the dry-erase marker back into the box I got it from and picked up my wine. How I was going to avoid the best player on the Chicago Cougars that I was absolutely going to have to interview multiple times this season, I had no idea. But having the plan written down soothed the part of me that was beginning to believe my mother and that I'd never achieve my dreams—always the failure in her eyes.

With a sigh, I turned my television on. Only to have a jump scare when Nick O'Connor's face appeared.

Was Nick truly deserving of the hate that I harbored for him? Probably not. It wasn't his fault he'd been born with a silver spoon in his mouth. But every day I went to work, I reminded myself I was the better reporter. Nick's questions were unoriginal and surface level. His interest in the person he was interviewing came across as forced and he'd gotten his information wrong on more than one account.

I sipped my wine as I watched him stumble through the statistics of the player he was interviewing, finding a sort of sick joy at the way the athlete raised his eyebrows at him questioningly.

No, I deserved to be sitting at a desk while I talked through the biggest stories across sports. And I wasn't going to let someone like Nick O'Connor get in my way. There was only one person who could possibly derail my plans and his name was written on the dry-erase board hanging on my wall.

Chapter 8

Jamil

Tommy had called for an emergency meeting between the three of us before showing up at my house after the game with arms full of snacks, ignoring my instant protests that I was fine.

"Please tell me you have beer," Derek said as he followed behind.

"Guys, I'm fine. It's late. I just want to go to bed." *And forget the cold glint in Harper's eyes as she looked at me tonight, stomping on my heart in the process.*

Neither of them listened to me as Tommy vaulted over the back of my couch and emptied the contents of his arms on my coffee table, while Derek searched my refrigerator for a beer.

"I'm busy tonight. Nico has me doing something for a new brand deal." The lie rolled easily off my tongue. It was one I used often when the noise got too loud, and I didn't want to be around anyone. But they weren't buying it.

"You're just going to let her go?" Derek asked me. "Just like that?"

"What if seeing her again is a sign?" Tommy added.

"You told him?" I stared Tommy down as he ripped open a bag of Skittles and emptied a third of its contents into his mouth.

"What else was I going to do?" he asked me around a mouthful of candy.

"I'm so pissed I missed out on seeing her. I knew I should have gone to one of the home openers. I remember doing an interview with her once last season." Derek sank into one of my armchairs and cracked open his beer. "Did you like her?" he asked Tommy.

"She would totally give this asshole a run for his money."

Tommy and Derek high-fived.

"Can we not talk about Harper?" I asked because the only person running was her away from me apparently.

"I've never seen you happier than during those days after you met her," Tommy told me. "I would be a shit friend if I let you wallow in pity just because she clammed up at the sight of you."

Tommy was right. Harper had silenced the noise in my head for longer than the night we spent together. I played looser, the worries about my brother and the media slipping to the back of my mind.

"She could be regretting it." My heart might crack in half if that were the truth of the matter. "I'm not going to corner her and force her to talk to me if she doesn't want to."

"For the record," Derek told me, "I think the biggest mistake of your life will be letting that woman slip away from you again. And if you let it happen, I'm reserving the right to call you an idiot until we die."

The idea of Derek having something to hold over me for the rest of our lives had me reaching for the Twizzlers Tommy was now snacking on.

"Harper seems really nice, J. Especially if she knew who you were and never once mentioned a thing to you that night," Tommy added, handing me another Twizzler.

"She was really nice—*is* really nice," I told them. "But that means nothing if she didn't want that night to trickle into the next day. She left before I even woke up. That's telling enough."

"The Jamil I know doesn't quit." Derek's words echoed in my brain later that night as I stared up at my bedroom ceiling.

"The Jamil I know doesn't quit."

*

The second Tommy made the last out of the final game of the series, I finally let myself focus on Harper in the stands. She was scribbling furiously in her notebook as her crew began to prep the camera for the postgame interviews. Was she serious about interviewing me after the game? Or would she try to avoid me again? Just like she had at yesterday's game when she barely spared a glance in my direction.

My stomach twisted in on itself as I drew near the dugout where she was making her way out onto the field. She looked beautiful in a teal suit jacket, black pants that hugged her curves, and a pair of Jordans. My mouth watered just at the sight of her. Tommy and Derek were right. I wasn't going to leave this stadium until I had the one thing I'd wanted since I woke up alone—another chance to spend time with her.

As Harper got into position in front of her camera crew, I moved before my brain could catch up and warn me not to. The first thing I noticed once I was close enough to her was that she still smelled like cinnamon.

She was just about to step in front of the camera and go live when she noticed me standing close enough to her that I could reach out and touch her. "Can I help you?"

The look she gave me made me want to wither away on the spot, but I summoned up an ounce of my normal flirtatious personality. "I'm here for the interview you wanted from me. I couldn't find you though after the last two games. Maybe you forgot?"

I swore I saw Harper's eye twitch.

"Right."

For the first time since I saw her again, a thought occurred to me.

Did she regret our night together? Was I making this worse by reminding her of that night?

Before I could come up with an excuse to bail from this awkward situation, I noticed Tommy giving me two thumbs up. Olivia and Maggie were perched on the roof of the dugout, sharing a bag of popcorn.

I narrowed my eyes at Tommy. He must have told them about Harper. He grimaced and gave me one of his signature "what will you do" shrugs before dipping into the locker room.

Traitor.

"Are you ready then, Jamil Edman?" Harper asked me. Gone was the easy smile that she gave me as we laughed over our margaritas. Only professionalism and a firm wall she had shuttering her feelings were left.

I flinched. "Ouch, not the whole name."

Harper looked at me like I'd lost my mind. "That's your name."

"My friends call me J."

She raised an eyebrow at me. "And we are friends?"

It felt like a standoff was beginning to form between us and the last thing I wanted was to push her further away. "Actually"—I signaled for her crew to give us a moment—"can we talk?"

The cameraman removed his equipment from his shoulder and lifted a questioning eyebrow in Harper's direction. She waved a dismissive hand, letting him know he was fine to step away, and a few moments later it was just the two of us. It was the first time I could take every piece of her in. She looked different than when I saw her in Florida, but I couldn't put my finger on it. It wasn't the makeup or the styled hair or even the professional clothing. It was in the stiffness of her shoulders and the tight smile she was giving everyone. There was no trace of the free spirit I met that first night.

I rubbed my hand down the back of my neck nervously. "I'm not sure where to really begin."

I was afraid I was making a fool of myself standing here in front of her when she thought our connection was only cut out for that one night.

Harper regarded me for a few moments before catching me off guard. "I'm Harper Nelson, the new field reporter for the Chicago Cougars." The smile she offered was small and cautious. She also realized the tightrope we were walking on. We were stepping out of the snow globe we'd created in Florida and back into reality.

"Jamil Edman, starting centerfielder for the Chicago Cougars."

"It's nice to officially meet you." Her voice was still small, but that girl from the bar was starting to make an appearance.

"I guess I know why you were in Florida now."

A deep flush bloomed on her neck and crept up to her cheeks. "It appeared that you wanted a break from baseball that night and, honestly, so did I."

"Thank you for that."

Harper's eyes shot up to mine when she realized I wasn't upset that she hid who she was. How could I be when I was doing the same thing?

But I no longer wanted either of us to hide ourselves away. I wanted to learn everything about her. Not just the pieces that I had already. The moment I'd traced those tattoos, now hidden under her top and blazer, I knew there was more than met the eye. More importantly, I wanted her to know me.

"Would you want to get a drink so we can maybe introduce ourselves properly?"

Harper glanced down at her shoes as her finger fiddled with the switch on her microphone. "I'm not sure that's the best idea, seeing as we will be working with each other this season. It may be better to keep things professional. I feel like that's breaking some journalism code of conduct."

"It's not a date, Harper." I flashed her a small smile with the hope of reassuring her. "It's just a drink."

I noticed the way she pulled her bottom lip between her teeth as she weighed her options. Not long ago I had those very same lips between my teeth.

"Just a drink?"

I nodded, hoping she could see the sincerity in my eyes. "Just a drink."

"I have to finish packing up," she trailed off and hiked a thumb over her shoulder toward her things.

"I've got to get changed anyways. I'll meet you by the player locker room. Do you know where that's at?"

She nodded. "Great game, by the way. That was a phenomenal performance."

"Was that a compliment?" I asked her, faking disbelief.

Harper rolled her eyes and laughed. "It was."

"What are you doing?" she asked me as I placed a hand to my chest and closed my eyes.

"Savoring the moment. Who knows when I'll get another Harper Nelson compliment again."

Her mouth formed a perfect circle. "You're a real piece of work."

I winked before I turned to head back to the dugout, only stopping when I heard her call after me.

"I'm happy I ran into you again, Jamil. Truly."

Truth was, I wasn't sure why we had crossed paths again. Maybe the universe was giving me a gift after everything it had put me through. There was no denying there was some sort of chemistry between us back in Florida. Tommy and Derek were convinced that she could be the one. But that wasn't what made me want to ask her out for a drink. I craved another night of sitting with someone who didn't care about the stats or the fame and only cared about *me*.

"Me, too, Moon," I told her with the barest hint of a smile. "Me, too."

Chapter 9

Harper

Moon.

That nickname nearly sent me to my knees when I heard it. Then he walked away like he hadn't left me speechless.

The hallway outside of the team's locker room was empty, which I was thankful for, as I paced back and forth. It wouldn't be out of the blue for a reporter to be lingering, waiting for a comment. But how would I play it off when someone caught me leaving the stadium with Jamil Edman? And one drink couldn't hurt, could it?

"Are you ready?" I whirled around to find Jamil standing in the doorway to the locker room, now dressed in a pair of jeans and a black crewneck, that same Chicago Bobcats hat pulled low over his eyes.

"Where are we going to stay away from prying eyes?"

"I have a place," Jamil told me as he pulled a set of keys out of his pocket. "Are you okay with leaving your car here?"

"I actually walked," I told him. "The network got me an apartment just down the street so I could be close. It was a sudden reassignment."

"You don't mind if I drive?" I was touched that he cared to even check with me.

"Not at all." I motioned for him to lead the way.

Jamil took off at a leisurely pace. It was the same relaxed pace he had back in Florida, except this time I noticed the way his eyes cut around corners, as if he were scared someone would jump out to ask something of him.

"What do you mean by a 'sudden reassignment'?" he asked me.

There was still a chill to the air when we emerged from the stadium out into the player parking lot and the smell of rain was setting in.

"I was originally assigned to the DC Capitols." Jamil nodded, remembering I had told him I was from Washington DC. "But this position had an unexpected vacancy, and it was important for the network to prioritize filling it."

"Maybe that's a stroke of luck." Jamil stopped in front of a black sedan and opened the passenger door for me.

I caught his eye as I slid into the awaiting seat. "Maybe," I agreed.

As soon as he was in the driver's seat, he turned to look at me. "So, Harper Nelson, field reporter for SC News, do you line dance?"

Jamil had a wicked gleam in his eyes.

"Should I get out while I still have the chance?" I asked, joking . . . mostly.

His only response was to give me a wink and tell me, "Don't worry, I've got you."

That wink had the bottom of my stomach dropping out. This was the same man that kissed nearly every inch of my body and told me how perfect I was at least a dozen times during the night we spent together. And he had the audacity to *wink* at me?

"How long have you been in Chicago?" He was driving us west out of the city. Tall buildings slowly gave way to open land and cornfields.

"I got in the morning of the first game of the last series." It had taken nearly the entire weekend to pack my life up into three suitcases. Most of the stuff in my apartment had to be boxed up and shipped out to meet me here. Plus, my parents insisted on one more family dinner Sunday night before I was busy for nearly the remainder of the year. I brought a bottle of whiskey with me.

Jamil's shoulders fell. "And I'm the asshole that asked you out for a drink. You must be tired. Do you want me to bring you back to your apartment?"

I shook my head furiously. "Absolutely not. I'm used to traveling. A long day on the road is nothing."

"If you're sure."

"I'm positive," I told him as I reached over to put my hand on top of the one he had resting on his leg. His eyes flickered down then back up to the road and I thought I saw a bit of color in his cheeks.

Jamil cleared his throat before changing the subject. "Do you ever get tired of the travel?"

"Do you?"

He wasn't expecting me to throw his question back at him, but the lives we both lived weren't any different. He was on the road just as much as I was.

He spoke so quietly. I almost missed his response. "Sometimes."

Every word I had died on my tongue. My heart clenched when I saw his internal struggle so clearly displayed all over his face.

"We're here," he told me before I could reply.

We pulled in front of what looked like a rundown barn with neon signs hung outside a door. I could make out the sound of music from within the car.

Gone was any trace of the pain I just saw on Jamil's face as he tipped his head in the direction of the entrance. "Come on."

Together we walked toward the entrance, the music growing louder the closer we got. By the time Jamil placed his hand on the door to push it open, I could make out the lyrics to a famous country song and the sound of excited hollers from the patrons inside. This was the second time I found myself in a secluded bar with Jamil Edman, but this time he wasn't trying to fade into the background. He seemed to feed off the energy in the room, glancing excitedly toward the dance floor where people were doing an intricate line dance that I knew would have my uncoordinated feet tripping over themselves.

The walls were covered in old road signs and the only lighting in the entire place was the neon signs and the lights that were strung across the dance floor. Some of the tables were old wire spools with various mismatched chairs around each one. The bar looked like it was made from old pallets and galvanized metal. It wasn't the kind of place I thought I would ever find someone like Jamil in. But he moved through the crowd to the bar in the back as if he were right at home.

"How'd you find this place?" I asked him once we found an empty spot near the end.

Jamil waved down the bartender. "You know Adam Steel, right?"

I nodded as Jamil asked the bartender for a rum and soda and a beer.

"After we won the World Series, he brought me and Tommy here as his last hurrah before he was officially retired. The guy never went out with us, not even in the off-season, but he agreed to one night. We told him he could pick the place, and this is where he took us. Not a single person recognized us, and we came here the day after we won." Jamil accepted the drinks from the bartender before handing me mine. "I loved it immediately. It's like my own little getaway now."

"You come here by yourself?"

Jamil shook his head. "No, I always have someone with me. Most of the time it's Tommy."

I took a sip of my drink, relishing in it after a long day. "But tonight, you brought me."

"Tonight, I brought you," he replied. "I find you good company."

"Let's see if you still think that after you get me out on that dance floor," I told him. Jamil wiggled his brows playfully before he downed his drink and held a hand out to me. I was unable to keep a smile off my face with how infectious his was. How full of *life* he was.

I downed the rest of my drink and slammed the glass on the bar, feeling invigorated as I put my hand in his and let Jamil pull me out onto the dance floor.

Everyone had some kind of boot-denim combo and were all doing the same dance without any sort of prompt, but none of them batted an eye as Jamil and I found an empty spot for us to follow along.

"Do you know this dance?" I asked as Jamil attempted to follow the people around us. He moved gracefully, even as he was blatantly wrong with half of the steps.

"No idea," he shouted over the music. "Does quantity over quality apply in this situation?"

"I don't think so," I told him as I attempted to follow along and ended upside-stepping right into him.

Jamil's arm wrapped around my waist to try and steady us. "Careful or you'll take us both out."

My body reacted the same way it did in Florida when his fingers splayed out over my stomach—hot and needy. This was dangerous what we were doing. Now that I knew what Jamil tasted like, what he *felt* like, my liquid courage threshold was significantly lower.

Once I was back on two feet, Jamil's hand disappeared, and I mourned the loss of it. Completely oblivious to the fact that I was now frozen like a statue, Jamil hollered with the crowd as he spun ninety degrees.

There was something intimate about watching him in this moment. This was the Jamil Edman the world had fallen in love with, but they were slowly leeching away the very essence that they loved about him.

If I didn't put some space between us soon, there was no telling what I would do—professionalism be damned.

"Maybe it's best we get off the dance floor then, so I don't hurt you and you have to explain this to your coach."

There was a flash of disappointment in his eyes, and I tried to ignore the pang in my chest as we walked over to an open table in a secluded corner where only the neon lights reached. Jamil disappeared to the bar to grab us another drink, giving me enough space to think properly.

"So why did you want to be a field reporter?" he asked once he returned with two glasses of water for us, relief filling me. Maybe I'd be able to hold off any further bad decisions tonight.

"Because I love chasing after a good story and being the one to highlight it for the world." I wrapped my hands around the water glass and stared down into it. It had been months since I'd thought about why I started this career, and it made my heart clench.

Was I really doing anything important?

"Getting to cover the Chicago Cougars must be a big step up."

My shoulders dropped with the breath I blew out of my nose. "It's not where I had hoped to be."

Jamil stayed quiet and patiently waited for me to elaborate.

"I've been with the network for four years and I had hoped that I would have done well enough to earn a host spot on one of the daytime shows. But here I am, still living out of hotels for most of the year, flying to wherever they want me to be." Suddenly the floodgates opened. I hadn't spoken about this to anyone before. My lifestyle didn't leave room for many friendships. Or any relationships at all, really. Never having time to prioritize someone else made it difficult to sustain a relationship with them. "I never get the kind of stories that would make the executives notice me and I'm beginning to wonder if I just need to move on. Maybe this was never meant to be."

Jamil leaned back in his chair, and I tried to pretend I didn't see the swath of skin that was exposed just below the hem of his sweatshirt when he laced his fingers behind his head. "I wouldn't have pegged you as someone who would ever throw the towel in."

My eyebrows pulled together as I narrowed my eyes at him. "I'm not. Hence why I am still here."

When he flashed me one of those smiles that had nearly brought me to my knees back in Florida, it felt more like a challenge. "Then what are you going to do about it?"

I crossed my arms over my chest. "I have a plan. I worked on it last night. If I can cover some big interviews over this season, then my boss would have no choice but to recognize my worth. It's the *how* I get those interviews that I'm stumped on."

"Sometimes you just have to be creative, Moon." That smile made it exceptionally difficult to be angry at him. Especially when he called me that nickname. The ghost of his fingers burned a trail across the tattoo on my chest. "What if I could get you feature stories with some professional athletes to bring you more attention?"

My pulse slowed.

Was he being serious?

Maybe it was the fact that everyone in my industry never did anything from the goodness of their hearts that my first instinct was skepticism. "Why would you do that?"

"Because it would help you?" Jamil's gaze was sincere and a small voice in my head told me to believe him, but I couldn't. Not yet.

"Why would you do that, though? Why would you help me? You don't even really know me."

Jamil rubbed at the back of his neck as he debated on what to share next. "I think this is actually mutually beneficial."

I stared at him, wondering if I should be regretting coming here with him.

"If you cover stories on different athletes and they get good coverage, maybe it will take some of the heat off of me." Jamil looked sheepish as he finally admitted to what he was thinking.

When I still didn't make a move to reply to his rather weak reasoning, Jamil pressed on. "My life has quickly become not mine anymore in the past six months. There's always someone expecting something of me. Expecting me to smile, expecting me to sign autographs, expecting me to stop and talk when all I want to do is go home for peace and quiet, expecting me to say yes to another deal. There's always something. So maybe if someone else had some light shined on them, the media would leave me alone for just a bit. Until something else happens that reminds them I'm still here."

It was obvious that Jamil was tired of everything that came with being a famous professional athlete besides playing the sport, but I hadn't realized that it was affecting him this much.

With his help, I was sure to knock off the steps of my plan by the end of the season. Successfully interviewing other athletes was exactly the kind of thing that would solidify my prowess for the network. It could showcase my talent for in-depth interviews that were longer than the few seconds I normally got on the sidelines as a field reporter.

But was I playing a dangerous game partnering and working with Jamil Edman? Can I control my feelings around him? Would it be so bad if I didn't?

My brain told me no as I stuck a hand out for him to shake, but my heart squeezed the moment his skin touched mine.

Chapter 10

Harper

Ding.

The sound of my phone buzzing across my nightstand brought me out of a dream where I was tangled up in white sheets and a pair of hazel eyes were looking at me in a dark room, worshipping every inch of me.

Ding.

I searched for my phone. The only thing that could be going off this early in the morning was updates on previous stories that were covered by SC News and that could wait until I had a cup of coffee in me. I wasn't lying to Jamil that travel rarely bothered me anymore, but packing up most of my life and moving halfway across the country to cover a game all within seventy-two hours must have been my limit. I felt like I was waking up after a one-hundred-year nap.

Ding.

"What could possibly be this popular already this morning?" I mumbled as I finally found my phone and pulled it toward me.

The light nearly blinded me as I clicked the screen on. Maybe I needed two cups of coffee this morning if I was going to be in any shape to cover the next series tonight. Once my eyes finally adjusted, I scrolled through the notifications on my lock screen.

"This can't be right," I whispered into the quiet of my new bedroom.

Every notification was a colleague praising an interview that came out late last night while I'd been failing at line dancing with Jamil. The interview was everywhere by this morning. My stomach was in knots and if I hadn't remembered I only had one drink last night I would have assumed I was hungover.

The news everybody was raving about was Nick O'Connor, my newfound nemesis, interviewing Nate Rousch, the NHL darling, on the breaking news of his trade from the Chicago Lynx to the Texas Rattlers yesterday. All I could hear was the blood pounding in my ears.

That should have been mine.

Nick O'Connor's smug face mocked me on my screen as I watched him ask Nate about what went wrong with the Chicago Lynx and why he'd requested a trade from the team that had been working toward a championship with him at the focus of it. His questions were predictable and safe. He never pressed Nate on any of the rumors of his girlfriend cheating on him with a teammate. Or even the rumors about the locker room needing new carpet after the fight that ensued between him and his teammate. Nick was only there as a tool for Nate to paint the picture he needed as he moved to a conference rival of his former team.

Triple Play

"You've got to be *fucking* kidding me!"

The covers went flying as I stalked out to my kitchen, suddenly wide awake. I angrily tapped at my coffee maker, thankful the network was nice enough to have this place fully furnished before I arrived.

"When will it be my turn?" Some of the coffee sloshed over the side of the cup as I grabbed it a little too forcefully. "Why couldn't *my* dad get me a leg up in my job?"

You never would feel like you earned it if that was the case.

My shoulders slumped as I set my coffee down with defeat and pressed my hands into the counter on either side of it. Every inch of my body was filled with rage that needed to be released and if I wasn't in an apartment, I would have let out a scream. But before I could go through with the idea blooming in my mind of taping a picture of Nick O'Connor's face to a dartboard, my phone started to ring. My boss's name flashed on my screen, as if I'd summoned him myself. I glanced at the clock—it was barely past seven in the morning, but that was eight his time.

After about five rings, I finally found the courage to answer. "Good morning, Mr. Wilson."

"Harper! I was just calling to check in on you and see how everything is going. Did you get settled into the apartment?" I wanted to hate this man, but I couldn't scrape an ounce of loathing together when he acted this nice.

"The apartment is great. Thank you and to whoever else set this up," I told him, the interview with Nick and

Nate still replaying in my mind. This call felt like pouring salt in the wound.

"Of course. That territory is obviously very important to us and we wanted to make sure that you were accommodated . . ." Terry trailed off for a second. "I actually have something to discuss with you this morning besides checking in to make sure everything is going smoothly."

The beaten down wings of hope fluttered in my heart. Maybe I was a fool for still having any.

"There is a lot of attention on the Chicago Cougars this season," Terry started.

My mind flashed back to the tortured look on Jamil's face as he told me all he wanted was the media to give him a break.

"And we are hoping that we can get a feature story of someone on the team."

Wait? Was he suggesting what I thought he was?

"The spotlight has been bright on Tommy Mikals, but especially on Jamil Edman. The network wants to get a sit-down story with him. Something with substance that other networks won't be reporting on."

All those little wings of hope fluttering around disappeared and plummeted like a heavy rock sinking straight to the bottom of a lake. I wanted to believe that my intuition was misguided, but my gut was never wrong.

"You are more than deserving of this opportunity, Harper. If you can break a story on Jamil Edman, I think this could give you the attention that you've been so deserving of."

A month ago, I would have jumped at the opportunity without any hesitation. Now it felt like a potential betrayal of Jamil's trust. But who said I couldn't highlight something great about him? Something harmless that wouldn't bring any further hysteria.

"Thank you for this opportunity," I told Terry. "I'll work on having something hopefully before the end of the season."

"That will do," Terry agreed, already disengaging from the conversation. "Keep me updated if you need anything, Harper." Then there was only silence and the voices in my head asking what was wrong with me if I was second-guessing being handed something like this over someone I barely knew.

Before I had even taken two sips of my coffee, my phone was ringing again. This time my mother's name was staring back at me. I steeled myself for what was about to come. The last thing I wanted this morning was to have a conversation with my mother where her entire objective was to pick apart how my new job was going. The clock on my stove told me I had a few hours before my flight that I was expected to be on to Arizona, where the Cougars would be playing next. I mentally prepared myself to rush to finish packing after this call.

So this is how this day is going to go.

"Good morning," I answered, forcing cheer into my voice.

The sounds of hushed voices and papers shuffling in the background came over the phone. "How is Chicago?"

No good morning. Not even a check-in to see how I was doing.

Typical Maria Nelson.

"I've only been here a few days and most of that has been spent inside the ballpark," I reminded her as I downed the rest of my coffee. I was going to need it to make it through this conversation. If I had time this week to go to the store for more than the essentials, I would have added a serving of Baileys to my coffee for good measure.

"This is what I mean when I say that job doesn't allow you to have a life. How are you supposed to meet anyone?" I could hear my mother's assistant trying to fill her in on the next committee meeting she had on her agenda in the background.

I gritted my teeth as we started down the same merry-go-round of a conversation that we always had. "That's not a priority for me right now, Mother."

"It's not good to always be working. Even a social life would be good."

How rich coming from you, the blueprint that they made the word workaholic after.

"I will let you know when I get around to that," I replied as if this were a business discussion between two colleagues.

"I did see that your coworker had an interview come out."

All the breath in my lungs pushed out through my nose. I didn't want to give her more of my time than she deserved so I walked back into my bedroom to attempt to pack while having this conversation. "I saw that."

"That looked like a pretty big interview for someone who hasn't been there as long as you have." I wanted to scream at her that I knew this and that she didn't need to remind me of it, but that was the entire quest she was on.

"I would say so."

After years of experiencing this, I slipped into autopilot as I threw clothes I would need for this next away series in my suitcase. I had learned long ago that there was nothing I could do or say that would make my mother happy besides stepping into the life she had always planned *for* me.

"Does this finally make you realize your employer doesn't value you?"

This made me pause.

"Why? So I can move back home and start working on your campaign?" I asked, not even bothering to hide the venom in my voice.

My mother let out an exasperated sigh as if I was missing the entire point, as if I should know that she's always cared about what I wanted. "I just want you to work for somebody that sees your talents and uses you to your fullest potential."

The worst part about this conversation was that I couldn't immediately write off what she was saying. It was everything I'd been telling myself for months.

"I've got a new assignment from the network. It's a good opportunity."

"An interview?" My mother perked up.

"They want me to secure one, yes."

The line stayed silent for a few moments before she responded. "This may be your last shot at your goals, Harper."

"No need to remind me," I mumbled low enough so she wouldn't hear me and then loud enough so she would, "I'm going to give it my best shot."

"That's what us Nelsons do, honey. I must head off to my next meeting. We will talk again soon."

The line went silent before I could even say goodbye.

With my apartment silent once more and a suitcase completely packed, I padded back out into the kitchen to fill up a second cup of coffee. When I flipped on my television, the first station it opened to was SC News and the face I was greeted with was none other than Nick O'Connor.

I let out a disgruntled yell as I turned the television off and stalked back toward my bedroom to get ready for my flight. I would rather sit in an airport terminal for longer than necessary than watch Nick O'Connor discuss his interview with Nate Rousch.

Times like this I wished I had friends I could text to express my frustrations. People who would listen and encourage me that I wasn't on the wrong track, that I was meant for this. Someone who would meet me for a cup of coffee or come over and watch a reality television show while drinking too much wine as a distraction.

I felt like I was at a crossroads wanting something at the end of both roads that I was being forced to choose from. It didn't matter if I wanted them both.

Chapter 11

Jamil

"How much longer do I need to keep this on?" I asked Olivia. She and Maggie were sitting on either side of me. Tommy was stretched out in the chair next to the bed as the four of us watched a movie in my hotel room. Olivia and Maggie had begged me and Tommy for a movie night once we'd checked in and then produced face masks when they showed up at my door.

"Just a few minutes longer," Olivia told me, her words stilted as she tried not to make any sudden movements with her face.

Tommy had his eyes closed and looked like he was enjoying a nice spa day. "This is ridiculous."

"You sure look like you believe that," Maggie told her boyfriend.

"I stand with Canon. You look like you're enjoying this more than the rest of us," I told my best friend. Tommy simply lifted one hand with a single finger extended in my direction. But I watched him open his eyes enough to toss a wink at his girlfriend before he closed them again.

"So, are you going to tell us about that reporter?" Olivia asked me as she peeled her face mask off.

I rolled my head over so she could see the look on my face. If I told Olivia about the history Harper and I had, even limited as it was, she would launch herself off a cliff to make something happen.

"There's nothing to tell," I replied nonchalantly.

Tommy coughed next to me, and I shot him daggers, willing him to keep his mouth shut. He knew as well as I did that Maggie and Olivia would be relentless about this.

"It definitely didn't look like *nothing* the other day after the game." Olivia's smile was like a cat that had cornered a mouse for dinner.

Maggie's hand slipped into mine to give it a quick squeeze. "She is really pretty, J."

"You two are terrible," I muttered as I leaned my head against the wall behind the bed.

"I knew I never needed to say anything. They would get it out of you one way or another. They always do," Tommy added.

"What's her name?" Olivia continued.

I sighed, realizing that there was no way out of this situation. "Her name is Harper Nelson."

"That's a pretty name," Maggie replied thoughtfully.

Olivia cocked one eyebrow at me. "And how do you know her?"

"We met back in Florida." I didn't need to tell them that between the ocean breeze on my face and the way I'd smiled fully for the first time in months, that night had been one of the happiest moments in my recent past. Those pieces I could keep for myself.

"Did something happen between you two?" Maggie asked cautiously.

"Oh, boy, did it," Tommy said quietly. Maggie snagged a pillow from behind her head and whipped it at him.

"You knew? You knew and didn't tell me?" Tommy barely batted the pillow away before it connected with his face. "I thought he was just smitten with the new reporter!"

"I don't tell you all of Jamil's escapades. I didn't think I needed to share this one."

"Even after she showed up as a reporter at the game?" Maggie crossed her arms over her chest. The look in her eyes had me worrying for the well-being of my friend and I felt obligated to bail him out since I was the cause of him potentially seeing Maggie's wrath.

I threw my hands up to silence everyone. "Before this gets out of hand, I have a question for you, Olivia."

She pointed an accusing finger at me. "You do not get to change the subject, J."

Instead of addressing her comment, I forged on with my mission. "Do you think Derek would sit down for an interview with Harper?"

The room went silent.

Tommy and Maggie glanced between me and Olivia like a tennis match as the tension in the room grew. Not only had I brought forth even more questions about Harper, but now I'd dropped Derek Allen, the tight end for the Chicago Bobcats, into the mix. Over the past year, Olivia and Derek had grown into fast friends, but to everyone except Olivia, it was obvious that Derek was pining after her. She just refused to acknowledge it.

"Why are you asking me if he would do an interview?" Olivia crossed her arms over chest defensively, ignoring the way Maggie had pressed her lips together tightly to keep any giggles from escaping.

"Because you're friends with him . . .?" I cautiously replied, afraid that I had lit a stick of dynamite with my question.

Olivia stared at me for a few seconds before she picked up her phone. Her thumbs moved quickly over the screen before she set it back down. "I asked him."

I caught Tommy trying to hide a smile out of the corner of my eye.

"She must be important if you're doing something like this for her," Olivia volleyed back at me.

The room went silent once more as they waited for my response.

Part of me wanted to defend my actions and push my friends' questioning stares away. But how was I supposed to explain that I was doing something like this for someone I barely knew? "I'm just helping her out."

A laugh saved me from having to endure any more of Olivia's stares as Tommy bent over in the chair next to us, clutching his stomach. "You keep telling yourself that, J." Tommy stood up and reached for Maggie's hand. "Let's wash these face masks off and grab some dinner."

Once each of us had used the bathroom, we made our way down to the lobby. Any more questions about Harper had been pushed to the wayside, as everyone discussed the upcoming Chicago Bobcats season. That was until we walked into the hotel's restaurant, and I spotted the subject of all my thoughts sitting at the bar.

My steps slowly came to a halt as the rest of my group continued to an open table. Olivia finally realized I wasn't behind her and turned to find me still staring at Harper sitting at the bar. A knowing smile spread across her face once more. She held up her phone to grab my attention.

"Derek said he would do it," she called across the dining room. Then she tilted her head toward Harper before sitting down to join Tommy and Maggie.

I hesitated for only a moment before I walked over to her. She was nursing a drink that I could only assume was a rum and soda as she watched the latest news on professional sports.

"Is this seat taken?" I asked as I hovered next to the open chair beside her.

Harper's shoulders froze as she realized who was talking to her.

"It's yours."

My breath caught in my throat as I wished that were the case. The bartender came by as I settled in next to her and I ordered a burger with a water. I could feel Harper's eyes on me the entire time.

"Did you just get in?" I asked her, suddenly clamming up. Something I seemed to do around her often.

"An hour or so ago." Her shoulders were downcast as her finger traced the rim of her glass.

"Rough travel day?" I asked.

Harper shook her head. One shoulder went up in a shrug. Her eyes were back on the television when she let out a groan. SC News was on and was replaying the interview from earlier today that aired where Nate Rousch announced his departure from Chicago. I glanced between Harper and the interviewer.

"Is that one of your coworkers?"

She let out a sigh before she nodded her head. "He's only been with us for a year. His dad is an executive."

My brain slowly connected the dots by reading between the lines of what she was saying and judging from the fact that she was nursing a drink alone at the bar, asking her to elaborate wasn't the smartest path to take.

So instead, I tried to lighten the mood some. "Derek Allen agreed to an interview."

She immediately perked up. *Mission successful.* "He did?"

I nodded my head and watched that infectious smile of hers come back. Excitement burned in her eyes. "We will have to hammer down the details with him. But once we are back from this stretch of away series, you can do a sit down with him. I think this would be the perfect chance for you to showcase your range and appeal to the entirety of Chicago sports fans. So much so, that SC News won't be able to ignore it."

The wheels in Harper's head were already turning as she started to think about what she would ask him, the interview on the screen forgotten. Then in a split second, her arms were around my shoulders as she pulled me into her.

"Thank you," she whispered into my ear.

Triple Play

Without even a second of hesitation, my arms wrapped around her waist. My hands were itching to touch her again. Every time I had the chance to, no matter how short, I was going to take it. The voices in my head finally went silent and I was awarded peace for just a moment. I also didn't miss the way that my friends were watching us from behind their menus a few tables away.

"Of course," I replied, trying to keep my voice light. "I will work on who else we can line up for you."

The ringtone of my phone broke up the moment. I reached into my pocket and froze when I saw who was calling. It was the facility my brother was currently staying at. The only times they ever called were if I was getting close to the next payment or if there was something wrong with my brother. Sometimes it was even my brother calling from the facility's phone rather than his own. It was never for something good.

"Excuse me," I told Harper before I stepped back out into the lobby of the hotel to answer the call.

"This is Jamil." The moment I was suspended in, waiting to hear the bad news every time I answered the phone for one of these calls, never got any easier.

"Jamil, this is Dr. Lanought." There was a long pause before my brother's doctor continued. "I have some bad news."

My heart squeezed in anticipation for what he would say next, as if it could protect itself from breaking. But it had learned long ago that when it came to my brother, there was no armor that would keep the hurt away. There were scars decades old and some as fresh as a few weeks ago all over my weathered heart. I wondered how it could still function at this point.

"What is it?" I asked when the silence lingered for too long.

Dr. Lanought cleared his throat. "Your brother is missing."

"What did you say?" I asked, feeling all the blood drain from my face.

Not again, Jordan. Please don't do this, I begged to the sky.

"His room is empty, and we logged a security guard's ID being used last night without his knowledge."

I took the phone away from my face, clutching it tightly. "Fuck!"

The desk worker looked over at me questioningly, wondering if they were going to have to intervene. Some of the guests glanced in my direction curiously, more interested in whatever drama was happening in my life than being concerned for the distress I was in.

"So, you have no idea where he is?" I asked when I brought the phone back up to my ear.

Jordan had only lasted two weeks this time. It was his second time departing the treatment facility. The first time he had been there for nearly two months before he had walked out and right back onto a riverboat to gamble the remainder of the money I'd given him when he first came to Chicago.

"No, sir," Dr. Lanought told me.

"You told me this wouldn't happen again." Part of me knew that I shouldn't be blaming him right now. The blame was solely with my brother, who wanted nothing to do with anyone who wanted to help him.

"Yes, sir. We did say that." Dr. Lanought's voice quavered.

I let out a long breath as I dragged a hand down my face. "Is anyone looking for him?"

"We have people out looking for him. We are aware you are out of the state right now, so we will keep our people on it until you return. Then we can reevaluate if we haven't found him."

I was tired. A younger brother wasn't meant to be the one to keep the older brother in line. He was meant to look up to his older brother. To view him as his hero, his role model, his blueprint. He wasn't meant to be picking up the pieces that his older brother was destroying, hoping to put them back so his brother would be whole. But this was the burden I carried daily.

"Okay. Thank you, Dr. Lanought." I clicked off the call and pressed the phone into my forehead.

There were few moments in my life that I regretted the path that baseball took me on and the fortune it had brought me. It was hard to regret something that brought such abundance into your life and your family's life.

But this was one of those moments.

Chapter 12

Harper

I had spent nearly the entire series replaying the images in my head of Jamil pulling at his hair while on the phone in the hotel lobby. The sound of him screaming "fuck" still echoed in my ears.

What I hated the most was my curiosity of the conversation. Was it something worthy of a story? Was it what the network wanted to cover?

Every time I watched him joke with Tommy or smile when he crossed home plate after another home run, I wondered what was hiding behind it. Then there was a small part of me that wanted to know because I *cared*.

I jotted down notes as the final half inning of the last game of the series played out. While sitting in the media section next to the Cougars' dugout, Jamil had caught my eye only once this entire game and that one look had turned the bones in my legs into jelly.

I tracked him as he ran out of the dugout, hoping for another chance to see those hazel eyes, when someone slid into the seat next to me.

"Who are you interviewing after tonight's game?" Olivia Thompson said as a way of introduction.

It had been years since I had any kind of girlfriend, so when she gave me an arresting smile like she was interested in talking with me, I clammed up. Do I compliment her? Do I ask her how her day is going? Do I ask her about her pictures? Why am I acting so weird?

"Uh—"

"I'm Olivia Thompson," she swooped in to save me as I sat there gaping at her with an open mouth like a fish.

Olivia extended a hand toward me and I worked up enough courage to take it. "Harper Nelson."

"Are you covering the team this season?" She and I both knew that she already had the answer to that question. It was just her way of treading lightly into the conversation.

"I am. Last-minute change with the network."

Maggie Redford claimed the seat on the other side of Olivia a moment later, her camera hanging around her neck. "Hi! I'm Maggie. I hope Olivia isn't grilling you too hard."

Olivia rolled her eyes. "I hadn't gotten to that part yet. You spoil all the fun, Mags." I watched the two girls share a smile just between the two of them as if they were speaking their own language.

Is that what it was like to have a friend?

"Are you interviewing Jamil?" Maggie asked as she brought her camera back up to her face, completely unaware that Olivia had already been questioning me on that topic.

"I hadn't decided yet," I told them just as Jamil made the final out with a diving catch that sent the stadium into a frenzy. Olivia jumped up from her seat to cheer while

Maggie snapped away, attempting to get the perfect shot. Judging by her previous work, she probably did.

"I think he just decided for you," Maggie replied as she brought her camera down from her face.

My crew stood up to get ready and I followed suit after I consulted my notes on the game one more time. I'd been avoiding interviewing Jamil these past few series, for fear of looking like a fool on camera, but now it seemed I couldn't any longer.

Postgame interviews were normally a flurry of moments. As the teams ran into the dugout, the stadium began to empty, and the families were allowed out onto the field, my crew and I had to weave through the chaos to corner the player I was hoping to get a quote from. I called this the hunt.

Normally the hunt gave me a thrill. But as I worked my way through the crowd with my camera crew following behind me, I only felt nerves latch on to my throat and squeeze the closer I got to the dugout.

All the players with families at the game were in the outfield with their wives and kids. The others were packing up their things and heading into the locker room to get ready for the plane ride tonight to the next series in Seattle.

Jamil was putting his glove into his bag when I walked up to the edge of the dugout. I cleared my throat to grab his attention. He glanced over his shoulder and smiled when he saw it was me. "Have a moment for an interview?"

"For you?" he asked. "Always."

I ignored the crackling sensation erupting in my stomach. *He's just a flirt. That's what he does,* I told myself.

I smoothed down my hair and checked that my mic was on before stepping into the camera's frame next to Jamil. Our hands smacked into each other's, and I went to pull mine back, but was stopped by his fingers looping around mine for a split second before they disappeared.

Dear God, it's me again. Please let me make it through this interview.

"Jamil, congrats on another great game. After today's win, the Cougars have put themselves two wins above the Milwaukee Crows, who are currently second in the league. Eleven runs put up in today's game and you contributed to over half of them. Talk to me about how you feel the team is doing coming off a World Series win." I extended the microphone toward Jamil who was looking at me with rapt concentration.

"Thanks, Harper. You look beautiful today by the way." He smiled as he watched me attempt to control my facial expressions. Surely, he had lost his mind greeting me that way, but he powered on as I stood there floundering. "We lost some key pieces off last year's team, but I think we've filled those gaps well. We are just now hitting our stride."

"You've also been on a tear at the plate so far this season. What's your goal?"

Jamil's eyebrows shot up. I knew most interviewers had been asking him if he was gunning to break his own record this season and I noticed the way his shoulders tensed at the pressure that question implied. I wanted to give him the space to claim what he wanted—whether that was anything at all.

"I'm just having fun this season. Which is easy to do when there's such good company around."

The cheeky smirk was back, and my mouth grew dry. From the look in his eyes, he knew exactly what he was doing. Every person watching at home probably saw the flaming red coloring in my cheeks.

"Uh, thanks for your time," I rushed to finish before turning my microphone off, and Neil took the camera off his shoulder. "What are you doing?"

That stupid smirk remained on Jamil's face even as I came nose to nose with him. My crew slowly backed away to pack up, leaving us in a standoff. The picture we painted was probably a treat—Jamil staring down at me trying to contain his laughter and me staring up at him with hands on my hips ready to go down swinging.

"I don't know what you're talking about, Moon."

I wanted to be mad that Jamil thought it was necessary to flirt with me in an interview that would be seen nationally, but all I could focus on was the unguarded look on his face. The lack of heaviness pulling his shoulders down. The mask that he had been wearing for months was gone. He looked *happy*. So instead of letting the fuse of my anger burn to ignition, I took a step back to put space between us. "You can't do that," I told him simply, my steady voice a juxtaposition for the racing beat of my heart.

"I did nothing but state facts."

The space between us didn't feel wide enough as Jamil brought me back to that night in Florida.

You are perfect.

Moon.

Something unsaid flickered in his eyes. A question from Jamil to me of if there would ever be a chance we could pick up where we left off.

"Harper!" Olivia's voice fizzled out the tension building between us as she approached. "Will you be in Seattle tonight before dinner time?"

With one more sparing glance in Jamil's direction where I noticed him still admiring me, I turned to Olivia. "We land at seven tonight."

"Would you want to do an eight o'clock dinner? With all of us?"

Any other season I would have landed and ordered room service to my hotel room with only reruns as company. This season was anything but normal. Apparently, everything about the Chicago Cougars was thrusting me out of my comfort zone. "Sure?" I replied hesitantly.

Olivia smiled triumphantly. "Great. Let's exchange numbers and you can let me know when you get to the hotel."

It was a foreign experience exchanging numbers with someone who wanted to have some form of communication with me outside of business purposes. When my phone dinged with the notification that Olivia had texted me back with her name and a smiley face, I was walking into new territory.

"I guess I'll be seeing you tonight," Jamil told me as he walked past me to the locker room, his voice low and sultry. "For dinner."

Standing alone in the middle of the outfield grass, I wondered if this season was fate or if it was quicksand that would render me immobilized.

Chapter 13

Harper

"Are you a fan of tacos?" Olivia jumped up from a couch in the lobby when I walked in and linked her arm through mine. Maggie was sitting next to Tommy, deep in a conversation that belonged only to the two of them. Jamil stood off to the side wearing that same old Chicago Bobcats hat. My eyes caught his at Olivia's question and a smile passed between us.

"I love tacos," I told her as the five of us exited out the front of the hotel.

"I knew I liked you," Olivia told me as our group turned left and headed toward our destination. "There's a restaurant just around this corner. Supposedly they have the best tacos."

A hand brushed the backside of mine and I looked over to see Jamil there, his eyes trained on the road ahead. I was trying my best to keep him at arm's length, but how was I supposed to when he continued to tease me?

"We will have to see," I told Olivia. "That's a tall order to beat."

The smallest chuckle was barely audible from Jamil.

A waitress showed our group to a table in the back, secluded and private. Everyone slid into a seat, caught up in a conversation about if chips and queso was better than chips and salsa. But before I could claim my own, Jamil stepped in front of me to pull my chair out.

"After you, Moon." He leaned in close enough for his lips to graze the shell of my ear. The ghost of his words nearly sent me into a wild tailspin that had me wishing I could drag him into a dark hallway just to show him how out of control he made me feel. His fingertips brushed my ribcage as he helped me push my chair close to the table, everybody else oblivious of our exchange.

Control yourself, Harper. He's an athlete. He's the topic of your research. He's surely heartbreak you don't want.

"I hear you're going to interview Derek Allen," Olivia said once we were all seated. A strong, muscular leg pressed against mine and I had to fight the urge not to jump in surprise.

"That's what I'm told from Jamil," I said to her between sips of water. On my second sip, I nearly choked when I felt a foot run up the back of my calf. As nonchalantly as I could, I pressed my heel down into Jamil's other foot. The hiss he let out drew a questioning look from Tommy across from him.

"Jamil took credit for that now, did he?" Olivia asked, a sickly-sweet tone to her voice as she narrowed her eyes at her friend.

"He did . . ." I trailed off as I looked over at Jamil, who was returning Olivia's glare.

"Olivia may have helped me with this one. She's good friends with Derek," Jamil amended.

Maggie coughed. "Yeah, *good friends*." Olivia threw daggers at Maggie.

My head snapped back and forth, missing some kind of inside information that only a group of friends knew about each other after living life together.

"I'm excited for it," Tommy added to break up the tense silent stare downs.

"Just promise me you won't make it an easy interview for him," Olivia added. "I love watching that man squirm."

"I never give my interviewees an easy way out." Olivia leaned back in her chair as she sipped on her margarita, satisfied that I was about to make Derek Allen's day potentially a little difficult. "Excuse me," I told them as I pushed away from the table to go to the bathroom before our food came.

As soon as I stepped into the bathroom and turned the lock on the door, I pressed my back into the cold metal. It was amazing how someone could sneak in through a cracked window of your mind and begin to plant roots there when you'd only known them for a few weeks, but here I was wishing I could get one more night with Jamil Edman just to experience how he made me feel again despite my better judgment.

After I'd dried every last drop of water from my hands and felt like I would be able to control myself at a dinner table next to him, I opened the door to go back. Only to see a shadowed figure leaning against the wall just outside the bathroom. He was wearing a ball cap pulled low over his eyes and a smirk.

"What are you doing back here?" I asked.

Jamil didn't answer at first. "Do you ever think about that night?"

His gaze burned into me as he waited for me to answer, even while I stood there gaping at him, knowing his friends were sitting out in the restaurant waiting for us. For someone who normally loved words, they were all failing me right now. Finally, I managed to nod my head, despite the pounding in my chest as I waited for what would happen next.

Jamil pushed off the wall and prowled toward me, slowly backing me up until I was cornered. "Do you ever think about that night, Moon?"

"Yes."

Shock that I answered and *admitted* how I was feeling sat between us for one moment . . . two. Then it was a flurry of hands and teeth and mouths as he pressed his body against mine. Despite the desperation of our touches, there was a softness as he cradled the back of my head in his hands. It was a balance of tender seduction and an animalistic desire sweeping between us as we devoured each other. His teeth nipped at my bottom lip. I twisted his shirt between my hands. He left a trail of kisses over every sensitive spot he'd learned on my neck.

The cap had been unscrewed on a pressurized can and there was no hope of shoving any of this emotion back in. My mouth slanted over his, wild and free. His fingers dug into my ass, grasping for purchase as he lit every single inch of me on fire.

Jamil was like a drug that I couldn't get enough of, and I pressed myself into him further, demanding more, every rational thought of someone walking up on us nowhere near my mind. With a curse, he ripped his mouth from mine and I wanted to plead with him not to stop. Plead with him to keep going or I would melt onto this very floor. "We should go back to the table before anyone comes looking for us."

"Right," I said, still trying to catch my breath.

"You go first," he suggested. "I'll follow shortly after."

I nodded, my brain still trying to catch up to the present. Just as I turned to leave, Jamil took my hand in his. "I'm not done with you."

Those words hung heavy between us as the reality of what just happened in this dark hallway sunk in. It was clear that what happened in Florida was never meant to be a one-time situation. "How do we always find ourselves in this position?" I asked.

Jamil only gave me a smile as if he didn't want to know the answer and honestly, neither did I.

Chapter 14

Jamil

Edmanfans11: *Did anyone catch that between Jamil and that interviewer? That man is on top of the world.*

JZ2020Cougars: *Jamil Edman proving he can score on and off the field tonight. I kind of dig this.*

BaseballProfessorx3: *I came here to watch baseball. I didn't realize I had tuned in to the Hallmark channel. But I'm into it.*

ChelsealovesEdman11: *I declare myself the president of this ship. They are so CUTE together!!!*

By the end of the series, my interview with Harper was all over social media. We had barely been around each other over the past three days. The Cougars lost all the games in Seattle and Harper had focused on interviewing the starting pitchers, barely sparing a glance in my direction. What happened in the hallway was like a heavy rock sitting with neither of us making the first move to push it out of the way. The court of public opinion didn't do anything to make matters any better.

Paired with the stress of my brother disappearing from rehab, my mind had been completely preoccupied. The facility was still looking for him, but I knew he'd turn up eventually. This wasn't the first time he'd disappeared from treatment. I had only hoped that when he checked himself back in it wouldn't happen again. I should have known better than to believe him. But there would always be a seed of hope that he would finally put the work in to fix himself.

It was beginning to become difficult to erase my worries for him from my mind when I stepped on the baseball field, which was evident in the uncharacteristic seven strikeouts I had over this series. I could almost hear the sports analysts debating what they thought was distracting me, all of them agreeing that I was letting the attention get to my head. The truth was none of them knew what was really going on in my life, despite how hard they were trying.

The interview Harper was going to do with Derek was a welcome distraction from that reality. Today would be the first day we would *have* to interact. I even had to get Harper's phone number from Olivia so I could figure out how we were going to meet. Harper had simply sent me her address and asked me to pick her up at noon. The flip from how hot that hallway was back in Seattle to how cold the distance was growing between us was jarring.

I should have been nervous as I pulled up to the apartment Harper was staying in, just down the street from the stadium, because we were dancing around the fact that we'd jumped each other's bones in the restaurant in Seattle. The chemistry between us was visible enough that people were even catching it in our interview. But I wasn't nervous. I only wanted to be near her again.

All I could think about was that kiss in the hallway. It was one kiss. But it had been an electrifying, mind-blowing, one-for-the-record-books kind of kiss. There was clear chemistry now between us. That first night couldn't be chalked up to the heat of the moment or a need for a distraction no matter how hard she was trying.

It was only a couple of minutes before she walked out the front doors of her building looking like a powerhouse. She wore a navy pantsuit and her hair fell in tendrils down her back. The look on her face was of someone who was ready to conquer a battle that was on the horizon.

Oh, Derek. You're about to be utterly unprepared for this woman. You and I both.

I quickly jumped out of the car and came around the front to open her door. "You look fantastic."

Harper paused as her eyes remained on the open car door rather than meeting mine. Conflict clashed on her face before she sucked a breath deep into her lungs and turned to face me. "Thank you," she said, a hint of a smile pulling at the corners of her lips before she slipped past me into the car.

"So . . ." I trailed off once I'd gotten back in the driver's seat. "I'm assuming you've seen social media these past few days."

There was only a moment of silence before Harper began to laugh. It started off as a soft chuckle before it devolved into a full belly laugh. I cast her a concerned look to see tears streaming out the corners of her eyes. Once she'd finally collected herself, she nodded her head.

"I have and so has my boss." She swiped at the rivulets of tears with a smile of disbelief on her face. "And apparently it was his favorite interview of mine. I barely asked you two questions, and they weren't anything more than surface level and *that* ended up being his favorite interview. Isn't that fucking hilarious?"

There was a deranged look in her eye as she waited for me to respond, so I trod cautiously. "Your boss wasn't upset or anything? I never would have done it if it was going to get you in trouble."

"Oh, he loved it. The clip is nearly at a million views and their ratings have even gone up on some of their shows today." Harper leaned her head against the headrest of her seat. "All this time I've wished to be appreciated at my job. I guess you really do have to be careful what you wish for because you may get the result and hate how you got there."

"Well, now that you have their attention, use today to show them all that you are."

Harper let out a breath of disbelief as she turned in her seat to look at me. She was staring at me like I had crept inside her mind and read exactly what she was thinking. "I'm sorry about the last series," she said once she sat back in her seat. "It was a hard one to watch."

I gave her a shrug. "That's part of the season. It's a marathon, not a sprint."

"I'm also sorry for not talking to you after the restaurant," Harper replied quietly as she gazed out the window, watching the Chicago skyline slowly fade away as we drove toward the Chicago Bobcats' practice facility.

"That's okay."

"I don't regret it," she told me after another moment of silence.

"Me neither."

Before we could continue our conversation any further, we pulled in front of the practice facility. Only a few cars were in the parking lot, and I recognized Derek's as one of the few. Harper's crew was also waiting for her. Together we studied the building as we walked up to the entrance. I'd only been once before to work out with Nolan Hill, the retired quarterback and now coach for the team, Derek Allen, and Hawthorn Smith, the team's kicker. Even I had to admit it was an impressive feat of architecture with the massive glass structure reflecting the green on the trees surrounding the facility.

"Welcome everyone to my humble abode," Derek greeted us just inside the main entrance. I rolled my eyes at my friend. The two of us had bonded after being brought together by Nolan Hill's relationship with Olivia's sister, Lottie. We were like twin flames always set to destroy wherever we went together, a guaranteed good time.

I took up the rear of the group as Harper greeted Derek and then introduced the rest of her crew. It was the perfect opportunity to observe her without being caught. It had been obvious from the moment I saw her at the bar that she had a magnanimous personality. The kind that would have people hung on every word of her interviews.

"And this is last year's Super Bowl trophy," Derek said as we stopped in front of the trophy case leading to the locker room where the interview would take place. There was a picture of the entire team next to the trophy and then one of the captains—Derek was being held up by Nolan and Hawthorn.

"Do you think you can manage back-to-back?" Harper asked him as we walked into the immaculate locker room where Derek already had two chairs set up in the middle.

"I'm not sure. We're young, but we've got a lot of talent and a lot of fire."

"Are you ready to get started?" Harper asked as she took one of the open seats. Her crew set up quickly—seasoned professionals that they were.

"Please," Derek told her, motioning for her to go ahead.

I moved to stand behind her crew so I could watch the interview through what the camera was capturing. The overhead lights had been turned off and only the lighting Harper had brought in was illuminating the two people in the middle of the room, everything else cast in shadow. Her navy suit popped on the screen while Derek's white button-down shirt complemented. Visually it was perfect.

"Derek Allen, it's a pleasure to have you in the hot seat."

"I'm excited to be here." Derek rubbed his pants nervously. On the outside he always came off as extroverted—the funny one—but anytime the spotlight was solely on him, he had a hard time with it. Yet another thing we both had in common.

"Let's start on the night of the Super Bowl. Take me back to those final few minutes. You and Nolan Hill had connected on ten passes with you racking up one hundred and thirty-five yards. It was an unbelievable performance the two of you put on after a rocky first half of the season. What were you thinking there in the last quarter being up nearly three touchdowns?"

Harper hadn't even glanced down at her notes once as she spit out those statistics.

"It was bittersweet," Derek started. "We were about to win another Super Bowl after three years. It was going to be my second one. But as those minutes ticked off the clock, I realized once we walked off the field, Nolan and I would no longer be teammates. He was going to be done."

"That chemistry the two of you had is like no other tightend and quarterback pairing in the league," Harper continued without even missing a beat. "What do you think made that partnership so special?"

Derek cocked his head thoughtfully for a moment before replying. "I think our playing styles aligned well. I never feel like I'm stuck with a specific route, and I can always find a way to get open. Nolan had this innate ability to know where I was going to try to go, even when it wasn't a part of the planned route."

Harper smiled. "Magic."

"Like magic," Derek agreed.

"Do you think that can be replicated with Caleb Willis as he takes over the reins of the team this year?"

I was hanging on Harper's every word. The way she commanded the room and created chemistry between her and Derek that made the conversation easy—it was something you couldn't teach. It was pure talent.

"With Nolan's mentorship as a coach, I think anything is possible."

"None of that has to do with you?" Harper asked with a cheeky smile.

Derek blushed. "I'd like to think I'm a good leader for my teammates. I hope I am. If I do my job to help motivate the locker room, then you'll see us back at the Super Bowl this year."

Harper pressed on. "The critics have been talking about how they don't see a clear leader out of the Bobcats' locker room this season. What do you say to that?"

"I'd tell them that they aren't looking hard enough. The leadership in the locker room has been learned from players past and the younger players are buying into our mission."

By this point in the interview, I knew that Harper had knocked it out of the park. She'd sent this out of the stadium and into the parking lot. There were few interviewers that could make an athlete feel comfortable the way she was for Derek and I'd been around my fair share of them.

"Have you taken any time to think about your own legacy? You speak so highly of Nolan, and rightfully so, but you are a first-round draft pick with two Super Bowl championships and on the cusp of breaking countless records in the league. How do you reflect on that and what's next for you?"

Derek let out a long breath. "I try to keep on an upward trajectory every season, always trying to take it one step further. But as for what happens next, I'm not sure yet. Maybe I'll end up in your seat."

"Good luck with that. I put up a good fight." Harper and Derek exchanged a smile that had the green hands of envy wrapping around my heart.

"In all seriousness," Derek continued. "I enjoy the reporting and media side of things. So maybe I'll venture into that space when this is all said and done. Do a podcast or something like that."

"I will absolutely tune in to your podcast, so you've got at least one listener," Harper told him. "Derek, thank you for sitting down with me today and good luck going into training camp."

"Thanks, Harper. It's been a pleasure."

When the camera finally clicked off, Derek let out one of his boisterous laughs. "Now *that* was an interview. It really is great to meet you."

Harper stood up to shake Derek's hand and I could sense the adrenaline rush fading as I watched her trembling hand slip into his. "Olivia told me not to let you off easy," she told him, and I nearly choked because she had no idea what she'd just walked into.

Derek turned scarlet. "Did she now? Well, you sure didn't. Thank you for asking me to do this. I feel honored."

"I should be thanking you," Harper told him as she packed up her notes.

Derek's eyes slipped over to me, and the saccharine smile he gave me filled me with dread. "I heard this was truly all thanks to Jamil, though."

Harper turned to me with the kind of happiness that reminded me of the first time you felt warm sunshine on your skin after a long winter. "He's pretty great."

My best friend's eyes bounced back and forth between us like he was watching one of his favorite reality television shows.

"You owe Derek," Harper added as she brushed past me out of the locker room.

"You sure do," my friend agreed as he clapped me on the shoulder. "Like box seats."

"Can't you ask Olivia for those?" I asked, throwing the dig at him with a smile that told him I knew exactly what I was saying.

"Be careful, Edman. It looks like I may have just got my own ammo to use against you now."

I have no idea what you're talking about, I wanted to call after him, but the words died on my tongue, my eyes shifting back to Harper as we left the locker room.

Harper was floating in the clouds the entire drive back to her place, completely drunk on the feeling that interview had just given her. "I think people will eat up being able to see Derek Allen in a new light. I feel like we got to see him from more of a leadership role than we normally do." Harper's fingers were flying over her keyboard as she constructed an email to her boss.

"I agree. That was a unique interview for him," I told her. "And that was all due to you." The complete look of elation on Harper's face as she glanced over at me was almost contagious, as if I could get high on life by just looking at how happy she was.

A text popping up on my car's entertainment system was the only thing pulling us out of this cloud of euphoria. My brother's name was at the top and my blood ran cold. All traces of happiness sucked away.

Jordan: *Are you home? Was wanting to drop by to see if you could help me get out of some trouble—*

It was the first time I'd heard from him since he left rehab. The rest of the message was cut off, but I could see Harper reading it out of the corner of my eye. Without even opening my phone, I knew exactly what the rest of the text would say. I'd gotten similar ones over the past few years since we both arrived in Chicago. He would tell me that he owed money to a bookie that was coming around to collect, yet he didn't have anything to give him. He'd turn to me to help him get out of trouble.

My stomach soured as I thought about all the possibilities that must be swirling in Harper's mind. I'd worked so hard to keep this reality of mine from everybody else—not because I was ashamed of my brother, but rather because I dreaded the looks of pity I got when someone realized the truth of what was happening with him. Only pulling up in front of Harper's apartment seemed to save us from sitting in the awkward silence for longer than a few moments.

"Congratulations," I told her as Harper reached for the door handle. "Being in that locker room today was like being one of the first people to witness the beginning of a star."

A strange look crossed Harper's face as she stared at me for a second before she said, "Hey, J, thank you." Then she slid out of the car and walked back into her apartment triumphant, while I pulled away feeling more beaten down than ever before. I barely registered that she'd called me by my nickname for the first time.

Chapter 15

Harper

Ding.

"I need to turn this thing off," I muttered as I fiddled with my phone. It had gone off throughout the entire game today with notifications from people tagging me on various social media platforms and text messages from contacts I hadn't spoken to in the industry in years congratulating me.

Ding.
Ding.
Ding.

SC News had posted my interview from a few days ago—now completely edited and apparently getting picked up by multiple other news outlets. It had gone global as people discussed this different side of Derek Allen that they'd never seen before. With so much speculation over what the Chicago Bobcats would look like this season without their veteran quarterback returning, this interview provided some insight to fans and analysts on what was happening with the leaders in the locker room. The number of notifications that were flooding my phone was proof of the hunger for a story like this one.

A giddy warmth had pooled in my stomach when I first woke up and I saw the interview on my television with nearly everyone talking about it. This was what I had been waiting for—when my work was finally recognized after all the years of sacrifice and determination.

Ding.

This time an email from my boss popped across the top of my phone. My fingers froze with hesitation for only a moment before I clicked into it. It took me nearly three read-throughs before the praise over my interview finally sunk in. The only drop of disappointment I had was when I read the final line and realized that this interview still wasn't enough.

Keep up the hard work. This interview is just the start. The network really liked the expansion to the Chicago Bobcats during the off-season. It was a risky decision . . . but it paid off. Any insight into a story on Jamil Edman? We want something more than just typical interview questions after a game. We really want to get to know him.

"Just the start?" I whispered, realizing that the four years of sacrifice and doing what I was asked was not realized in his eyes. All the times I took on something else voluntarily didn't matter. Only after bringing this kind of success to the company did it matter. Suddenly I no longer wanted to look through any more notifications I was tagged in, the triumph I had been celebrating now spoiled.

What else do you want me to do?

Not to mention the stark reminder of what I expected of me this season. The network wanted an inside scoop on Jamil and dread filled me at the thought of writing anything that could put him in a bad light. If I didn't write something like that, would that mean my job was on the line?

To make matters worse, a text from my mother came in.

Maria: *You would have made a great politician. Great interview.*

It was the closest I was ever going to come to a compliment from my mother. With a sigh, I tossed my phone into my bag to avoid looking at it for the rest of the day. The stadium was still emptying out. Workers were walking through the aisles cleaning up the trash that was left behind and the players were long gone. My crew had left a half hour ago, but I had stayed after my final interviews of the night to finish typing up my notes on the series.

"Why does someone who should be on top of the world look so downcast?" I glanced up to see Jamil standing next to me, dressed in a pair of workout shorts and a sweatshirt.

"You changed fast," I noted as I closed my laptop and shoved it into my bag with my phone.

"I love early afternoon games because the night is still young. I can still do something rather than dedicating the entire day to baseball and I'm wanting to do something with you."

Jamil and I hadn't had the chance to speak since the day of the interview with Derek. Between him playing and my job, we were only able to share a few smiles and waves—which only made me miss being around him more. I wanted to tell myself it was because he was one of the few people that I knew here, but it was more than that. I enjoyed being around him.

"I could use a bit of a distraction today," I told him as I stood up and slipped my bag onto my shoulder.

"And why would that be?" Jamil reached out and took my bag off my shoulder to throw it over his own. "Like I said, you should be on top of the world right now."

"My boss congratulated me on the interview," I said as we climbed the stairs of the stadium.

"And that's a bad thing?"

"I guess it's because I was expecting a big interview like this to launch me into a new stratosphere. Like he would have offered me a promotion on the spot after realizing my talent."

We walked down the tunnel that led to the player parking lot. "You shouldn't let that dim this accomplishment," Jamil told me with deep sincerity that made my heart squeeze. "Plus, you aren't done yet. You got their attention and now they're watching. Show them what you really can do."

No matter how many times Jamil supported and encouraged me, it always took me by surprise. I'd never had someone support my interests the way he had—not even my parents.

"So instead of a night of distraction, I personally think tonight should be one full of celebration." We stopped in front of the passenger door of Jamil's car. He opened it for me, motioning for me to get in before handing me my bag. There was a mischievous twinkle in his eyes as he smiled at me. "Because I'll be damned if you don't celebrate being the center of conversation on every sports network channel on television."

I hesitated. Every smile he gave me and every minute we spent together was distracting me from my goal. *Hello? Rule number four!* But my ability to resist his smile was non-existent. "Okay. What do you have in mind?"

"I'm going to take you to the best restaurant in the city," he told me as he pulled out of the parking lot. "You're going to love it. You don't mind a few extra people though, do you?"

*

Turned out the best restaurant in town was Jamil Edman's kitchen and a few extra people really meant a small party. The moment we pulled into a driveway that already had five other cars in it, I narrowed my eyes at Jamil.

"Did you plan something for me?" I asked him, already knowing my answer from how pleased he looked with himself.

"My mom always said you should celebrate your success with all of those that care about you, and I realized that you've had to uproot your life so you can't really do that. But every person in there wants to celebrate *you*, so I feel like it's a close second to celebrating with your friends and family from back home."

My throat constricted as I fought the emotions fighting to break free. I didn't want to tell him that a celebration back in Washington DC would have consisted of going to a local wine bar I loved by myself, so this was already more than I would have ever expected. My heart squeezing in my chest reminded me how out of my depth I was. I'd sworn off men to focus on me. But now I was beginning to realize I might have done myself a disservice thinking that opening myself up wouldn't allow me to fully reach my potential in my career because from where I was currently sitting, having a support system felt *really* good.

We got out of the car together and walked up to his front door.

Jamil lived in one of the more affluent suburbs of Chicago. The kind that had long driveways, perfectly manicured lawns, and expensive cars sitting out front. His house was large with five bedrooms and three bathrooms. Even more surprising were the textured rugs on the floor that provided contrast to the furniture, tasteful artwork on the walls that added pops of colors, and pictures of Jamil with who I assumed were his family from the striking resemblance. Worn books lined shelves on either side of a fireplace. Everywhere I looked, I saw more pieces of Jamil that made up the greater picture.

This wasn't just a house. This was a home. It was a sanctuary.

Tonight, that home was full of life as Jamil and I walked inside. Olivia and Derek were the first people to realize that we'd made it and let out a cheer that was soon amplified when the rest of the group joined in. Everyone I'd met was here—Maggie and Tommy, Olivia and Derek, and Nolan Hill. And there were people I recognized that I hadn't met yet.

Tears threatened to spill out as I watched people I barely knew, and people that I didn't, be so excited for me. It made the struggle I'd endured thus far feel worth it, only because I had others to celebrate overcoming my struggles with now.

"Are you surprised?" Olivia asked as she and Maggie came over, with Olivia's sister, Lottie, in tow.

"Definitely wasn't expecting any of this," I told her as I took in the room full of small children running around and people laughing while enjoying good company. It felt like a family gathering—something completely foreign to me.

"Jamil got this all together last minute before the game today," Maggie told me, her innocence completely missing the implications of what she just divulged. Olivia's eyes gleamed as she watched me glance over to where Jamil was conversing with the Chicago Bobcats players.

My head couldn't sort through how I was feeling as I watched him laugh at something Derek had just said. I was beginning to pick his laugh out in a group of people, the sound hitting my ears like a favorite song.

"He was so determined to help you with the interview," Olivia said as she sipped on her beer. "Now I see why. It was one of the best I've seen in a long time."

"You should be proud of yourself," Lottie finally spoke up. "I've never seen Derek that comfortable in an interview. He normally uses humor as a defense mechanism without giving the interviewer any real substance."

"It's nice to officially meet you." I stuck my hand out for her to shake. We had been in the same vicinity in the few games I covered of the Chicago Bobcats last season but had never formally met. "Your resume is quite impressive. Especially with what you did with Nolan Hill last season."

Lottie gave me a small shrug. "He just needed someone to push him and stop coddling him."

The Chicago Bobcats had claimed their newfound relationship as their own and considered Lottie as the secret ingredient that helped them win their last Super Bowl.

Nolan and Jamil migrated to the kitchen together to begin preparing the meal for tonight. Jamil had turned his hat backward and was reaching for an apron when I excused myself from the group of girls.

"Can I help you?" I asked Jamil as I rounded the counter over to where he was cutting up an onion. The muscles in his hands and forearms flexed with each precise cut he made. His movements were just as sure and full of confidence as they were on the baseball field.

"If you want, you can assemble the kebabs," he offered as he dumped the onions into their own bowl before starting to cut up some peppers.

"Harper," Nolan cut in as I began sliding the meat and peppers onto the kebab sticks. "Can I just tell you that I loved your interview."

The last time we had spoken to each other had been after his Super Bowl win. When the network had asked me to cover that game, I was certain more opportunities would come my way. In the sports industry, getting to cover as big an event as that was a career highlight. But I was once again disappointed when I was still assigned to the DC Capitols come this season.

"It's nice to talk to you outside of the football field," I told him. "And thank you. Derek made it easy."

Nolan scoffed. "Derek doesn't make anything easy. Don't discredit your own talent."

I looked over to where Derek was sitting with Hawthorne Smith's girls as they dressed him up in a fake tiara and earrings from the game they were playing. "I think Derek is realizing the role he is about to step into," I told Nolan. "He knows the shoes he has to fill."

Nolan studied me for a moment, his eyes darting between me and Jamil before he nodded toward the kebabs I put together. "Are those ready for the grill? I'll take them."

Then we were alone in his kitchen, as Jamil began cleaning up.

"Thank you for doing this," I told him, as I put everything we'd used to prepare the food into his dishwasher. "This is one of the nicest things someone has done for me in a long time."

Jamil looked at me, his eyebrows pulled together in concern. "If this is one of the nicest things someone has done for you in a long time, Harper, then you haven't been around people that value you."

I swallowed hard. Jamil didn't realize how close to the mark he'd just hit. Between my parents' disapproval of my job and the lack of friendship in my life, there was nobody else who cared about me in that way. All the text messages I got full of congratulations today from peers in the industry were social climbers trying to position themselves with others that were currently in the spotlight.

"And you value me?"

Jamil dried his hands off on a towel as he stared at me. "I don't make a habit of ignoring the blessings life puts in my path."

My lips parted.

"Dinner is ready!" Nolan called from out on the patio where the grill was.

"Come on, Harper." Jamil inclined his head toward the door. "Let's go eat."

I barely registered the hand that gently pressed on my lower back, encouraging me to start walking. My mind was still wrapped up in the mess of emotions, tangled like a ball of yarn.

Only one question persisted.

Did I like Jamil Edman?

What was even more confusing was how sure I was of the answer.

Chapter 16

Harper

The party was still carrying on and had migrated outside. The kids were splashing around in the pool in Jamil's backyard with their moms, while the rest of the guys were lounged out on the patio furniture to watch Nate Rousch's first game as a Texas Rattler. After dinner, I was quickly reaching my max for social interaction for the day, so I had snuck off to the fire pit to recharge. The lazy licks of the flames mesmerizing me and quelling all the racing thoughts in my head.

How would I top this interview?
Who would I interview next?
Would any of this be worth it?
Would I feel achieved after having to scratch and claw my way to the top?
Was this truly what I wanted to do?

Around and around they went—melting into each other before it became one big ball of anxiety.

"So how are you doing?" Lottie asked as she slid into the chair next to me, Maggie and Olivia following shortly after into the remaining open chairs.

"Just taking a moment away from it," I told her as I stared into the fire. "I'm not used to any of this."

Lottie nodded her head as if she understood. She took in everything—the kids screaming happily in the pool, the guys cheering for the hockey game on the television, to all of us sitting around the fire pit with wine in our hands.

"We're like a weird family unit. But it's comforting knowing that every single person here would do anything for me if I needed it." Lottie glanced over at me. "And we are welcoming you with open arms."

"I'm not sure why, though," I told her. I was used to high expectations and perfection, especially being the only child of my parents. They celebrated big accomplishments and questioned poor decisions. I had never grown up feeling like I had unconditional support from them and to have a group of strangers give me that while barely knowing me was hard to digest.

"They once did the very same thing for me," Lottie told me with a soft smile and an understanding look in her eyes.

"A common denominator brought us all together—professional sports. We take care of our own," Olivia chimed in. "And it is extremely clear that you're important to Jamil."

Wine immediately went down the wrong pipe. I coughed and spurted out a mouthful onto the ground. Maggie threw a hand over her mouth to try and hide her laughter. "I'm not sure about that," I told Olivia, turning in my chair to glance over at the group of guys in fear that they had heard our exchange or were concerned someone was dying over here.

Olivia placed her hand on top of mine. "Honey, Jamil is one of my best friends. I've known him for almost five years now. He is one of the biggest flirts that I know, but since you've shown up, all he cares about is the next chance he will have to hang out with you."

I considered what she said and glanced back over my shoulder to catch Jamil in the middle of laughing. His head was thrown back and his eyes were crinkled nearly closed. There was no denying Olivia's observations. Any free chance the two of us had, we always seemed to want to spend it together.

"I think we've found a mutual solace in each other. We both have a love-hate relationship with our careers now and I think we've found a friendship in each other with that commonality."

"Do friends make out with each other in restaurant hallways?" Maggie asked with an innocent look on her face.

My free hand flew up to cover my face out of embarrassment. When I peeked back out at the three of them through my fingers, they were all looking at me with amused expressions. "You guys knew?"

"Let's just say that Jamil's lips were a deeper shade of red when he came back than when he left," Olivia snickered, clearly enjoying watching me shift uncomfortably in my seat.

"Well, that's embarrassing." I downed the rest of my wine. "I don't know what you guys see, but I enjoy hanging out with him. I'm not sure I can confidently say much more than that."

"Something's holding you back," Lottie observed.

Only the fact that I need him to help my career between these interviews and a story he has no idea I'm going to be writing about him.

"I don't know if we are meant to be more than friends," I told them, ignoring the accusatory voice in my head.

Lottie shook her head as she gave me a sad look, like I was more delusional than Nolan had been about his career coming to an end last season. When her sister opened her mouth to try to convince me otherwise, Lottie just shook her head to silence her. "What will be, will be," she told everyone before standing up from her chair. "I think it's time we head home. I've got to get the old guy to bed."

The four of us wandered over to the patio where the guys were watching the final seconds of the hockey game tick off the clock. Lottie folded herself into Nolan's side and placed a gentle kiss on his cheek before whispering in his ear. He nodded and told her it would be only a minute longer. Maggie perched herself on the arm of Tommy's chair, only for him to pull her into his lap and wrap his arms around her protectively. Olivia took an open chair next to Adam and I stood toward the back of the group. With only ten seconds left on the clock, Nate Rousch scored one more goal to give him four of the five goals of the night.

Hawthorn walked over with two of his girls in his arms, his wife following closely behind with their third one in hers. "Alright everyone, we are getting out of here to get these princesses to bed."

"Those aren't princesses," Derek called out. "Those are three queens in your arms. They dubbed me their princess."

Nolan let out a groan as he and Lottie followed Hawthorn and his wife toward the driveway.

"Thanks for coming," Jamil called after them.

Adam stood next to help his wife wrangle up their boys. "We should head out, too. It's a school day tomorrow and I'm on carpool duty."

"Retirement looks good on you, buddy," Tommy told his friend as he and Maggie also stood to leave.

"Is there anything we need to help clean up?" Maggie asked as she hesitated to leave.

Jamil waved her off. "We already got everything put away before the game started. Be safe driving home."

Derek glanced over at Olivia. "Are you going with them or me?"

Just like at the restaurant when Maggie brought Derek up to Olivia, everyone's gazes ping ponged between the two of them. Olivia acted as if she didn't notice it.

"I'll just go with you. My place is on the way to yours. There's no point in making them drive out of the way to drop me off."

Maggie looked like she wanted to burst as she watched the two of them head toward the driveway together. "Bye, guys! And congratulations again, Harper. I can't wait to see what you do next." Then she turned around and slipped her arm through Tommy's before disappearing around the corner.

The silence that swooped in after everyone left was so much louder than the chatter of voices earlier. I walked over to the open spot next to Jamil on the sofa and sank into the cushions with a thud. Exhaustion made every limb feel ten pounds heavier. "Thank you for planning this," I told him as SC News came on the television to talk about tonight's sporting updates.

Jamil slung an arm over the back of the couch, so it barely touched my shoulders. "You should celebrate such a big achievement with more than just yourself."

It was almost uncomfortable for me to acknowledge the way Jamil was looking at me with unfaltering support. "It was overwhelming," I admitted to him softly. "In a good way," I hurried to add when I saw concern etch its way between his eyebrows.

"I'm sorry," Jamil said, his eyes searching my face. "I should have asked you if this was something you wanted."

I reached a hand over to gently place it on his leg. "It was perfect."

Jamil visibly relaxed and the thought of how nice it was to have someone care about what it was that *I* truly wanted was a nice change.

"If I were back home, I would have probably gone out to dinner with just my parents, and we would have celebrated with a nicer bottle of wine than they normally would have gotten. Dessert would have been loaded with questions about how I was planning on topping such an achievement."

My eyes tracked the television and the analysts on the screen. I had never felt so close and yet so far away from my dream than I did today.

"Are you not very close with your family?" Jamil asked, his full attention on me.

I shrugged. "When I'm back in DC, I spend time with them at least twice a week. But do I feel like my parents really know *me*?" I paused as I considered the heaviness of that question. "I don't. I think they have an idea of a life for me but haven't taken into consideration if that's what I really want."

Jamil chewed on his lip before he finally responded. "I think that's a shame because they're missing out on getting to know the kind of person that comes around once in a lifetime."

I didn't dare take a single breath—afraid that the smallest breeze would blow this moment away. "And what kind of person is that?" I asked.

Jamil turned his body toward mine, his arm still across the top of the couch but now his fingertips brushed my shoulder. "Someone who wants to take everything that the world will offer her and won't stop until she has it in her grasp." Jamil's fingers were now playing with my hair as his eyes stayed locked on mine. "People like to tamp out a flame that burns that bright, but they don't realize that those people are the ones you want to keep close because that same determination they save for themselves, they typically give everyone else in their life, too."

Every word Jamil spoke was ringing in my head like a gong. But he wasn't done yet.

"They're missing out by trying to fit you into a box that makes them feel comfortable. But you should never have to bend yourself into a person that is easily digestible for someone else. That's their problem, not yours."

Now I understood why Jamil hadn't crumbled under the pressure of the expectations that everyone else had for him. He'd surrounded himself with people that celebrated him and were part of his very foundation. They made it nearly impossible for the world to knock him down because they reminded him of the person he was—carefree, loving, and full of so much joy that you couldn't pull your eyes away from him. And he was trying to provide me with the same support system that he'd surrounded himself with.

"Do you always spill out such deeply personal observations to everyone?" I asked.

"Only with people I care about," he replied, his eyes soft as they traced every curve of my face.

If I were my mother, I would have shut down where this was heading. My mother would want me to prioritize the opportunity this interview with Derek was bringing and capitalize on it by doing what Terry was asking of me. She would hate that I was getting distracted by the earthy tones of Jamil's eyes or the dimple that highlighted his crooked smile. But when had I ever done what my mother wanted?

I worried on the inside of my cheek as I felt his gaze like a caress. "Do you think we should talk about whatever this is between us?"

"Do you?"

Take courage, my heart.

My grandmother's words echoed in my head, reminding me that I didn't need to play things safe all the time. Not everything could be defined or planned. So just like that night in Florida, I leaned forward and let myself fall into Jamil.

Strong arms wrapped around me as he met me halfway, like he'd been ready to react the moment I made the first move. He captured my mouth with his and that same sense of euphoria I'd felt before came rushing back in.

In one swift move, Jamil swept me up into his arms and walked us back into his home. I was barely aware of my surroundings as we passed through the dining room, the kitchen, the living room, and down a hallway I hadn't seen yet. All the while Jamil held me against him with one arm while his free hand roamed over the curve of my cheekbone with abandon.

I knew what was coming. We'd been here before. Except this time there was no liquid courage coursing through either of us. This was a decision we were making in good faith. Something that neither of us could supply an excuse for when the morning came.

The last time I'd let Jamil take me to bed, I knew before I even walked through his front door that I wouldn't be waking up next to him. That it wasn't going to be more than a one-night stand. It had felt impossible for it to be more than that. Now I was beginning to wonder how it could have ever been just once.

Jamil tipped me backward until I was lying on bedding that felt like a cloud and was silky smooth against my skin. "Why do you have such nice bedding? You have nicer bedding than I do." I ran my hands over the comforter, as the first sign of nerves made their appearance.

"Is this your bedroom talk, Harper? Do I need to mention the thread count to really get you going?" That teasing smile that rarely showed on his face nowadays made an appearance as he reached for the hem of his shirt to pull it over his head.

I looked everywhere except at the chiseled planes of Jamil's torso as he walked closer to where I was lying.

"Why are you so nervous?" Jamil teased as he tossed both of my shoes behind him.

"The last time we did this I had some extra courage from my good friend, Jose."

Jamil's fingers trailed up my legs softly, amusement written all over his face as he watched me squirm. "I should thank him for that night," Jamil whispered as he undid the button on my jeans and leaned over to place a gentle kiss to the bare skin that was now exposed. "He played an integral role in one of the best nights of my life."

I scoffed. "That couldn't possibly have been one of the best nights of your life."

Jamil hesitated to place another kiss against my stomach and I watched as his eyes slowly lifted to meet mine. "Eventually you'll understand what I mean, but tonight isn't the night to argue over how I feel, Moon."

That goddamn nickname sent butterflies erupting inside of me like some sort of aphrodisiac. The moment my shirt disappeared over my head and his fingers traced the tattoo on my chest reminded me where it came from.

When Jamil's lips fastened back on to mine, I was floating. I fisted my hands in the bedding to keep me grounded—here in this moment with him. "You're already holding on for dear life and I haven't even gotten started yet, Harper. What am I going to do with you?" His smile was practically devilish.

"You have quite the mouth on you today. Where was this back in Florida?" I squeaked out as Jamil traced a line of kisses from my mouth downward, feathering across every piece of sensitive skin on my body.

"I was in awe of you that first night. At a loss for words. Gobsmacked. I might have to pull a dictionary out to really capture what was going on." Jamil's teeth nipped at the inside of my leg, eliciting a soft yelp from me.

"And you aren't in awe of me anymore?"

Was banter considered foreplay? I'm starting to think it might be.

"Quite the opposite, actually," Jamil replied as he leaned down over top of me. The muscles in his arms flexed as they held him up. "I'm just prepared now."

Now it was my turn to be wholly unprepared.

Chapter 17

Jamil

A warm body snuggled further into me, reminding me that what happened the night before hadn't been yet another dream, and that this time she was still here when the sun rose.

I forced my eyes open despite their protest just to prove that I wasn't wrong. There burrowed in my arms was Harper, with her long hair pulled up into a messy knot that she must have done in the middle of the night and mascara smeared under her eyes, sleeping peacefully. My heart clenched at the sight of her. I let myself relish the moment for a few minutes before I slowly peeled my body away from hers and padded into the kitchen.

For the first time, a quiet morning in my kitchen didn't feel oppressive when I knew Harper was sleeping down the hall. I ignited the flame on one of the burners on my stove before tossing a pan over top of it. After grabbing all my ingredients from my fridge and pantry, I got to work making my mother's pancake recipe.

A realization dawned on me as I went to brew a pot of coffee. I had no idea if Harper was a coffee person or a tea person. I shuffled around my cabinets until I found the only box of tea that I owned. I pulled creamer and milk out of my fridge, along with butter and syrup. By the time the pancakes were done, my entire pantry was out on my island, and I was staring at it as if it would tell me how Harper liked to take her breakfast.

"This is quite the spread for two people," Harper said on a yawn as she emerged from the hallway. One of my t-shirts was hanging off her shoulders. My breath caught in my throat at the sight of her. That same messy bun sat cockeyed on her head, but she must have snuck into the bathroom to wash her face.

Even though this was fulfilling a fantasy in my head I'd imagined multiple times over the past weeks, disappointment leaked into me. "I was going to bring you breakfast in bed."

She hiked a thumb over her shoulder. "Do you want me to go back?"

I sighed and shook my head. "No. I realize I don't know if you like coffee or tea in the morning. Or how you like to eat pancakes, so I would have had to drag the entire fridge into the bedroom to make sure I got it right."

Harper giggled at the thought. Before last night, I thought I had a handle on my attraction to her. I wanted to spend time with her because of how relaxed she made me, but I was always able to control myself before. Now there were cracks that showed, like at the restaurant in Seattle, that were becoming uncontainable.

"I like coffee with creamer," she told me as she climbed onto one of the barstools and eyed the spread.

"Doesn't matter what kind of creamer and it doesn't matter how much."

I poured the creamer into both cups of coffee before placing one in front of her, following it up with a kiss that I pressed to the top of her head. Harper wrapped her hands around the mug and breathed in the scent of freshly brewed coffee, looking rested and completely content.

"Oh, someone texted you a bunch of times or a few different people. I thought it was important, so I brought it out to you," Harper told me as she produced my phone and slid it across the counter toward me.

My notifications said I had five text messages. Four of them were from the facility where Jordan had been and one of them was from my brother. It had been over a week since my brother had walked out of treatments and today was going to be the final day the facility was going to search before they deemed him as vacated.

All the text messages from the facility were updates telling me that my brother had checked himself back in and was now back under their care. The single one from my brother had my chest tightening with each word I read.

Jordan: *I still need your help to get out of my debt. Please. I'll pay you back. I've only got a month to pay it back.*

I noticed Harper watching me carefully as I tossed my phone back on the counter with a sigh. I shouldn't be surprised at this point, but those text messages would never get easier to read. It was more uncomfortable when I was confronted with the reality of my brother's life in front of someone that didn't know because that was usually when the questions started. Except Harper stayed quiet as she watched me, waiting for my lead.

"Thanks. It's just some personal stuff." I wasn't sure why I didn't feel comfortable with telling her the full story about my brother yet. I was fiercely protective over Jordan and his situation because I didn't want people to wrongfully judge him for a handful of mistakes he made in his life.

Addiction was a difficult thing to understand if you had no personal experience with it. It was difficult to watch a loved one battle with something that had wormed its way into their life and had such a stranglehold on them that they couldn't escape it.

I tried not to notice the single moment of disappointment that crossed Harper's face before she busied herself with stacking her plate up with pancakes. The last thing I wanted was for her to feel like I couldn't trust her—which was the farthest thing from the truth. I already felt safer with her than I had with anyone—besides my friends—in years.

But I wanted to keep Jordan close to my chest for a little bit longer.

"Do you have plans today?" It was an evening travel day for a ten-day away series trip, and we had the rest of the day to ourselves.

Harper shook her head. "I just need to pack for the trip at some point. I've mastered the art of last-minute packing."

Spending nearly every free second I had with Harper was beginning to become a habit, one that I didn't mind having. Coming up with any possible excuse was becoming second nature just to keep her near me and today I could use her positive energy.

On the long list of things I hated most, brand deals and commercials were at the very top. My agent had scheduled a quick filming day for today at the stadium before I had to travel, and it was exactly the last thing I wanted to do with my free time. I would have much rather spent it lounging around my living room with Harper until it was time for us to leave, but that was the price of playing professional sports that made me wonder if it was worth it.

"I have a commercial I'm filming at the stadium around lunch time. I can drop you off back at your place so you can pack and then we could go to the stadium together. Having you there would make the entire experience much more enjoyable."

Harper screwed her mouth to the side as if she were debating her answer before giving me a playful smile. "Are you adding me to the payroll as an assistant?"

"I can think of a particular form of payment you'll find acceptable," I told her with a wink before I sauntered off toward my bedroom to change. I heard a sharp intake of breath that had me chuckling all the way to the shower.

*

If I could cease to exist at this very moment I would.

If I could throw it all away and not have it affect my family, I would.

If I could play baseball without all this extra shit that was expected of me, I would.

The thoughts inside my mind were loud as the photographer's assistant coached me into different positions for various shots. "Now, let's get a smile," the photographer shouted over to me, and I had to force my eyeballs to not roll all the way to the back of my head.

We had only just begun and I was already losing patience from being asked to pose and then repose multiple times. Harper was standing off to the side of the photographer next to my agent. Catching her gaze while the makeup artist did touchups to my face under the lights lifted some of the overall anxiety I had for things like this. I tried to muster the best smile I could, and the photographer began snapping away while shouting out more instructions.

"Wider!"

"Less forced!"

"Think of something funny if you have to!"

They were all useless instructions and with each one shouted in my direction, my blood pressure rose. Eventually the smile fell completely off my face.

"Maybe we should take a break?" the photographer suggested.

"We don't have time for a break," Nico jumped in. "He has to be at the airport in two hours."

"I'm not sure that the brand is going to want pictures of Jamil looking like he would rather be anywhere else, would they?"

"The photoshoot is only supposed to be a portion of today's content," Nico fired back.

"If we don't get the shots we need, it will take the entire time."

Nico opened his mouth to respond but was cut off by Harper. "Hold on."

She slipped in front of the photographer and made her way out onto the field where I was standing, pulling all my attention to her instead of the swarm of people waiting for me to do what I was asked.

"You okay?" she asked quiet enough so only I could hear.

"I just hate this stuff," I murmured, fighting the urge to kick at the dirt and ruin the field for this shoot.

"Then reschedule," Harper replied, as if that was the easiest thing in the world.

"It's not that simple," I said with a sigh. I would give anything to be done with all of this and just get on the plane.

"Why isn't it?" Harper pressed. I recognized the bite in her voice. It was the same one she used when she was about to drill down on one of her questions and herd the person she was interviewing toward the answer she was looking for.

"I have obligations—contracts that I signed. I can't just walk away from that." Annoyance edged its way into my voice. How could she not see that?

"You are the commodity here, Jamil. If you need a break, you have every right to ask for that. Reschedule if you have to. If you can't stand here and smile, then you can walk away from it today."

The set of Harper's shoulders was strong and maybe even a little stubborn, like she was prepared to argue with me if she had to. Maybe she was right. I'd never had someone tell me that was an option before. Could I just walk out of here right now? Nico would lose his mind. Before I could decide if that was something I truly wanted to do, Harper leaned in close to whisper something in my ear.

"Or you could picture me naked, my hands fisted in those thousand-count sheets from this morning, and get this over with."

I barely had time to register what she said before she disappeared out of the shot. My mouth dropped open. It felt like a cold bucket of water washing over me before I caught the wink she gave me over her shoulder—much like the one I gave her this morning. A laugh burst out of me at the sight.

"That's perfect!" The photographer began capturing shot after shot. I barely even noticed the flash of the camera as I watched Harper blush, like she couldn't believe what she'd just done. In a stadium full of people, it was just the two of us enjoying our own inside joke.

After a few minutes, the photographer looked up from his camera. "I think I've got it!"

"Fantastic," Nico exclaimed as he clapped his hands together. "Thank you, everyone!"

Harper met me halfway as I began to walk off the field. She reached out to give my shoulder a small shove. "See, you always had it in you. You just need to loosen up a little bit."

Neither of us mentioned *what* it was that made me loosen up. If I did, I was worried that she would shutter herself off again and whatever was happening between us would end altogether. Only the quickest squeeze of my hand told me that she was thinking about it, too.

Chapter 18

Jamil

"It just doesn't feel the same without you here, old man," Tommy told Adam. We had video called him after getting to the hotel for our first away series of the trip and had propped him up in the corner as we ate dinner.

"When I thought about retiring, I had assumed I would be retiring from these gatherings we always seem to do," Adam replied. He was out in his garage, working on another unnecessary project he'd come up with for the house. After every project he'd completed so far, he sent me and Tommy a picture in our group chat. He was just as proud of his DIY projects as he was of one of his performances with the Cougars.

"You know you miss us," I told him as I took a bite of the sandwich that I'd ordered from room service. "If you didn't, you wouldn't pick up our calls."

"Maybe I should start ignoring your calls. I'd have fewer interruptions during my projects." Somewhere in the background, Adam's boys were yelling at each other about whose turn it was on their electric scooter. "Seriously? What did I tell you two? If you can't share, then you both lose privileges!"

Tommy nearly choked on his fry from seeing Adam morphing into dad-mode.

"Is that Uncle Tommy and Uncle J?" Adam's youngest asked as he walked into the view of the camera.

I waved. "Hi, bud!"

"Uncle J, can you tell Daddy that it's my turn on the scooter?" Adam's youngest puffed out his bottom lip and gave me his best puppy-dog eyes.

"Oh, no!" I shook my head vehemently. "I'm not getting in the middle of that. Your dad would not be very happy with me."

Adam's youngest sighed in defeat before stomping back over to where his older brother must be with the electric scooter to try again.

"How's the domestic dad-life treating you?" Tommy asked Adam, both of us amused at seeing a hall of fame pitcher being outsmarted by his two little ones.

"I'm running out of things to upgrade with the house." Adam brushed his hands off on his pants before reaching to pick up his phone. "Nora has been on me to get out of the house. I think I'm driving her crazy. I've been given the responsibility of coaching my eldest's t-ball team and practices don't last very long when they only have an attention span that lasts about thirty minutes."

"What if you got into coaching like Nolan?" Tommy asked. Adam and Nolan were close friends and were the main reason our friend group had grown into what it was. The two clearly had very different ideas about how to approach retirement.

"I've thought about it, but I don't think I'd do professional. I've had a few of the local colleges reach out to add me to their coaching staff, but I haven't decided yet."

"Wait," I interrupted, a new idea dawning on me. "Would you do an interview about your life post-retirement?"

Tommy paused mid-bite into his burger when he realized where I was going with this. It took Adam only a moment before he was catching on, too.

"Are you asking me to do an interview with Harper?" Adam cocked an eyebrow and gave me the smallest upward tug of his lip—which was Adam Steel's signature smile.

I tossed my hands up in mock surrender. "I'm just saying that if you and Nolan sat down to do an interview with her to talk about your experiences, I think it would be an incredibly unique interview and maybe help a few athletes at the same time. We all know that Nolan would have killed to have someone do that for him."

Tommy finished chewing before he asked the question I knew was on everyone's mind. "Why are you doing this for her? Really?"

Both had been around me long enough to know that I didn't need a reason to help somebody else. If I saw a way that I could help, I was going to do it.

"When I made this deal with Harper, I told her that I thought it would take some of the heat off of me," I explained. "But I really just wanted to help her and figure out a way I could keep hanging around her, if I'm being completely honest."

"Why is it that I always end up having to give one of you two relationship advice?" Adam asked.

"Because you're the oldest, so that makes you the wisest?" I joked, earning a dry chuckle.

Adam rubbed a hand down his face. "I can't wait until you two are the oldest on the team and some young rookies come to you with the most idiotic problems. You two must make everything difficult, mustn't you?"

Tommy leaned forward with a hand on his chest, feigning hurt. "That hurts, Adam."

"I'll do the interview, Jamil. But only because my wife will probably think it'll help get me out of the house. Just send me the details." The sound of cries that were quickly turning into full-blown wails could be heard in the background. Adam sighed and set his hammer down. "I know, I should've bought two scooters. I'll talk to you guys later."

Then the line went dead.

"Are you going to call Nolan?" Tommy asked me as he rolled off the end of the bed to throw the remains of his dinner away.

"I probably should. I don't want him hearing about it through Adam first." I thumbed through my contacts until I landed on Nolan's name.

"I'll leave you to it. I'm going to get some sleep before the games tomorrow. You should, too." Tommy started toward the door before drawing short and turning back around. "It's nice seeing you happy again, J."

A heaviness settled between us for only a moment. Tommy had watched me go from the happiest guy in the room and on the field to someone people were used to seeing wear a frown. The sudden change from last year to this year had turned my world more upside down than getting called up to the league had. When I first started, I could still go to a restaurant without the fear of being hounded for an autograph or a photo. I could go to the grocery store like a normal human being. Now I had my groceries delivered and if I wanted to eat out at a nice restaurant in Chicago, I was asking for a private table.

Tommy was one of the highest paid players in the league, but he didn't have the kind of fanfare that I had. He didn't have what felt like pieces of his humanity stripped away from him. He wasn't living in a glass cage.

"Thanks, Tommy," I told him before waving goodnight.

After shutting the door, I dialed Nolan's number and waited for him to answer.

"Jamil! Shouldn't you be traveling to your next series?" Nolan's voice came over the speaker—straight to the point, just like him.

"We got to the hotel a few hours ago. How is everything?" The Bobcats were facing down the NFL Draft which was on their doorstep and after the season they had, they were going to have to be tactful with drafting new players. I knew Nolan was neck deep in game film of young quarterbacks he could pick up that could play behind his new starter, Caleb Willis, who took over after he retired.

"Lottie got sick of watching football, so we're taking a break tonight and watching one of her favorite reality television shows."

"With wine!" I heard Lottie shout in the background. "You would love it, J."

"You'll have to invite me next time," I told her. "Look, the reason I'm calling is to see if you'd like to do an interview with Adam about your lives post-retirement."

There was a pause. "Are you asking me to do an interview with Harper Nelson?"

I sighed. "Why is that so surprising for everyone?"

"Adam asked you the same thing, didn't he?" I could almost hear the smirk in Nolan's voice.

"I swear if I get shit from you, too, I will hang up this call and find someone else." I had no idea who else I would call to replace Nolan. But at the very least, Harper would have Adam to interview.

There was the sound of someone being smacked, followed by a yelp of pain from Nolan before I heard Lottie on the other end. "He'll do it!"

"Great, thank you. I'll send you the details once I have them." I hung up before Nolan could talk himself out of it and sent a quick thank you text message to Lottie before I settled back in my bed. Only for my phone to go off once more. With a groan, I picked it up without looking at the caller ID.

"J?" The sound of my brother's voice on the other end of the line was both jarring and reassuring all at once.

"Jordan?" I shot up in bed. This was the first time I'd heard his voice since the opening series of the season.

"I wasn't sure if you were asleep yet," Jordan said. There was a cautiousness to his voice that I wasn't used to hearing.

"Not yet."

"How's the hotel?"

The conversation felt awkward and uncomfortable—like two strangers and not two brothers who'd known each other their entire lives. But it was also the first conversation that I'd had with Jordan in a long time where it didn't feel like it was leading toward him asking for more money or for insider information that he knew I couldn't give him so he could gamble.

"It's nice. We're in Boston tonight and then we go to New York to play against the Reveres and then Brooklyn."

"That's a long away series trip," Jordan exclaimed. He'd clearly been preoccupied with other things than my whereabouts recently.

"I'm off next Wednesday. Would you want to have lunch together? I can bring something by?" I was fully expecting Jordan to brush off my offer. He hated when I visited him at the facility, like he was ashamed for me to see him there. Despite the countless times I'd told him how proud I was that he was making the effort to work on himself.

"I'd like that. Could you bring some South Side pizza?" I wasn't sure what shocked me more—that he agreed to lunch or that we were having a normal conversation.

"You bet," I told him. "Meat lovers, right?"

Jordan laughed. The sound felt like an electric shock to my heart. "You remembered."

"Would never forget it. What are you up to tonight?"

I could hear a faucet turn on in the background. "I just got back from the gym. My therapist suggested I try to find a few different hobbies that are healthier than . . . what I currently do."

"What else did they suggest?" I tried not to sound too excited. I learned that lesson a long time ago. The second I got excited that Jordan may be turning a corner, my brother would clam up and bail—breaking my heart in the process.

"Video games, if you can believe it. He said I can work my way up to playing sports games, but that for right now it's best if I avoid them."

It almost felt like old times with the two of us sharing our interests with one another. "I'll send you my gamer tag. We can play together when I'm home."

This time when Jordan laughed, I filed it away as I tried to replace all the memories over the past few years.

"That would be awesome. I can introduce you to some of the friends I've made playing online." Jordan paused. "I should let you go so you can get some rest. We can talk again when you're free. I'm proud of you, J."

I pulled the phone away from my face to muffle a sob that crawled its way up out of my chest. "I'm proud of you, too, Jordan."

Chapter 19

Harper

The cursor on the blank page blinked, each flash mocking me. I'd been staring at this white screen for nearly an hour already with no luck. With a groan, I dropped my head down on the desk in my hotel room.

I'd woken up to an email from my boss, asking if I had any update on the story I was supposed to write on Jamil. He offered to read over anything I had so far, even if it were a few bullet points. I was sure he wouldn't be happy to have a blank page sent to him.

That email had filled my stomach with a sense of dread. He mentioned that the story didn't need to be delivered until the end of the season, so I'd assumed I'd have more time before he came knocking. We were nearing a month into the season.

There was only one thing I could write on this paper, but my fingers hesitated every time I tried to type the words. The only place those words existed were on a sticky note I'd scribbled my thoughts on after leaving Jamil's house that day of his photoshoot.

1. *Jamil Edman*
2. *A rehabilitation center*
3. *Someone named Jordan?*

I had yet to connect the dots with how those three things were related. Between the call Jamil got back in Seattle to the text messages he got from Jordan, I'd contemplated nearly every possibility and none of them felt like something Jamil would want out in the world.

The only problem was what that left me with for this damn story—nothing.

"What kind of journalist do you want to be, Harper?" I asked myself as that cursor continued to blink at me. "You want to cover big stories, but at what cost?"

But how else will you get ahead?

Defeated, I closed my laptop and pushed away from the desk. I was sure to drive myself crazy if I sat there any longer. It was clear no story was coming out of me today. What I needed was a distraction, so I took the elevator down to the lobby on the hunt for something to take my mind off my boss's email.

With no idea where to go, I started to wander toward the entrance to the hotel with the hopes of exploring Boston. It had been ages since I'd taken the time to see the city I was visiting while working. I'd been so wrapped up in trying to advance my career that I never took the time to enjoy where my feet were, always looking toward the future instead of staying in the present.

"Harper?"

I pulled up short of the doors at the sound of my name. Standing over by the coffee bar was the one person I'd just been debating on writing a hit piece on upstairs. Jamil accepted his coffee from the barista and walked over to me, but not before dropping a large bill in the tip jar.

He wore a Chicago Cougars sweatshirt with a pair of sweats slung low on his hips. There was no doubt in my mind that any sports fan would recognize him instantly wearing those signature blue and gold colors.

"What are you doing?" he asked me with that brilliant smile that had women fawning all over him at ballparks.

"I was going to go for a walk. I needed to take a break from my work . . ." I trailed off, suddenly feeling like I was keeping something from him.

"Getting ready for tonight's game?" Jamil asked as he walked with me toward the hotel entrance.

"More like trying to figure out my next story." We emerged out onto the street, already catching the eye of passersby with Jamil looking like a walking billboard for the Cougars next to me.

"I have great news then," Jamil replied after he took another sip of his coffee. "I've got your next interview."

"With whom?" I asked.

The smile on Jamil's face told me that he was quite proud of himself. "Nolan Hill and Adam Steel."

"Two people post-retirement?"

He nodded his head, his excitement growing. It made the sinking pit in my stomach feel so much worse. Here I was with a sticky note stuck to my computer upstairs contemplating secrets that Jamil was obviously trying to keep while all he was doing was helping me.

"That could be interesting. Especially with both having the careers that they had." A part of me hoped that if I delivered enough of these interviews and they did well enough, my boss would forget entirely about the story he wanted me to cover on Jamil.

"We can schedule it for one of our days off coming up. I know we have one the day we get back from these away series, but I was hoping to steal you for something else."

We continued down the street with no destination in mind, just two people enjoying each other's company.

"And what would that be?" I asked.

"There is a charity gala that day. It's for the Boys & Girls Club. Tommy has been a large donator and supporter of them, and he invited me to attend. They're auctioning off various items to raise money, so he asked me to donate a few jerseys and other memorabilia with my signature on it." Jamil turned sheepish as he paused, debating on what he was going to say next. "I was hoping I could bring you as my date."

I stopped in front of an antique shop that wasn't open yet, mostly because my brain suddenly forgot how to walk and to buy some time before I responded.

"A gala?" I asked. "As your date?"

"If you're busy, I totally understand," Jamil rushed to add, politely giving me an out. I had to admit that watching him get mildly flustered was rather cute. So instead of answering him right away, I pretended to ponder a response.

"I would love to." Jamil looked visibly relieved. "It would probably be good if I got out of my apartment for more than just work and the occasional meal run. I can't remember the last time I put on a dress for a fancy event."

Jamil's eyes filled with heat. "I'm sure you're going to capture every person's attention the moment you walk in the room."

The way he was looking at me with such sincerity made me want to believe him and maybe a small part of me was beginning to. "Jamil, why are you doing all of this? With the interviews? Why are you helping me?"

I'd asked this question once before and at the time, under the neon lights of that country line dancing bar, I'd believed him. Now, I wasn't sure if any of what I was doing was actually helping him. So why would he keep helping me?

He looked at me for a few moments before he spoke again. "Because I enjoy spending time with you. Does it help me in the long run? I don't know. It was the easiest explanation to get you to agree." Jamil walked a few paces in front of me before turning back around. "When we met back in Florida, you took me off guard. I don't normally meet people like you."

"What do you mean?" I asked when Jamil didn't elaborate further.

"Everyone I meet nowadays acts like they know me—Jamil Edman, the hall of fame guarantee. But you didn't act like that. You've never acted like that. You don't treat me like a commodity or some oddity to try and decipher. That public persona isn't me." Jamil paced back closer to me and stopped mere inches in front of me. If he breathed in deep enough our chests might even touch. "You didn't seem to care about any of that. You took the time to let *me* show you who I am. When I saw you again, I figured that was my chance at keeping someone like you around in my life. And for what it's worth, I like helping you. You don't give yourself enough credit for how good you are at your job."

When he finally stopped talking, his chest was practically heaving with each intake of breath. Those hazel eyes were shining down at me, reminding me of drops of starlight in the night sky.

I wanted to tell him that I didn't feel like I deserved his kindness. I wanted to tell him that maybe he didn't know me as well as he thought. But I didn't say any of those things. Instead, I reached up on my toes and pressed my lips to his in the middle of that sidewalk in Boston. For once I wanted to be the girl someone wanted. I wanted to be someone worthy of the goodness that was Jamil Edman. I was beginning to grow sick of the way my job was hanging over my head like an axe that was going to fall at any moment. Instead of prioritizing my work as the most important thing in my life, I wanted to put my *life* first.

Jamil's arms encircled my waist and held me to him. Somehow this man was sneaking in to nearly every piece of my life. But for once, I didn't seem to mind. The moment I slipped my arms around his neck and pulled him in even closer, I debated on inviting him back up to my room before either of us would have to leave for the game today.

But before the words could get out of my mouth, my phone rang.

"I'm not sure this would be considered saved by the bell," Jamil said as he took a step back from me.

When I glanced down at the name on my phone screen, I groaned in agreement. "It's my mom. Just give me one second."

After taking a few steps away from Jamil, I answered the call. That familiar sense of fear for wherever this conversation was about to go filled my mind. "Hello?"

"Harper! How are you?" My mother sounded cheerful and that only made me tense in anticipation.

"Good, we have the first game of our next road series today. We're in Boston," I told her.

"I know! My assistant told me this morning. You wouldn't believe it, but so am I. Do you want to grab lunch?" I glanced over at Jamil, who was watching me with concern. I was positive I probably looked like I was having a mild panic attack at my mother's request.

"Like today?"

"What else would I mean?" My mother asked incredulously. "I'll meet you at The Whistlestop in an hour."

The line went dead. I blew out a breath to try and diffuse the anger building inside of me. I was used to my mother dishing out orders for everyone to follow. But I thought I'd escaped that the moment I left Washington DC.

"What's going on?"

"My mother's in town." I slowly looked up from the phone in my hands to meet his gaze. Jamil was trying to understand, like the saint that he was, but was grasping at straws. "She wants to meet for lunch in an hour at some restaurant."

"Okay, let's go," Jamil replied, like it was the simplest answer.

"I don't think you understand what you're agreeing to. The last thing I want to do is subject you to a lunch with her."

Jamil pursed his lips. "If you don't want me to go, you can just say so."

I shook my head, rushing to stop his train of thought. "No, that's not what I'm saying. I just really don't want to go to lunch with her, but there's no way of backing out now."

"Then we go. I'll be your backup." It was clear there was no way I could talk him out of going with me.

Poor Jamil had no idea what was coming for him.

*

"So you two are"—my mother glanced between the two of us—"friends?"

The moment we sat down at the table in the corner my mother had selected for us, her attention immediately zeroed in on Jamil.

"Yeah," I told her, trying to keep my attention on the menu in my hands rather than see the way my mother was scrutinizing us. "He plays for the new team I'm covering."

My mother narrowed her eyes, and I felt Jamil shift uncomfortably next to me. He was right to prepare for impact because whatever was about to come out of my mother's mouth next was sure to hit its mark. "Do you think that's professional?"

"Actually, Jamil was the one that helped me get the interview with Derek Allen and we're currently working on another one." I'd hoped that the news of another interview would pique my mother's interest. But her eyes became glued to her phone as she typed away yet another email for her job.

Disappointment sank in me like a brick. Suddenly I was twelve again, vying for my mother's attention while she was too preoccupied with politics. A hand squeezed my leg and I glanced over at Jamil to see him giving me an encouraging smile. His sincerity was the only thing keeping me from wanting to disappear into the booth I was sitting in.

"That's nice, sweetheart. Maybe this one will get you that promotion you've been wanting." My mother finally put her phone down. I could already see her attention moving away from my life.

"What are you doing in Boston, Mom?" I asked.

"Well"—my mother cleared her throat as she pushed the salad around on her plate that the waiter had dropped by—"I'm meeting with a few potential donors."

My brows pulled together. "Donors? This isn't your district."

"It isn't," my mother agreed. I watched her eyes flick questioningly to Jamil before she decided he was harmless. "I'm testing the waters for a presidential run."

Her words doused me like a bucket of cold water. There had been whispers of a presidential campaign over the years, but nothing ever serious. It still didn't make the reality of it any less jolting.

"I'm stopping at a few different cities to meet with some potential donors to see if this can even be possible, but it's promising." My mother lit up as she began to detail out her plans. That look meant this lunch was about to be hijacked by her. "Do you think you could pencil in some appearances if I do a campaign trail?"

Jamil's pinky slipped around mine as he watched my accomplishments get pushed to the side to make room for hers once more. "I'll have to check my work schedule when the time comes," I managed to reply as I focused on the way Jamil's fingers were slowly wrapping around mine until he was squeezing my hand.

The rest of the lunch was much of the same. My mother filled us in on various bills and meetings she was leading in congress while I attempted to feign interest. Jamil was apparently much better at it than me and by the time our plates were being cleared, my mother was enjoying Jamil's story about the final World Series game.

When he placed his card down to pay for the lunch despite my mother's protests, I caught the wink he sent my way that loosened the claw being in my mother's presence normally placed on my throat.

"Thank you," I told him when we emerged back out on the street. "For being . . . a buffer back there."

Jamil slid his hands into the pockets of his sweats, looking more relaxed after a lunch with my mother than

I felt. After being in Chicago for a month, away from my parents, I'd forgotten just how overwhelming being around her could be.

"You didn't mention your relationship with your mother being quite like that." He tossed me a glance, but there wasn't an ounce of judgment in his eyes.

"I think that's because I don't know what to say." Jamil stayed quiet as he waited for me to elaborate, just a steady presence next to me that I could rely on. "Both of my parents are exceptional at what they do. They're the definition of a power couple."

"And that's a bad thing?" Jamil asked cautiously.

"It is when they expect you to follow in their footsteps and live up to their own standards. The level of success they expect has felt like a moving goal post my entire life. Then when I do have something good happen, it's suddenly overshadowed by a new campaign or a surgery with low success rates that my father was able to do."

Now that I'd gotten started, I wasn't sure I could stop. An entire childhood worth of anger and trauma was bubbling up out of me.

"Sometimes I feel like my parents had a kid just to check a box and they have this idea of the perfect family that they expect me to mold myself into to fit. It's like I'm fighting for my life trying to get them to appreciate what I do or at least to support me. I wish I had half the support it seems like your family gives you. The way you talk about your family in Florida made me realize just how far from a family mine feels."

Jamil placed his hand on my arm to pull me to a stop. There was a sadness in his eyes that hadn't been there before, and I knew that it wasn't for me.

"My family isn't as perfect as you think it is." A muscle popped in his jaw as he ground his teeth together. "Trust me when I say I know it's difficult to accept what it is our family members are telling us. We turn a blind eye to it and expect that they'll be different, and they won't keep breaking our hearts. Eventually we need to decide if it's worth sacrificing our own happiness because of someone else's lack of it."

I searched Jamil's eyes, surprised to find such anguish in them. It seemed I continued to underestimate the weight that he carried on his shoulders. Sometimes the deepest sorrows hid behind the happiest of smiles.

Chapter 20

Jamil

After a little over a week of sleeping in a hotel room, I was happy to wake up in my own bed and go about my normal routine of breakfast, a nice workout, and sorting through my emails from my agent. When I first started in this league, I thought the grandeur of it all would never get old—traveling six months out of the year, seeing a new city or two every week, all while playing for a stadium full of people cheering for you. Somewhere in the mix of it I'd taken my rose-tinted glasses off. I watched my teammates show up to work and enjoy their time playing the game, but when things got too hard, they got to go home to their families. No matter where I went, whether it was home or the field, there was no reprieve for me.

Maybe today that would change.

Jordan had already called me earlier this morning to let me know he'd gotten approval to leave the facility today for lunch. He'd asked if we could order pizza to my place and play video games together, just like we'd done on Friday nights in high school.

I had just hung up with South Side after placing an order for delivery when Jordan emerged from the facility.

I still remembered the first day I watched him walk in. It was a Monday morning I'd never forget. Jordan had managed to pick the lock on my safe I kept in my house with extra cash and my emergency credit cards. He'd taken everything to Vegas and had gone on a bender, only to end up on my doorstep three days later with tears in his eyes as he fell into my arms. I had booked him in to this place by that evening.

Now here we were almost three years later. Jordan had been in and out of this place twice, never staying long enough for anything to really stick—earlier this season being a perfect example. But this time felt different. This time *would* be different.

"Congrats on the three series sweeps." Jordan and I were nearly carbon copies of each other, down to the smile. Our mother used to say I was so enthralled with him as a kid that I must have learned every one of his mannerisms.

"Thanks, man," I told him, reaching over to give him a hug. "The pizza will probably arrive just after we do."

Jordan rubbed his hands together with excitement. "Nothing like South Side, I'll tell you that. I saw Tommy post about a charity event with the Boys & Girls Club tonight. Are you going?"

"I am. I'll have to start getting ready around four, but that should give us plenty of time to hang out before I need to get you back."

The edges of my brother's smile dimmed at the mention of having to go back this afternoon, but the disappointment was gone as quick as it had come. "Bringing anyone?"

"Actually, I am." I rolled my eyes at the look of surprise on Jordan's face. "What?"

"You're just not normally one to go to public events with someone like that. You're more the meet-someone-in-a-bar-and-take-them-home type or you'll flirt with a girl outside of the stadium long enough to be satisfied."

I cringed at being painted in such an unflattering light, but I couldn't argue that he was wrong. I'd never been that serious when it came to relationships because my job, my friendships, and my family had always been enough for me. But now the cracks were showing in two of those three things.

"We met in Florida during spring training." I didn't miss the raised eyebrow of judgment he sent my way or the assumption clear as day in his eyes. "Yes, it was a one-night stand."

"And she's in Chicago now?" Jordan asked me.

"Coincidentally, yes. For work."

"And you like her?"

I looked over at my brother once we'd come to a stop at a red light. "Yeah, a lot actually."

"Who would have thought you'd be the first one to get serious with someone?"

His face was stricken with pain. "You'll find someone, Jordan." The light turned green and I turned away from him.

"I've got to fix myself first, J." Jordan's eyes looked almost hollow when I glanced over at him.

It was strange watching someone you love continue to hurt themselves the way my brother had, even when all they wanted to do was stop.

I pulled my car into the garage and cut the ignition. "As long as you continue to take rehab seriously and we've got to do something about your debt."

The air in the car grew heavy with everything he'd been through hanging between us. Jordan cleared his throat. "Let's go get the console set up while we wait on the pizza."

The sound of the passenger door slamming echoed through the garage as my brother disappeared inside of the house. I let out a long breath and forced myself to count to sixty before following him. It felt like it was always one step forward, three steps back when it came to him, and the climb was becoming exhausting.

My brother, however, was not in the living room where my gaming console was when I followed him inside.

"Jordan?" I called out.

No answer.

"Jordan?" I tried again.

But this time, the doorbell rang before I could start looking for him. Standing on my front porch was the pizza delivery guy—a young teenager that looked like he'd had his license for maybe a week.

"You're Jamil Edman," the kid stammered as he clutched my pizza in his hands.

I sighed. "Yes, I am. It's nice to meet you. Do you want an autograph or something?"

"I—I—I . . .," the poor kid floundered like a fish out of water as he tried to untangle his thoughts while he

Triple Play

stared at me with eyes as round as that pizza I desperately wanted to eat.

"Do you have a phone?" My brother appeared behind me and reached an open hand toward the delivery guy.

"Yeah, yes. I do. Here, one second. Let me get it." The kid fumbled to find his phone and I reached out to grab the pizza box from his hands before it ended up on the ground.

Jordan took the pizza and the kid's phone that he offered up. "Alright, get in close."

I looped my arm around the kid's shoulders. Did I like having to take pictures outside of my own home with the delivery guy? No. But I knew every fan I met supported me, cheered for me, and paid their hard-earned dollars to come to games. No matter how I was feeling on the matter, I wanted to make sure the few seconds or minutes they got with me were worth it.

"Here, hold on." I turned over the back of my copy of the receipt and scribbled my signature on it before thrusting it into the kid's hands along with a large tip that made his eyes go even wider. "This is for you."

"Oh, man. Thank you!" The smile on the kid's face as he backed off my front steps made the entire encounter a little less painful. "Good luck at the next home game. I've got tickets. My friends won't believe this. You're the best!"

Each sentence blended into the next until he'd shut himself inside his car and drove away.

"I'm not sure I'd ever get tired of that," Jordan mused as he turned around and walked toward the kitchen to grab some plates for the pizza.

"You would think it wouldn't," I told him, trying to hold back another sigh.

Jordan put a few slices of pizza down on both of our plates. "People would kill to be in the position you are in."

"You don't think I know that?" My voice came out deadly low as I walked over to the island to grab my plate. "Everything looks amazing when you're only looking at it all from the outside through a keyhole. But there's more than just that small view that makes up the job."

"Life could be so much worse, J," Jordan continued as we walked over to the living room.

Heat rushed to my face as anger grew inside of me. Who was Jordan to tell me what I could and couldn't be tired of? And why wasn't he on my side?

"Let's just play video games," I ground out, trying to keep any outbursts from happening. The last thing I wanted to do was ruin the little time we had together. "Where were you earlier when you first walked in? I called out for you."

Jordan took a bite of his pizza and lifted one shoulder in a shrug. "I was in the bathroom. Here's your controller."

I took the controller from him and settled back into my couch, ignoring the voice in my head that questioned if my brother was lying to me. It wouldn't be the first time, not even close. Jordan had broken my trust a long time ago and had yet to prove to me that he was attempting to rebuild it. I hated myself for assuming Jordan was up to something the moment he disappeared. Today was proof he was trying to change his life.

"How are things going?" I asked cautiously. It was never clear how Jordan would react to the mention of therapy or the work he did at the facility. Often it ended up with him shutting down completely.

"I'm starting to not hate going to therapy, so I feel like that's a start." Jordan's attention was already on the video game, but I knew that was the only way to get him to talk about anything serious.

"Have you thought about what you want to do after you get through the program?" These conversations felt like I was walking through a war zone with bombs waiting to go off at any time.

"I've debated on moving back to Florida."

The admission wasn't what I had been expecting. Jordan had left Florida with me the moment he could, feeling trapped within our hometown with nothing for him to grow into. I never thought he'd want to go back. Mom would be excited to have her baby with her again. She'd never admitted it, but having two of her kids halfway across the country from her was like she was operating with only half of her heart.

"Is there something down there that you are wanting to do?" Jordan had never gotten a job when he moved to Chicago. He relied solely on me and, somehow, I'd allowed him to. The only way Jordan was ever going to move forward with his life was if I stopped enabling him.

My brother screwed his mouth to the side as he contemplated my question. Even the small bit of hesitation sent fear through me that he was going to go down to Florida and put our parents in the same situation he put me in. "Dad said I could come work for him if I ever wanted to."

Our father owned a lumber yard down in Tampa. It was one of the largest lumber yards in the area. The work was often physically demanding with long hours—the exact opposite of what I pictured Jordan wanting to do. But I only wanted him to start living a better life, no matter what he chose to do with it.

"That's a great idea, man. Dad would probably love to have you around, so would Mom."

I tried not to read too much into the sag of my brother's shoulders or the faraway look in his eyes that stayed long after our conversation ended.

*

"He said he'd come work for your father?" my mother asked incredulously. I'd dialed her the moment I'd dropped Jordan back off at the facility. I left out how I wasn't completely sure if Jordan was all in with his treatment because my mother had already gone through enough disappointment when it came to her eldest child, I didn't need to give her another reason.

"That was what he said," I told her as I drove back to my place. I glanced at the clock on my dash, mentally calculating how much time I'd have to get ready before I'd have to pick up Harper for the gala.

"And he was serious?" The shock in her voice mirrored how I felt when I'd first heard Jordan's plans.

"I think so, Mom."

There was a long pause, long enough I thought the call had dropped before she spoke again.

"He seems happier?"

My stomach clenched. I hated the pain she was going through, and I hated my brother for putting her through this.

"He was in the best mood I'd seen in months."

My mother let out a sigh on the other end of the line. It felt like she was releasing years of pent-up worry she had over Jordan right in that very moment.

"Maybe I should come visit him for a little while. Do you think you could give your mom one of your spare bedrooms for a week?" I rolled my eyes at her question. She knew I had more rooms than I knew what to do with in my house and that she could have one at the drop of a hat.

"I'd love to have you. Maybe you can come see a home game if it lines up with when you want to come out." I loved my mom and sometimes it was nice to just have her around again, like old times.

"What about the rest of this week? You have a string of home games over the next two weeks. I think I can catch a flight up to Chicago tomorrow."

"You know where the key is, Mom," I told her as I pulled back into my driveway.

She laughed and it sounded like music to my ears to hear her happy. "I'm so proud of you, baby. And so excited to see you soon. You've been shouldering everything with Jordan by yourself for too long. Maybe it's time all that effort pays off and he turns his life around."

"I hope so, Mom. I really do."

Chapter 21

Harper

The dark green silk of the dress I'd found earlier today ran through my fingers like water. I'd spent all morning hitting different shops around the city in search of the perfect dress for tonight's gala with Jamil and I'd nearly given up until I'd spotted it in a boutique window on my way back to my apartment.

Giving it one more shot before I lost all hope and resorted to panicking, I'd walked in the store only to find the final dress they had in stock was the one on the mannequin and it just so happened to be in my size. I'd called the boutique owner my fairy godmother before rushing back home to get ready.

Now, freshly showered and standing in my robe, I trailed my fingers over the material of the dress. When Jamil had asked me to go to this event with him, it had felt different than the few dates we'd been on or the cookout he'd thrown for me at his house. It was sitting in the grey area between friends and something more.

As I shaved my entire body in the shower, I thought about how this outing wasn't going to be just us or only with our friends. We would be walking into an event together full of the city's wealthier residents that lived off trading information. This felt more serious.

Why wasn't I scared about that?

Normally I would have come up with some valid excuse at this point as to why whatever was going on between me and Jamil wasn't worth it. Lord knew there were plenty of reasons if I just looked hard enough.

It was completely possible that my brain was running me astray, failing me when I needed it most, and I'd find myself destroyed at the end of all of this. Jamil had found his way into nearly every part of my day—between waking up to a text from him first thing in the morning, to focusing on his performance while covering games, to wondering if we would be hanging out afterward.

I should be running for the hills right now. Or putting up boundaries that pushed him away. But instead, I was slipping a dress over my head and working to get the back zipped up by myself, fully committing to a night of being Jamil Edman's date.

I took my time curling my hair and applying my makeup. Being on camera, glam was a part of my job. Tonight, I didn't want to look like Harper Nelson, the field reporter. I used a deep maroon lipstick that I rarely wore. The color paired well with the deep green of the dress. After I applied the last swipe of color to my lips, I took a moment to look at myself in the mirror. The woman staring back at me was unfamiliar. She looked luxurious and sultry. The dark eyeshadow I went with accentuated my golden-brown eyes and made them look larger than normal.

A buzz echoed through my apartment and I cursed, realizing that Jamil was already here. I hurried out of my room to buzz him in. "Come on up! I'm almost done. I'll unlock the front door for you," I said into the speaker before hurrying back into my room to put on jewelry and find a pair of shoes that would go with my dress.

"Harper?" I heard Jamil call from my front door as I failed at putting on the bracelet I wanted to wear tonight for the third time.

"In here!"

I wasn't prepared for what I would see the moment he rounded the corner into my room. Jamil in a black tuxedo with a bowtie nearly stole the breath out of my lungs. The tux was perfectly tailored to his lean frame, showcasing his long legs and broad shoulders. His hands were shoved in his pockets and the glint of a silver watch popped on his wrist. Those curls I loved burying my fingers in were styled and it even appeared like he'd gotten a fresh haircut for tonight. He looked like he belonged on a red carpet with his elegance and refinement.

Both of our faces were probably mirror images of each other's—mouths agape, eyes wide.

Jamil took his hands out of his pockets and gestured at my dress, his mouth working to form the words to describe what he was seeing. "You look . . . Wow. I'm not sure my vocabulary is wide enough to find a word to describe just how beautiful you look."

"You're a professional flirt," I joked.

"A professional?" Jamil scoffed. "I feel like an utter amateur when it comes to you."

Heat burned in my cheeks as I dropped my eyes from his. The bracelet I was trying to clasp was still dangling in my fingers. "Do you mind helping me put this on? I still haven't mastered the art of putting on a bracelet with only one hand."

His throat bobbed up and down before he closed the last few steps between us. I was enveloped by the cologne he was wearing. It reminded me of a summer night around a campfire—warm and cozy. Jamil carefully took the clasps of my bracelet from my fingers before gingerly hooking them together and dropping the chain around my wrist.

"There," he said, his voice low and husky. "Final touch."

His fingers wrapped around my wrist, his thumb moving back and forth over my pulse point. If I thought his cologne was nearly overwhelming, his thumb was making me forget that we were due to leave, or we'd be late to the gala.

"Thank you." I tucked a stray piece of hair behind my ear as a wave of nerves washed over me. We were like two high school kids about to go to prom, pretending to be grownups for one night.

"We should get going or we'll be late," Jamil said, but didn't make a move out of my room. His tall, lanky build was still taking up the entirety of the frame.

"We should." Our bodies drifted closer together, neither of us making a move toward the door.

"We'll be late," Jamil repeated. His lips were mere inches away as he curved his body around mine.

"You wouldn't hear the end of it from Tommy."

He scoffed. "Screw Tommy. He'll get over it."

"What about the kids?" I gasped, trapped in the depths of his eyes.

"I'll toss in a signed helmet for good measure. They'd understand, too, if they had a woman as beautiful as you standing in front of them."

Jamil's hands slid underneath the curtain of my hair as he gently gripped the nape of my neck. "Because it would be a shame if I didn't get to kiss you senseless before we walked into this gala together tonight."

"A complete shame," I whispered, my heart in my throat as I waited for him to close the distance.

The second our lips touched; Jamil went fucking wild. His teeth grabbed hold of my bottom lip and his tongue ran over mine. His hands fisted in my hair, and I knew we were really going to be late. Jamil's body pressed against mine, every hard plane of his taut torso forming to my soft curves. His hands slipped down my back, following the curve of my spine before they pressed into my waist. He walked me backward until my back hit the edge of my dresser, so my body was pressed between it and him. Everywhere Jamil touched felt like a wildfire, his hands setting off a blaze inside of me that scorched everything in its path.

How does this man know how to kiss so well?

Every time we found ourselves in this very position, it was like I was holding on for dear life. Jamil had a way of devouring everything—my insecurities, my hesitation, my worries about my job. All of it disappeared the moment his lips touched mine and with every swipe of his tongue.

I heard something crash and then I was being lifted onto the top of the dresser, my dress riding far enough up my legs so Jamil could step between them. My hands wanted to yank at the bowtie on his neck to pull him closer, if that were even possible, but I resisted if only to spare us the few minutes we'd need to get out of here.

"We're really going to be late," I mumbled against his lips as he kissed each corner of my mouth.

"I really don't care right now," Jamil whispered against my skin.

With a sigh of regret, I pressed my hands against Jamil's chest to push him back. I hoped a few feet of space would allow enough oxygen to both of our brains so we could start thinking clearly again.

"We should go."

Jamil's eyes were hooded as he stepped back from me, his lips stained the color of red wine from my lipstick. He was the picture of seduction, and I would have given anything to pull him into bed and shut out the world around us, but that would mean missing out on a chance to be seen on his arm. I hadn't realized how excited I was to spend an evening like this with him until we were faced with potentially skipping it altogether.

"You may have to reapply your . . ." Jamil trailed off as he motioned at his own lips.

I laughed as I glanced at myself in the mirror behind me. Nearly all my lipstick was wiped off, with the barest red still coloring my lips. "Looks like we exchanged makeup."

Jamil looked at himself in the mirror over my shoulder and let out a curse.

"Here," I slid off the dresser and walked over to a basket of towels to offer him one.

His eyes ran all over me—my hair, my face, my dress—a wry smile breaking out at what he saw. "No one will question if you're really with me or not."

"And that's something we want?"

Jamil finished wiping the lipstick off his face before he turned to look at me. "Why wouldn't it be?"

Instead of acknowledging that I *wanted* to be seen on Jamil's arm, I turned back to my dresser and picked up my hairbrush. "Let me reapply my lipstick and brush my hair. I'll be right out."

Jamil reached for me before shoving his hands in his pockets, like that would keep them from caressing me once more.

"I'll wait out in the living room." He gave me one more long look, like he was trying to commit this moment to memory, before he disappeared around the corner. But not before throwing me a wink.

Dear God, please let me make it through this night without climbing Jamil Edman like a tree in front of everyone.

*

"All ready," I announced as I entered the living room with brushed hair, a fresh layer of lipstick, and my clutch.

With a flourish, Jamil offered me his hand as he slightly bowed at the waist. "It would be my honor to take you as my date tonight."

"Are you flirting with me, Jamil?" I teased as I let him slip my arm through his.

"Since the moment I saw you again, Harper." Jamil laughed at the stunned look on my face and took advantage by placing a quick kiss on my lips. "I'm glad you're finally starting to catch on."

Dear God, I thought I asked you to help me make it through the night?

Chapter 22

Jamil

"That's a lot of cameras," Harper said as she looked out the window of my car at the paparazzi lined up on the other side of the red carpet, snapping pictures of the attendees for tonight's event.

"That's nothing. There's like ten of them," I told her as I pulled up next to the valet.

"It's more than I'm used to."

I glanced over at her, struck again by how beautiful she looked tonight. "Aren't you in front of cameras every day for your job?"

She rolled her eyes and leaned over to punch me in the arm.

"Ouch," I rubbed at the spot where her fist connected, surprised by how much strength she'd put behind it.

"This feels drastically different. I'm controlling the narrative at work. They are trying to create a narrative with a single picture. Potentially creating a narrative out of nothing."

The valet knocked on my window and motioned for me to step out. I held up a finger, asking for just a moment.

"There isn't a single bad thing they could write about you, Harper Nelson. I promise." I stuck out my pinky for her.

"A pinky promise?" she asked as she eyed my finger. "And how can you even give a promise like that and expect to keep it? They could write a million things about me. They could write about my parents, they could write about my job, they could write about *us*."

"And what would be so bad about that?"

Those perfect brown eyes widened. "You don't want to be in the press."

I dropped my pinky to slip my hand into hers. "I don't want to be in the press because I'm tired of the expectations that pile on top of me. Like saying I'm the next Babe Ruth, and those are some large shoes to fill that I didn't ask for. You're right in thinking the media likes to tell everyone who a person is. They've done it to me my entire career. So why shouldn't I finally give them a narrative I want them to share?"

After giving her hand one more squeeze, I lifted my pinky once more. Harper looked at it for a moment longer before she wrapped hers around mine. "Let's go give them a show then."

That tenacious energy that drew me to her that first night in Florida was back. I leaned over the center console and stole one more kiss while it was still just the two of us before I opened the door and tossed the keys to the valet.

"I've got it!" I called out to one of the event workers that reached to open Harper's door. The worker backed away so I could open her door and offer her a hand as she stepped out of the car. "Are you ready?"

Harper lifted her gaze to mine once she had both feet safely beneath her. "I think so," she breathed as I fit her hand into the crook of my arm.

"Let's go find Tommy and Maggie. Maybe even a shot or two of tequila," I told her as we started down the red carpet together.

I pulled us to a stop so we could get the obligatory photos taken for the event. "Tequila seems to get us both into trouble."

With a laugh, I leaned in close to her, "Isn't that the point?"

She rolled her eyes at me and threw her head back. I made a mental note to hunt down the photographer that managed to catch this moment, so I could display it somewhere in my home.

"Come on, let's get you inside before you say something you'll regret."

The event tonight was being held in an old factory building that had been recently restored. The floors were still the original wood and every wall was covered in brick. A stage was erected in the center of the room with white tablecloth covered tables surrounding it. The items that would be auctioned off later this evening lined the walls. I spotted the signed baseballs, uniforms, and glove I'd donated for the cause displayed on a separate table.

Normally I hated events like tonight, but Tommy had gone as far as sending me photos of him with the kids at the Boys & Girls Club on his visits there to convince me to help. Tommy Mikals did not play fair—he knew I was a sucker for kids.

"I can see why you hate events like these, rubbing elbows with people." Harper eyed the crowds, taking in the way gala attendees were trying their best to be seen and making sure they were seen with someone worthy enough to draw attention.

"We're not here for any of them," I told her. I placed a gentle hand on the small of her back and steered her toward the edge of the room as I looked for Tommy.

"Over here!" Maggie was waving like a madwoman at a table near the stage in the middle of the room. Tommy was in deep conversation with the president of the Chicago Boys & Girls Club.

Harper waved excitedly back at Maggie before taking the lead. Her delicate hand slipped down my arm and into mine as she started to pull me toward the center of the room.

I could feel the looks from people as we moved, wondering who my date was. This time, I didn't mind them. Only because I was being seen with her.

"You're here," Maggie exclaimed as she jumped up from her seat and wrapped her arms around Harper before pulling me into a hug.

"Hey, Canon. You clean up nicely." I took Maggie's hands in mine and gave her a spin, the silver dress she was wearing fanning out around her.

"So do the both of you," Maggie gushed. "This dress is stunning on you, Harper."

Maggie took Harper's hands and pushed her out at arm's length to get a good look.

"I agree," I added, not missing the deep blush that covered Harper's cheeks. "You two are the most stunning women in this room."

"You don't know how to be subtle, do you?" Tommy cuffed my shoulder as he joined our conversation.

"That's rich coming from you." I raised an eyebrow at him.

He laughed as he grabbed two glasses of champagne from a passing tray, one for me and one for Harper. "Maybe I'm rubbing off on you, J."

I gladly accepted the glass of champagne and motioned toward the room that was beginning to fill up. "This looks great."

"It does, doesn't it? I think this will be a successful night for the club. We have a lot of great items that people are eyeing." Tommy paused. "Thanks to you, man."

"It's the least I can do. I know how much this means to you and I've got a soft spot for this kind of stuff."

Tommy cleared his throat. "You two look really good together."

I followed his gaze to where Maggie and Harper were moving toward the auction items, arm in arm. "I'm just happy to see her friendship with Maggie taking off. She deserves someone like that in her life."

Tommy's gaze never left my face. "You didn't even acknowledge that I said the two of you look good together . . . like a couple. Are you okay?"

His hand inched toward my forehead slowly like he was going to test my temperature, and I reached up to swat it away. "Knock that shit off. I'm fine."

"Not answering my question is an answer in itself."

I wanted to wipe the smirk on Tommy's face right off. "What do you want me to say, Tommy?" I asked. "That I like her? You already know that I do. What else do you want me to say? That I want to date her? That's not up to just me."

By the time I was done, Tommy's eyes had drifted to something over my shoulder. I slowly trailed off and turned my head to see that Maggie and Harper had returned. Harper was looking at me with wide eyes. Maggie was trying her best to hide a smile, but the sparkle in her eyes gave her away.

"Uh, Harper," I started, rubbing at the back of my neck. My stomach felt like it was a brick sinking to the bottom of a lake as I stared at her, dumbstruck.

Neither of us had discussed what was going on between us. The only obvious part of it was the clear chemistry we had. There was an immediate attraction between us, but neither of us had made a move to be the first one to define it.

Hell, this was the first time I'd even thought about the idea of *dating* her.

Was that something she wanted?
Was I an idiot for not thinking about it before?
Was that even possible for us?

Harper rushed to cut me off before I could say anything else. "Let's sit down. I think dinner is going to be served soon."

A sigh escaped my lips as everyone moved to take their seats. Tommy tossed me a wink across the table that made me clench my teeth with annoyance.

"What are you going to get?" I asked Harper as we all looked at the menu placed in the center of our plates.

Harper's gaze stayed locked on the menu as she whispered, "Were you serious about what you said?"

The last time I'd felt gripped in the throes of panic like this was the first time I'd found out how bad my brother had gotten. I knew what needed to be done—needed to be said to him—but the moment I spoke those words aloud, I could never take them back. There was a before and there was an after. I was terrified of what the after would bring with Harper. I wasn't sure I could bear losing her and the time we spent together.

A waiter stopped by to take our orders and buy me more time while I weighed my options. Do I confess my feelings for her and my interest in exploring something more serious or do I keep things casual? As soon as the waiter left, the air grew heavy with anticipation.

Before I could overthink things, I turned to look at the woman next to me. Her eyes wide as she waited for what I was going to say. "I wouldn't say something like that unless I meant it, Harper."

"Oh," Harper replied before clearing her throat, although her eyes never left mine.

Oh?

"Is that . . . an issue?" I asked cautiously, but before she could reply, the host for the gala walked onto the stage to begin the evening.

"Hello everyone and welcome to the Boys & Girls Club of Chicago Gala. We are so grateful all of you wanted to be here tonight and are so thankful to every business and person that donated to tonight's auction. We will start the auction here shortly over dinner, but first we wanted you all to hear a few words from one of our premier donors, Tommy Mikals."

A polite round of applause sounded throughout the room as Tommy pushed back from the table and climbed the stairs up to the stage. The auctioneer handed the microphone off to him and he turned to address the crowd, giving everyone the full force of his charm that made up the fame he was still running from.

"I wanted to take a few seconds to thank all of you for supporting an organization like the Boys & Girls Club. They are making a difference every day in the lives of the youth in this city. The money raised here today could go toward our next great thinker, our next great artist, our next great inventor, or the next great athlete. We're thankful for your dedication to the next generations. Now let's get this auction started."

A roar took over the crowd as they applauded Tommy's speech. Maggie tried to inconspicuously dab at the corners of her eyes as she watched him walk back to our table. She stood up to give him a hug and my heart squeezed as I watched two of the most important people in my life share a tender moment, despite the pang in my chest at the uncertainty of Harper's response.

As soon as Tommy sat down, servers swarmed to deliver our meal and to give the auctioneer a moment to prepare.

The first item to be auctioned off was one of Tommy's World Series badged jerseys. The starting bid was five-thousand dollars and quickly went up from there.

Item after item was ushered across the stage until my own World Series badged jersey was presented.

"The bidding will also start at five thousand dollars," the auctioneer told the crowd. "We don't want to show any favoritism here."

The crowd chuckled as Tommy and I shared a smile. Someone in the back opened the bid before others joined in, raising the price faster than Tommy's.

"I'm looking for ten thousand dollars," the auctioneer pointed out at the crowd as he waited for the next bidder to raise their hand.

"Ten thousand." My body froze as I realized that voice had come from right next to me. I slowly turned my head to see Harper with her hand in the air.

"We have ten thousand dollars down in the front, do we have twelve?"

As soon as the sound of my blood rushing left my ears, I reached out to stop her hand from raising again as another bidder jumped in after her. "What are you doing, Harper?"

She dropped her head as she released a breath and gave me a small shrug. "I don't know. I wasn't thinking that far. I've just been sitting here thinking about how badly I screwed up by not saying anything earlier and I wanted to do something to make it up . . ."

"You were going to go into debt to get my attention?" I asked her, ignoring the way Tommy and Maggie were watching us.

"I also wanted your jersey." Harper gave me a sheepish smile, as she avoided looking at those around us giving curious glances.

"I have five other ones. You could have just said something, I'd give it to you for a lot less than ten thousand dollars." I was the first one to laugh at the ridiculousness of what she'd just done before Harper was joining in.

Tommy and Maggie were looking at us like we'd lost our minds completely and maybe we had. Between Harper bidding for a jersey that was worth an absurd amount of money and the way her green dress was sending all the blood away from my head, our cognitive thinking skills were nowhere to be found.

As the laughter subsided, Harper's eyes met mine. "I was trying to do one of those grand gestures people always talk about."

"Why?" I asked as the auctioneer sold my jersey for nearly fifty thousand dollars in the background.

"Because I froze earlier!" Harper exclaimed. "When you told me you meant what you said to Tommy earlier, I froze."

I reached out to take her hand in mine, admiring the way they looked together—her delicate fingers against my callused ones. "I hadn't really planned for you to hear what I said to Tommy, so I can't expect you to have a response for it yet. It's okay that you froze, Harper. We haven't had this discussion and I'm putting you on the spot. That's not fair to you. I want you to feel comfortable and ready for a conversation like that."

Harper nodded her head and turned her hand over in mine, so we were palm to palm. "Let's talk about it then."

I glanced toward the stage where the last item I'd donated was being auctioned off—a signed glove. Tommy and Maggie had attempted to turn their attention away from us, but I caught Maggie glancing over every few seconds. She gave me a guilty smile when she realized she'd been caught snooping.

"Right now?" I asked Harper.

"That's the last item." She pointed toward the exclusive vacation in Italy that was showcased on the screens around the room. The bidding had started to slow down, and the auctioneer was getting ready to slam his gavel down and declare the winning bid. "Maybe we can get some air?"

I caught Tommy's eye, who had gone back to staring at us like a nosy neighbor. He tilted his head toward three sets of doors just behind us that led out onto a patio.

"Okay, let's step outside."

We stood up as soon as the last bid was declared. I waited for Harper to go in front of me so I could stick close to her back as we moved through the crowd, eyes still following us as we walked past.

We walked through the open doors leading out onto the patio and the chatter of conversation drifted away. It was our own personal oasis, surrounded by tall bushes and flowering shrubbery. A fountain bubbled in the middle with curved stone benches on either side.

Harper moved to take a seat first and I sat down in the open space next to her. A breeze drifted through the air that sent a shiver down Harper's spine.

"Here," I told her as I shrugged out of my tuxedo jacket and moved to drape it over her shoulders. She looked so small with the jacket swallowing her slender frame.

"Thanks," Harper gave me a grateful smile as she snuggled into the fabric.

There was only the sound of the fountain and the leaves rustling in the shrubbery around us until Harper turned to look at me with those beautiful brown eyes shining through the night.

"I think we both should have realized this conversation was going to come eventually with everything we've been doing." Harper twirled one of my cuff links around as she avoided looking back up at me.

I laughed at the obviousness of it all. After flirting with her for nearly a month and sleeping with her again, the only place this was heading was this very moment.

"I guess so," I told her, waiting for her to take the lead. I'd already unintentionally made my feelings clear, there was no need to remind her.

"That first night back in Florida, I had no intention of anything that happened between us extending beyond another day." I tried to ignore the way my heart clenched at her honesty as I remembered the way my excitement had been extinguished when I'd woken up to an empty bed that next morning. "But when I got the news I'd be covering the Cougars, the first thing I thought about was that I'd see you again. Maybe I should have known then that there was more between us than just using one another to escape reality."

"I was wondering if the universe was bringing you back into my life after how hard these last few months had been," I told her, desperately wanting to wrap her hands in mine again, but I kept them curled into fists, so I didn't push this further than she wanted it to go.

"I was calling it serendipity."

"I like that . . . serendipity," I mused as I rubbed my jaw and looked up at the moon in the sky, nearly full and illuminating the night.

Harper finally let go of my cuff link and reached for my hands. "I'd hoped to keep my distance and remain professional or at the very least friendly, but you were quite insistent."

I leaned against the edge of the fountain so I could tilt my head back further to take in the stars twinkling down at us. "If there's one thing you should have learned by now it's that I'm relentless in my pursuit of something I want. And yes, I would like to date you, Harper. But if you want to wait and keep seeing each other the way things are now, that's fine, too. Because the last thing I want is to not have you around."

Everything in me desperately wanted to hear her say she wanted me, too.

Harper's stare was heavy as she studied my side profile. She sucked in a breath like she was preparing to tell me what I wanted to hear—that she didn't want things to stay the same. My heart dropped when she decided against it and followed my gaze up to the nearly full moon in the sky. "It sure is beautiful tonight."

I turned my head to look over at her, my eyes tracing the curve of her jaw and the slope of her nose. Every time I looked at her, I was taken by her beauty, and in awe of the luck I'd struck that she wanted to spend her time with me. Her hair spilled over her shoulders as she tilted her head back and basked in the moon's glow.

"Yes, it is." Harper startled as she looked over at me to see me staring right at her. "You both are."

Chapter 23

Harper

"Maybe I should drive," I told Jamil as I slipped an arm around his waist to keep him upright. After we'd come in from the patio, Tommy and Maggie had ordered a round of tequila shots that seemed never-ending.

After the first two shots and the rate at which Jamil was tossing them back, I'd asked for a glass of water knowing that one of us would need to drive home.

Jamil staggered slightly, his chest pressing into my shoulder with most of his body weight. If I hadn't had a good grip on his waist both of us would have been sprawled out on the red carpet.

"Alright then, let's get you in the car." Jamil waved to Maggie and Tommy who had slipped into a town car with their own driver.

Maggie blew me five kisses more than necessary as Tommy pulled her into the car by her waist and she disappeared. The valet opened the door for me as I tried to fold Jamil's body into the passenger seat.

"Thank you," I told him, earning a tip of his hat in return.

"Do you think you'll be able to remind me how to get to your house?" I asked Jamil once we were safely buckled into his car.

Jamil laughed again and reached over to pull on a stray piece of curled hair that had slipped out from behind my ear. "I'm not that drunk, Moon."

"You need to be more creative, Jamil. Calling me 'Moon' because I have a tattoo of a moon on me," I said, as I eased the car out of the parking lot and turned toward Jamil's house.

"No, Moon. I don't call you that just because of your tattoo. I call you that because you lit up what felt like the darkest of nights for me when I met you in Florida." Jamil was staring out the window and luckily didn't witness my heart nearly stopping. Completely oblivious that I was slowly slipping into a state of shock, Jamil continued. "Of course, I was attracted to you when I first saw you. Anyone who isn't doesn't have a pair of eyes. But what I couldn't get over was how calm you made me feel. You're the one person in my life right now that I can go to escape it all."

I could barely feel my arms reaching out toward the steering wheel as I pulled into Jamil's driveway and hit the button to open his garage. Tremors racked my hands as I threw the car into park and tried to unlatch the buckle of my seatbelt.

"Are you okay?" Jamil asked me, suddenly sounding much more sober than before. "Here, let me help you."

His hands reached down to cover mine and undid my buckle with ease before moving to undo his own.

Tell him you want him.
Tell him you want him.
Tell him you want him.
Say it.

My hair fell over my face like a curtain, keeping me from having to look him in the eye while I tried to collect myself. "We should get you inside and to bed. You're probably going to feel this in the morning."

If life were simpler, I'd give in right now and tell him that I wanted to date him. I wanted to see where this went. That I felt the same way he did. But life wasn't simple. If I didn't keep my distance, I could lose sight of the goal I'd had for four years. I could risk everything for someone I'd just met. I loved myself too much to do that, so instead I threw Jamil's arm over my shoulder as I helped him inside his home.

The house was quiet as I guided Jamil toward his bedroom. Pictures of him and his family lined the walls. Pieces of him were scattered everywhere. The familiarity of it all did nothing to stop the ache in my chest. Jamil thought of me as his peace, his escape from the world and all the noise. While I was over here with a blank document waiting for me to write something about him for the world to read, to disrupt his peace.

The guilt that swelled within me was nearly unbearable as I deposited Jamil onto his bed. He flopped down unmoving, his body bouncing on the bed. I worked to get both of his shoes off and then his socks. His jacket was still on my shoulders, and I laid it gently on his dresser before trying to undo the bowtie around his neck.

Jamil's hands came up to encircle mine. "Will you stay tonight?" His eyes were closed but the grip around my hands was strong. "If you don't want to, you can take my car home. I can come pick it up tomorrow. I'll have Tommy drop me off . . ."

His words fell off as he started to drift into sleep, his hands slipping from my wrists. With some effort, I managed to get his legs underneath the covers.

My hand lingered on the light switch as I debated on taking up his offer of driving his car back home. Part of me knew that I should leave. Especially after he'd laid out his feelings for me tonight, there was still so much that hadn't been said yet. Despite all of that, I turned around and walked over to his dresser as my hands worked to unzip my dress.

I slipped into one of Jamil's old t-shirts and a pair of sweats that were far too big for me before padding out into the kitchen to pour Jamil a glass of water for the morning and attempt to find some pain relievers.

It took me two guesses to find where the glasses were and another three to find a cabinet full of medication. As I poured the glass of water, my eyes caught on a photo of Jamil holding a baby, the biggest smile on his face as he stared down at the bundle in his arms like she was the light of his entire world. It was the same little girl in a photo on his wall leading back to his bedroom that was in the arms of a woman who looked similar to Jamil, and I guessed that was the niece he had shown up to spring training early to see. I took my time looking at each photo as I walked back toward the bedroom, studying the different images of Jamil's family. His two sisters were beautiful and looked so much like Jamil. He was almost a perfect mixture of his parents. He had his mother's hazel eyes and sharp cheekbones, but his father's complexion and curly hair. He was much leaner and lankier than his father, towering over his family like a giant.

When I spotted another man that hadn't been in any other photo so far, I paused. I remembered Jamil mentioning an older brother that had moved to Chicago with him when he was first drafted, and it occurred to me that I hadn't seen him at a single game this season or how Jamil had barely mentioned him to me—it was almost as if he didn't even exist.

If an older brother moved halfway across the country with you, I would think you'd have more than a single picture to prove his existence.

After placing the glass of water and pain reliever pills on Jamil's bedside table, I crawled into bed next to him thinking about the texts Jamil had received from someone named Jordan and the phone calls he'd gotten over the past month. There was clearly something going on in Jamil's life and the journalism instincts in me pointed toward his brother.

*

The following morning, I woke up to the sound of a blender running and I wondered how Jamil had bounced back so quickly after downing that much tequila. I groaned as I turned over in bed and attempted to give myself a pep talk to get up.

"I hope she's making a strawberry banana smoothie," I heard Jamil mumble next to me.

Wait.

I turned over to see Jamil still burrowed under the covers with a pillow over his head. If Jamil was still lying next to me, then who was in the kitchen?

"Jamil," I hissed, trying to get his attention.

He let out a groan.

"*Jamil*," I hissed a little louder.

Still nothing.

I reached over and yanked the pillow off his head. Jamil squinted at the few rays of sunlight sneaking in from between the slats of the blinds. "What?" he asked.

"There's someone out in the kitchen," I told him, trying to keep my voice low enough to not alert the intruder that we were awake.

"Yeah, that's Harper." Jamil's voice sounded like sandpaper. He reached out for the glass of water I'd placed next to him last night and downed half of it before popping the pills in his mouth and draining the rest of it. I had no idea how he was going to play in tonight's game, but I'm sure it wouldn't be the first time he played hungover.

"Jamil, I'm right next to you."

The glass paused, tilted against Jamil's mouth as he finally registered what was happening. His head slowly turned, as if he was afraid to see if I was telling the truth. Our eyes locked just as the blender stopped out in the kitchen.

"Who is here?" I asked.

His answer was exactly what I was afraid of. "I have no idea."

We both stared at the door together. "Should we go find out?" I whispered.

"Probably," Jamil whispered back. "I'm just letting my brain catch up before I walk out there."

But before either of us could get out of bed, the sound of footsteps coming down the hallway grew louder.

"Do you have a baseball bat or something in here?" I asked quickly, my eyes darting around the room.

"Just because I'm a baseball player, Harper, doesn't mean that I have a baseball bat with me wherever I go," Jamil mumbled, keeping his voice low. He moved his body, so he was positioned in front of me as we waited for the intruder to make themselves known.

"Jamil, honey, you need a new blender. That thing barely can hold enough for one serving." The door opened and an older woman walked into the room with two glasses full of a vibrant pink smoothie in her hands. She looked strikingly like Jamil and horror washed over me as I realized what was happening.

"Mom!" Jamil shouted as he stumbled out of bed, trying to block his mother's view of me.

"What? I told you I was catching an early flight out of Florida and Chicago is an hour behind. This is quite late for you to be getting up on a game day, don't you think?" I tried my best to sink as far into the bed as I could, mortified that the first time I'd meet Jamil's mother would be in his bed while wearing his clothes.

"Why are you still in dress clothes? Are you hungover?" His mother took his chin in her hands to turn it both ways as she inspected him.

"Mom, I'll meet you outside in the kitchen in a second." Jamil was gently trying to push his mother back out of his bedroom, but his efforts were fruitless.

Her gaze caught me attempting to disappear entirely from this moment. "And who is this, Jamil?" she asked her son as she studied me with one eyebrow raised.

Jamil let out an awkward cough as he glanced back at me over his shoulder. "This is Harper. Harper, this is my mother, Denise."

Denise reached out to smack her son on the back of the head. "You should have told me you had company, or I would have made more smoothie. Here, you two have these. I'll go make one for myself." She shoved both glasses into Jamil's hands before turning on her heel back toward the kitchen.

"That was not how I pictured meeting your mother. You didn't mention she was coming." I pulled the covers over my head and let out a groan. Jamil's smile was wolfish as he pulled the covers back.

"She called yesterday and wanted to come up, the tequila fog made me forget. When you meet everybody else, you'll understand that this went much better than expected. Come on, I'm sure she's cooking up a proper breakfast now that she knows you're here."

Jamil disappeared into his bathroom to change out of his clothes from last night, leaving the smoothies on his dresser. Realizing I had no other clothes to change into except for my dress from the gala, I picked up the smoothies from the dresser and bit back my embarrassment as I walked out into the kitchen.

The island was cluttered with eggs, milk, cheese, and various other breakfast items as Denise worked over a pan on the stove.

"Thank you for the smoothies." I started off cautious because who knew how his mother truly felt about finding a woman in her son's bed? My mother would have never let me hear the end of it and probably would have given me a lecture about how Nelsons are supposed to act. "I'm sorry we weren't up when you arrived. Jamil didn't mention you were coming."

Denise turned around with a wide smile on her face and the deepest warmth in her eyes. It was the opposite of what I'd expected. Her presence reminded me of Jamil's—laidback and good-hearted. I felt as relaxed with her as I did with her son, and I forgot for a moment that I was standing in front of her with bedhead and wearing Jamil's clothes.

"If Jamil didn't have Nico as his agent, that boy wouldn't know up from down when it comes to plans." Denise motioned to one of the empty barstools at the island. "Take a seat and tell me a little bit about yourself."

"Oh, sure," I told her as I glanced back toward Jamil's bedroom door where there wasn't a sign of him yet. "I'm a field reporter for the Chicago Cougars."

Denise laughed and the melodious sound reminded me of Jamil's. "I'm not surprised. I'm sure Jamil was struck by you the moment he first saw you at the stadium."

I could already feel the heat rushing to my cheeks. "Oh, no. That's not . . . That wasn't . . . He didn't . . ."

"Please"—Denise waved me off—"I know my son is a flirt. He gets that from his father. That man had talked me in circles all the way to a first date before I even knew what was happening. Jamil is much of the same."

Before Denise could catch me with my mouth hanging ajar, I grabbed the smoothie off the counter in front of me and downed half of it. "We actually met in Florida," I told her.

"During spring training?" She turned around with a spatula in her hand, both eyes wide.

"Yes, actually. We didn't think we'd see each other again after that." Denise stared at me for a moment longer, connecting the dots in her head about our journey thus far before she turned back to the stove and flipped two omelets onto separate plates.

"Life has a peculiar way of grabbing your attention. It makes it known when it wants you to notice something it's putting in your path." She turned around and deposited one of the omelets in front of me and the other in the empty seat next to me.

Jamil emerged from his room freshly showered and looking much less hungover than he had earlier. "Omelets? Mom, this is too much." Despite his protests, he slid into the chair next to me and dove into his food without anything further.

"I always made you omelets on game days. Today is no different." Denise swiped Jamil's smoothie away from him with a wink before taking a sip. "If I had known you had a guest, I would have maybe done something a little fancier."

He sighed. "I'll never hear the end of this, will I?"

Denise shook her head with a wry smile on her face. "Never. Harper, I'm guessing you're quite busy during the game for me to sit with you today?"

I glanced between Denise and Jamil. "Wait, you'd want to sit with me?"

Jamil's hand slipped onto my thigh and gave it a reassuring squeeze.

"Of course, sweetie. I'd love to spend time with you while I'm here this week." Denise reached out to squeeze my arm. "Both of you. And Jordan of course."

Jordan?

Next to me, Jamil's back went nearly ramrod straight. "When are you going to see him?" His words were short and clipped as he went back to staring at his plate.

"I think later today."

If Jordan was, in fact, still in Chicago, why hadn't Jamil talked much about him yet? Where was he? And why were they talking like he was in some kind of care?

Chapter 24

Harper

"This is where you normally sit?" Denise asked me as we settled into my usual seat right behind the dugout. My camera crew was getting situated behind us, fiddling with their equipment.

"This is it," I told her as I pulled my notepad out. "Away games differ depending on where that team has their media sitting."

Denise was wearing Jamil's jersey and had already stopped at the concession stand to order a hotdog, nachos, and one of those margaritas they put in a souvenir glass. She'd offered to get me one and if I hadn't been working, I would have taken her up on it. It was obvious from the moment Denise walked into the stadium where Jamil got his personality from. She greeted nearly every person that made eye contact with her, a wide smile on her face the entire time.

When she showed up to the stadium I tried to gauge how she was feeling. She had mentioned she wanted to see Jordan and would have gone earlier this afternoon. The question was if she had gone and how had it gone.

But it wasn't my place to ask, no matter how badly I wanted to know the answer. For the sake of considering if it was worthy of writing a piece on, I'd find the information out a different way.

"And you just watch the game and take notes about what you see for interviews later?"

I nodded my head. "We do interviews during warmups too, which I'll go do in a minute. But that sums it up on a basic level."

Denise took a sip of her margarita, the same look in her eye that Jamil got when he was about to say something cheeky. "You haven't interviewed Jamil much yet, I don't think. Or at least not that I can remember. Only once, yes?"

"Just once so far this season," I confirmed, not missing the quirk of Denise's eyebrow.

She looked like a cat who'd cornered a mouse as she waited for me to respond. After backing me into a corner with nearly nowhere to go, the only option I had was to either tell the truth or fabricate a lie that Denise would see right through.

I decided to play it safe and avoid telling her the complete truth—that I was too afraid to interview her son, because the one time that I had the chemistry was so obvious between us that the entire world had taken notice. Something I was sure she was aware of.

"I think Jamil has appreciated me giving his other teammates the spotlight this season."

Denise leaned back in her seat, her lips screwing to the side. "Jamil has had a tumultuous past few years. This last year should have been one of celebration for him, but it seems it's only brought him more stress than it should have." She reached up to run her fingers over her necklace with four different stones on it. Before I could figure out how to ask her what she meant, the crowd roared to life as the Cougars ran out onto the field for their warmups. I caught sight of Jamil finding the two of us in the crowd, the widest smile on his face.

"He deserves to be happy," I told her, unable to tear my eyes away from him as he went to play catch with Tommy.

"I miss seeing him look this free," Denise whispered more to herself than to me. Her eyes tracked Jamil as well, and I could feel the pride she had for all her son had accomplished edged with a sadness that was bone deep. "He and his brother both have carried so much sadness these past few years. I just want them both to find some peace."

This much I'd gathered already, but it was *how* Jordan fell apart that I was still in the dark on. The *how* I knew was connected to that night in the hotel in Seattle with Jamil yelling into his phone or the nervousness whenever a text from Jordan came through with me around. I was beginning to wonder if Jamil's hesitation of being in the limelight was due to trying to keep any extra prying eyes away from his brother, protecting him no matter what. Denise didn't move to expand on what she'd said, leaving me with more questions than answers.

"Harper!" I glanced up to see my boss, Terry Wilson, looming over me.

"Mr. Wilson." I'd never stood up out of my seat faster, nearly tumbling down the steps in the process. "You're in Chicago?"

Terry typed away on his phone, which was always glued to his hand for the constant stream of calls and texts that came in. "I'm here for some business for the network. I had some meetings today, but I thought I'd stop by the game once I was done to see how you were doing. I also wanted to check in on how that story is going."

The blood drained from my face as I rushed to stop him from saying anything further in front of Denise. "Terry, this is Jamil Edman's mother, Denise. Denise, this is my boss, Terry Wilson."

Terry gave me a curious look before he reached out to offer his hand to Jamil's mother. "It's a pleasure to meet you, Mrs. Edman. You have a very talented son. He seems to be all the media wants to focus on nowadays."

Denise, still completely oblivious to the way I was nervously glancing between her and Terry, grasped my boss's hand. "I try to take as little credit as I can for his success. He earned that all on his own. I'm just lucky enough to claim him as my son."

"We're actually hoping to feature him on our network by the end of the season," Terry continued, and I wanted nothing more than to disappear as Denise looked at me with surprise. "Harper is going to cover a story on him."

"Is she?" Denise's gaze felt like it was looking straight into my head and seeing exactly what kind of story Terry wanted me to cover. "Between the charity work that

Triple Play

Jamil does and his success on the field, there is plenty to highlight."

Terry reached over to clasp me on the shoulder, jostling me in the process and nearly sending me down the stadium stairs for a second time. "Harper has been gathering as much information as she can to do the story justice."

I startled once more when I felt Denise's hand wrap around my arm. "I know she will."

Another phone call came in for Terry, taking his attention away from me and Jamil's mother. "I'll talk to you soon, Harper. Hopefully about this story on Jamil so we can also discuss other business matters, along the lines of that promotion?"

Without another word, Terry walked back up the stadium stairs, his suit standing out in a sea of blue and gold memorabilia. I used to think that suit was a sign of success. But now as I watched it disappear into the crowd, it reminded me of a snake looking for the perfect moment to strike. This exchange felt more like a predator toying with its prey than a boss checking in on their employee. I was caught in the middle of a dream I'd had for years and a desire that had only just started to bloom over the past month.

"Harper, we may not have enough time for a pregame interview," my camera guy leaned forward to inform me.

I waved him off. "We will just do two postgame interviews then. Let's settle in for the game."

Denise offered me some of her nachos as I slid back into my seat. "Promotion?" she asked.

My heart was nearly in my throat as I debated on what to say to her. Her eyes were sharp, and I was certain she hadn't missed a single moment of my exchange with Terry.

"I've been hoping for a job as a host for the network," I told Denise. Her warm gaze made it nearly impossible for me to keep anything from her. "The traveling life has taken a toll on me."

The crowd roared as the Cougars ran to take the field. Denise curved her hands around her mouth and yelled out Jamil's name before clapping enthusiastically for the team.

"Life on the road is difficult, no matter if you have to bear it alone or if you have someone at home waiting for you." Denise settled back in her chair. "Would you have to move for that job?"

"It would be in New York City," I told her, not missing the intent behind Denise's pointed question.

"And that would be at the end of this season?" Denise kept her gaze forward as she watched Tommy turn a double play to end the top of the first inning.

"That is what I'm hoping for." The ultimatum my mother gave me before I moved to Chicago rang in my mind. If I didn't succeed in getting that promotion, I would very well be stuck back in Washington DC in a life that I didn't want. "I have a lot riding on making sure it happens this year. I'm not sure I'll be here next season either way."

Jamil walked up to the plate to lead off the Cougars' lineup. The crowd went wild at a simple tip of his helmet.

His megawatt smile was visible from nearly every corner of the stadium as he settled into the box to await the first pitch.

"I have a good feeling about this game," Denise whispered as she watched the pitcher wind up.

Call it mother's intuition—a crack sounded as Jamil made contact with the ball and sent it flying in the opposite direction. The first pitch to the Cougars, to Jamil, ended up over the right field fence.

"How did you know?" We both jumped to our feet as we cheered on Jamil. As he rounded third base, he looked up to the two of us. He raised a finger to point in our direction and I had to remind myself that his mother was standing next to me. That couldn't possibly have been for me.

"I can see it in his step today. There's something lighter about him. I noticed it this morning when you two came out for breakfast."

I coughed and glanced over my shoulder to see if anyone had heard her. My cameraman, Neil, was too busy trying not to make eye contact with me for me to believe he hadn't heard Denise. Luckily no one else appeared to have caught it. I enjoyed being the one in control of the spotlight and deciding who to direct it to. The last thing I wanted was the spotlight to be on me.

Chapter 25

Harper

Whatever Denise saw in Jamil today was turning out to be much more than either of us had expected. With three at-bats so far, Jamil had hit a home run, a single, and a triple. If he managed to hit a double before the end of the game, he'd hit for a cycle and potentially collect the most runs batted in thus far in his career. The stadium was on edge, the anticipation building as they waited for Jamil to come to the plate again for his next at-bat.

It was the bottom of the eighth, Jamil's last chance at making the unthinkable happen. It was now or never, with the stakes higher than they'd ever been this game. The Cougars were up by three runs. The game wasn't on the line, but Jamil's chance at etching his name in the history books was.

I never understood how athletes didn't crack under this kind of pressure. If Jamil was nervous, he didn't show it as he walked out of the dugout toward the on-deck circle to wait for his at-bat. Denise and I must have had enough nervousness for him as we clutched each other's hands. There was an unspoken rule in baseball that when something magical was happening, no one spoke of it. If a pitcher was throwing a perfect game, you didn't mention it. If a player was about to break a record, you didn't mention it. If a batter was about to bat for a cycle, you didn't mention it.

The unmentionable lay over the crowd like a heavy blanket as we watched the first pitch sail into the catcher's glove to be called a ball. Jamil stepped out of the box to redo his batter's gloves before touching the top of his helmet and stepping back in for the next pitch. He was the picture of steady patience—a strong tree never bending in the face of a storm.

The world slowed as the pitcher wound up to deliver the next pitch. If I was any closer to the field, I would have been able to see every rotation of the ball as it soared toward Jamil. The crack of his bat hitting the ball was nearly deafening as he sent it back in the opposite direction.

My heart pounded fiercely in my ears as I tracked the ball into the outfield. Denise's grip on my hand tightened as we watched the ball get past both middle infielders. Jamil rounded first base, his eyes locked on second. Just because no one spoke about a player on the verge of the unthinkable didn't mean the player was oblivious to what was happening.

Fierce determination was written all over Jamil's face as his arms pumped hard and his legs tried to carry him safely into second. The centerfielder had already chased down his hit and was rearing back to throw it to get him out.

Denise sounded like she was down a tunnel as she screamed for Jamil to run faster. For a moment, I stopped breathing as I watched him lean back to slide into second, just as the ball hit the fielder's glove and he moved to tag Jamil.

A pin drop could have been heard around the stadium as everyone waited for the umpire to make the call. Was he safe or was he out?

The umpire's arms extended out sideways, signaling that Jamil was safe.

The cheers that erupted were like a World Series or Super Bowl win. Fans were jumping up and down with their arms extended over their head as if the game had just been won in that very moment. Some were clutching each other. Others were high-fiving fellow fans around them. The only thing that everyone was doing collectively was chanting Jamil's name.

"He did it!" Denise exclaimed, her arms wrapping around my shoulders as she jumped excitedly. "He did it!"

"He did," I breathed, my eyes still locked on Jamil as he stood up on second base. His eyes were scanning the stadium, only stopping when they landed on me and his mom. He had yet to smile or celebrate the achievement he'd just completed, until he saw the two of us.

There was a sparkle in Denise's eyes as she reached down to squeeze my hand. I scribbled furiously in my notes, detailing exactly how Jamil had just completed this major feat as the Cougars took the field to close out the game.

My heart was still beating rapidly as the score was announced and the teams slowly started to filter off the field. The adrenaline running through me felt like I'd

Triple Play

been the one sliding into second and being celebrated like a god.

Jamil was lingering as my crew and I walked out onto the field. The moment I was within ten feet of him, his shoulders relaxed, and he turned around to face me.

"Congratulations!" I threw my arms out, unable to hide my excitement for his success. Without a second of hesitation, Jamil wrapped his arms around my legs and lifted me into the air. The laugh that bubbled out of him reminded me of a child with the joy that he was displaying. It was infectious and I was nearly in tears from laughing as he spun me in a circle, the breeze whipping my hair around my face.

"Another compliment from Harper Nelson? Has hell frozen over? Are pigs flying outside? Do I need to put in for a lottery ticket when I leave here?"

"I think you need to put in for a lottery ticket by your performance alone," I told him. If possible, I would have frozen us in that moment; if only I could stay in his arms just a little longer.

"Jamil!" I hit the tops of his shoulders. "You've got to put me down so I can do my job."

"Are you interviewing me?" Jamil asked as he gingerly put me back on my feet. "It's about time. The people would assume you were shying away from me after the sparks that flew last time."

"You are full of yourself," I told him.

"I'd like to call it confident." He stared at me with a wolfish smile.

My camera crew had already set up and had my microphone waiting for me once I'd turned to them. Players' families were mingling around the field, taking pictures, or watching the younger kids run the bases as I fluffed my hair and prepared for the camera to go live.

"Jamil, you've been on this upward trajectory with your performance and somehow, you've done the impossible and topped yourself once again. You broke the home run record last season, which cemented your name with the greats in baseball history. Now you're chipping away at other accolades. What are you doing to stay the course?"

He leaned in so he was close enough to my microphone to be heard. His body loomed over mine, the proximity between us mere inches, as people crushed around us. "I'm trying to keep my head down and continue doing what I've always done—work hard, improve my skills, and be a team player."

"The fans are so excited for your achievement," I continued, pointing toward the still mostly full stadium as they watched my interview with Jamil on the Jumbotron in the outfield. At the mention of them, cheers erupted once again. "What does the support from them mean to you?"

Jamil cast his eyes around the stadium, even giving the crowd a small wave, before leaning back into the microphone. "The only things that keep me going are my family, my friends, and Cougar Nation. There isn't another city like this one. I want to do right by all of you. Every time I get to celebrate, *we* get to celebrate together. I'm so thankful for the support and I think I speak on behalf of the team when I say that we want to make this city proud."

"The next game is giving away a signed jersey to a lucky ticket holder," I continued, trying to finish up the interview. "Rumor is it's standing room only because of that jersey."

"I know one person I wouldn't mind seeing my last name across their back." Jamil flashed a smile. "Thanks for the interview, Harper."

He turned and ran away, fully aware that I would throttle him later for making a comment like that which would only feed the fire on social media.

I twirled the microphone around in my hand as I watched him duck into the dugout and disappear into the hallway beyond. My eyes stayed on the spot I last saw him for seconds longer than necessary as I realized how far gone I already was.

Chapter 26

Jamil

"Jamil!" my mother called from the living room. I'd just finished up a remote interview for one of Chicago's local networks in my office. After my game yesterday, the requests for interviews had nearly tripled. Nico was sending me a new email almost every hour since the end of last night's game.

"Coming! I just finished up an interview," I called back as I came down the stairs.

The smell of my mother's famous biscuits and gravy was wafting from the kitchen. My mouth was practically watering by the time I walked in. She was just finishing preparing a plate for me as I slid onto a barstool.

"Maybe you need to come visit more often if I'm going to be surprised with food every time I venture into the kitchen," I told her as she set the plate down in front of me.

"I don't get to do this for my kids very often anymore. It's the least I can do for letting me stay here."

"Mom." I reached out to wrap my hand around her wrist before she could turn back around. "You don't have to feel like you need to pay me back for me letting you stay here. You can stay here anytime you want without feeling like you have to make up for it."

My mother gave me a soft smile and reached up to cup my cheek. "You've turned into a wonderful young man, J. I am so proud of you."

This was all I ever wanted when I got drafted—to support my family after all the years of sacrifices my parents made.

"How was Jordan?" I asked cautiously as my mother started to clean up the dishes in the sink. After I'd dropped Harper back off at her apartment yesterday morning, I'd gone straight to the stadium to start warming up. Which left my mother to visit Jordan before the evening game.

Silence stretched for longer than what was expected if the visit had gone to my mother's liking. Her lips pressed together as she debated what she wanted to say. "Jordan seems happier than the last time I saw him," she started, her eyes still focusing on the soapy suds she was washing away on a pan.

"I thought something similar when I had him over earlier this week," I agreed, still trying to wade the waters. When she didn't respond right away, I cut right to the chase. "Mom, what are you thinking?"

"I ran into his therapist on my way out of the facility. You should have run that facility past me and your father. It is entirely too much for you to be paying for on your own."

I sighed and set my fork down so I could focus on her. "Mom, that's not of your concern. Jordan needed help, so I helped. Don't worry about the money. Tell me what's bothering you."

She reached for one of the dish towels to wipe her hands off before she finally continued. "His therapist made a comment that Jordan still doesn't seem to be making much progress in their meetings. He was surprised to hear about how well his visit with you went and my short lunch with him. He's under the impression that Jordan hasn't made much progress with his addiction."

The news was like the realization of a ticking time bomb in our midst counting down, the seconds left unknown. Every worry I had about my brother was circling in my head, telling me that I was missing the signs again. I was missing *something* important and if I didn't figure it out, Jordan would only slip further away from us.

There was a harsh reality with professional sports. With the amount of money that was at athletes' fingertips, there was a risk for athletes just as much as there was a risk for their families. Between signing bonuses and the eye-popping numbers listed on the contracts, most athletes and their families were underprepared to manage those kinds of assets. My parents had tried to prepare me as best as they could for what was to come. But what I hadn't expected was for my brother to take advantage of my vulnerability for his own gain.

I had hoped that maybe one day, Jordan would care more about his relationships with all of us than the next big win.

"He never bothered to reach out to me before though," I reasoned, still not willing to accept that Jordan was just playing another game. "That has to mean he's making progress, right?"

My mother closed her eyes, the stress that all these years she'd had to worry about Jordan visible in the slope of her shoulders and the crease between her brows. Her hands wrapped around the edge of the sink with a white-knuckled grip.

"I hoped so when you called me, J. But now I wonder if I was being too hopeful at the time." The pain laced in her voice reminded me of that very first phone call I had with her in my first year in the league when I had to tell her that Jordan had gotten himself in some trouble with a bookie and was lying bloody and bruised on the floor of my bathroom. I could still hear the tears she had tried to hold back so I wouldn't hear them, but the wobble in her voice was unmistakable.

I stood up from the barstool and walked around the island to pull her into my arms. "I'll figure it out, Mom. I promise."

"*We* will figure it out, Jamil. I'm not letting you keep all of this from us anymore. Your father and I aren't weak. We can face the mistakes our son is making." My mother's arms wrapped around my torso and squeezed. Her words were like bullets tearing straight through the weak defenses I'd tried to erect over these past few months. Tears sprung at the corners of my eyes, and I tried my hardest to keep them from falling. "Eventually, Jordan will run out all the goodwill we're willing to give him."

Gingerly, I pulled myself out of her grip. "We can't give up on him."

My mother scoffed. "I would never say that. But we can't help someone who doesn't want our help."

"I *won't* give up on him," I told her fiercely as I slid back onto the barstool and picked my fork back up.

Jordan had been the one to teach me nearly everything I knew as a kid—how to ride a bike, how to swing a bat, even how to drive. He never gave up on me when I struck out nearly every at-bat I had during my first season in baseball, and I wasn't about to give up on him during the hardest moment in his life.

"Tell me about Harper." My mother was a master at eloquently switching subjects.

Whatever happened between the two of them during the game yesterday was still a mystery to me. My mother had teased me mercilessly on the way home from the stadium about flirting with Harper during another interview, but she remained close-lipped about if anything was discussed between the two of them.

"What do you want to know that you don't already?" I asked as I dug into my food. I was surprised that she'd waited this long to put my feet to the fire, but between yesterday morning and the game, there hadn't been time for her to question me yet.

"You like her."

I ignored the teasing smile on her face. "That's not a question."

"Don't be a smartass." My mother flicked water at me. "What are you wanting from her?"

That dreaded question. I'd hoped that after the gala, I'd have an answer. But by the end of the night, the only thing that was clear were our feelings for each other, which were now sitting out in limbo. I'd allowed her to take the reins to decide on what this was or what she wanted it to be. Apparently, that meant still being stuck in a constant state of unknown and I'd just gone with it.

"I don't know, Mom." I shoveled the remainder of my breakfast around my plate to avoid making eye contact. My mother always had a way of seeing the truth the moment she looked at you.

"Do you like her?" I wanted to roll my eyes at the triviality of the question. Anyone with two working eyeballs could see that I liked her, but I knew that wasn't why my mother was asking. Her strategy was to lead a horse to water. Now where that water was, I had no idea yet.

"Of course I like her. I think that much is obvious."

She leaned onto the island across from me, still trying to catch my gaze. "Then what's the problem, J?"

"There's just a lot going on in both of our lives right now." The response was flimsy at best and I knew with one rebuttal, it would topple over.

"There's always a lot going on in life, J. There will always be another story for her or another game for you. If that's what the *real* problem is, then you'll never be able to really commit to someone."

For only a moment I thought the conversation was already over, blissfully short. But I should have known better when it came to Denise Edman.

"You *do* want to commit to someone, right?"

My eyes trailed to the pictures on my wall, filled with memories with my family. A family that only existed because my parents had once been young and in love. They were the perfect example of a healthy relationship for me and my siblings growing up. Janessa had already followed in their footsteps, finding the love of her life and bringing little Kyla into the world. Jayden was still dating, getting closer every day to finding her person. It was only me and Jordan who struggled with relationships and I wasn't sure what that said about either one of us.

"You and Dad have been the best example for all of us kids. If we're lucky, we'll all find a relationship like yours."

My mother walked over to place a gentle hand on my cheek. "Honey, I'll stop prying. Just know that your father and I want you to be happy. Whoever that may be with."

I placed my hand on top of hers and gave her a smile. "Thanks, Mom."

"What do you have on your agenda for today?" my mother asked as she walked to grab the keys for my spare car.

"Should I be asking the same thing of you?"

"I'm going to stop by Jordan's again and talk more with his therapist. Maybe I'll sightsee some if it doesn't take very long. Don't you worry about me. What is it you're doing?" She breezed over her plans and redirected the conversation back toward me fast enough to nearly give me whiplash.

Triple Play

"Harper has an interview with Nolan Hill and Adam Steel that I helped set up. I'm going to . . . supervise." I didn't miss the smirk on my mother's face.

"You set the interview up for her?" she asked casually.

Alarms were going off in my head, telling me to stop now while I still could. The look on her face was the same one she gave us as kids when she was digging for information.

"It's part of an agreement we have." I tried to escape to my bedroom before my mother managed to get more information out of me than I was willing to give.

"And that is?" she called, stopping me before I could escape into the safety of my bedroom.

"I help her find interviews so she can impress her boss and get a promotion. Those interviews keep the attention off me and maybe will keep me out of the news as much as possible."

I could tell she didn't buy our arrangement for one second. Any sane person would see how lopsided it was.

"Are you sure Harper intends to keep you out of the news?"

My brow furrowed at my mother's question. "She understands why I'm trying to keep a lower profile if I can. What are you trying to say, Mom?"

"Harper's boss showed up at the game yesterday. He asked her about a feature story that he wants her to do . . . on you." She slowly trailed off as she registered the look of confusion on my face, realizing that she had stumbled on something that I hadn't known about.

"A feature story on me?" I asked her, wanting to make sure that I'd heard right.

"That's what her boss mentioned," my mother replied cautiously. "Has she not mentioned that to you?"

I chewed on the inside of my cheek. My mind spun its web of questions faster and faster until I couldn't get myself out of it, stuck in the center of it all.

"No. She hadn't mentioned it." Somehow, I managed to give my mother a smile. "Have fun today. If you need me, give me a call."

"Are you going to be okay?" she called after me, the familiar sound of worry that she normally reserved for Jordan laced in her voice.

"Sure, Mom. I'll see you at the game later." The words were hollow and both of us knew it, but my mother turned to leave without pressing the issue any further.

The truth was, suddenly I wasn't sure if I *was* going to be okay.

Chapter 27

Harper

"Will the lighting work in the living room?" Nora asked me as we studied the area.

Jamil and I had showed up, along with my camera crew, about ten minutes ago to Nora frantically trying to finish cleaning their home while Adam and Nolan attempted to wrangle the Steel boys downstairs for the duration of the interview. Jamil had disappeared to go help them.

During the entire car ride over, I couldn't put my finger on it, but the air between us felt off. Jamil was holding back, like he wanted to say something, but was biting his tongue. He'd still gotten out of the car to open my door for me, and I'd even caught him admiring how my legs looked with the skirt I was wearing. But the uncertainty was sitting in the back of my brain, and I was unable to shake it away.

"Nora"—I reached over and placed a gentle hand on her arm—"This will work perfect."

A stray hair fell from Nora's claw clip, and she desperately tried to blow it out of her face. "Are you sure? I can clean up the front sitting room. We don't use it much, but the boys have taken it over for their projects," she began rambling again.

Before she could spiral past the point of no return, I turned her toward the kitchen. "Let's go get you a glass of wine."

Nora sighed before breaking down into a fit of giggles. I eyed her warily, wondering what we'd just walked into this afternoon. "I'm sorry. Between the boys finishing up school and trying to get ready for summer break while also having Adam home all the time now, I think I'm going crazy."

The tiredness on Nora was everywhere—etched in her eyes, seen in the set of her shoulders, even in the shirt that had one too many mysterious stains on it. I wasn't sure what came over me, never in my life had I ever considered asking another woman to hang out. Nora and I were at two different stages in our lives, but that didn't mean she didn't deserve a night off. "Do you want to hang out? Maybe we can have a girls' night and grab drinks. I know we have a stint of away games coming up, but after we come back?"

Maybe being around Olivia, Maggie, and all the other women in this friend group was wearing off on me. Nora looked over at me like I was sent from the heavens above. "That would be amazing. I haven't had any socialization with someone sane since the party Jamil threw for you."

It was almost comical that Nora considered me sane. I felt like I was far from it nowadays. Between desperately chasing after a career that I questioned was worth it some days and navigating friendships for the first time in years, normal was far from what I was feeling. But the warmth I felt from surrounding myself with people who cared was almost better than the pride I felt when nailing the perfect interview.

"I don't think I have your number," I told her as I fished my phone out of my bag. "Why don't you punch it in here for me and I'll text you some dates. Maybe we can snag all the girls to come along."

Nora continued spilling her guts as her fingers flew over my phone screen. Now that the flood gates were opened, it didn't appear that they were going to close anytime soon. "It's been years since Adam and I have spent this much time together and it's a bit of an adjustment. I'm more afraid that he's going to grow resentful of retirement far earlier than he should. He's only forty. He still spends a lot of his free time following as many sporting events as possible. I wonder if he misses it, but he swears he was ready to be done."

Adam, Nolan, and Jamil emerged from the Steels' basement chatting about Jamil's game from yesterday. Adam was talking animatedly about Jamil's ability to hit nearly every pitch that was thrown his way, listing off statistics like he'd written them on the back of his hand.

"Has he ever considered broadcasting?" I asked Nora as the men stopped in the kitchen.

Nora glanced over at me, the wheels in her head turning as she weighed the possibility of something like that for her husband. "He'd be wonderful at that."

"I have some contacts in the industry. Let me write some numbers and emails down. Do you have a pen and a piece of paper?" Nora hurried off to the kitchen to grab a pad for me to write on.

"What are you two doing?" Adam asked as he watched his wife hand me a legal pad. "You've got the look of someone scheming."

"And if we were?" Nora cocked an eyebrow in Adam's direction, her arms crossed over her chest. Her husband raised his hands, clearly knowing after so many years of marriage what conversations he needed to bow out of.

"Harper, I think we've got everything ready," Neil called out from the living room.

"Perfect. Thank you." I turned to Nolan and Adam. "Are you two ready?"

As the three of us settled into our chairs, I made a point to make eye contact with Nolan first. "I only want to highlight the amazing careers you both had, while discussing what it's been like transitioning out of the uniform. You can share as much or as little as you want. I won't pry for more than you're willing to give me. If you want to stay surface level, like one of the previous postgame interviews I've done with you, that's fine."

His shoulders visibly relaxed away from his ears. "You didn't seem to cut Derek quite the same deal." The mirth in his eyes told me he'd appreciated seeing Derek answer the hard questions for the first time in his career.

"It's Derek. Don't you think he deserved it?"

Both Nolan and Adam doubled over in laughter. When Nolan picked his eyes back up to meet mine, there were tears streaming from the corners. "I knew I liked you."

I adjusted my jacket to make sure it was sitting properly before signaling to Neil that I was ready. "Are you both ready?"

My eyes cut toward the kitchen to try and grab Jamil's eye and encouragement. But instead of giving me a smile and a thumbs up like he'd done before, his attention was focused on his phone in his hands. My heart sank as I tried to tell myself his behavior had nothing to do with me.

But what if it does?

As soon as the camera started rolling, I fell into the familiarity of an interview, pushing my concerns for Jamil to the back of my mind. "Nolan Hill and Adam Steel. The two of you are both infamous for the success you had in your careers and even stirred up some conversation into how long your careers would last."

"Probably too long some may say," Nolan coughed, and the two men shared a lighthearted laugh together.

"The decision to lengthen your careers one more season seemed to pay off for you both. In fact, both of you ended with a win on the biggest stage of your respective sports, which many cannot say they had the opportunity to do." This was the part of my interviews which I enjoyed the most, the first question that would set the tone for the remainder of our time together. "Do you feel as though that decision was worth it?"

Nolan gestured for Adam to answer first. The retired pitcher cleared his throat, a thoughtful expression crossing his face as he considered my question. "It's never an easy decision to take the uniform off for the last time.

For many of us, we've been playing our sports for most of our lives. Playing has become interwoven into our very identities. I remember my father telling me that I'd know when it was time to finally make that decision. I wasn't chasing a World Series win. I was playing out every ounce that I had left in me. But I knew the moment I realized that my boys were growing up at a rate far too fast. I didn't want to miss more than I had to."

"And you, Nolan? Was playing one more season worth it? I do recall from our previous interviews that some of your desire to play again stemmed from wanting a Super Bowl win. I'm certain that was an extremely rewarding moment when you achieved that goal." I didn't miss Adam trying to hide a growing smirk that was directed toward his friend. During my research process, Olivia had told me that Adam's friendship had been long-standing, and his advice was highly sought after by Nolan.

"Many of my critics would have liked to have seen me retire two years earlier, but if I had listened to them, I wouldn't have figured out that I am more than the jersey and I wouldn't have met my wonderful girlfriend. Those two things are much more important than any Super Bowl win or line in a history book." I could practically hear the women across America swooning at Nolan Hill talking about his love for Lottie. Only one without a heart wouldn't find the notion sweet.

"The transition from on the field to off the field permanently is often quite difficult for most athletes, as Adam mentioned. How have the two of you been fairing?" I could already tell this interview would bring the masses of Chicago sports fans together. Between the friendship of Nolan and Adam and the cross-sport interview, this was sure to be as big of a hit as my interview with Derek.

"Coaching has been unexpectedly fulfilling," Nolan jumped in when he noticed the color drain from his friend's face. "I hadn't given much thought to what I'd do after my career was over, but with the guidance of my family, I decided to stay with the Bobcats to coach the next generations of quarterbacks. I've found coaching to be just as challenging, maybe even more so, than playing. It's exponentially more fulfilling and I can only hope that I make enough of a difference in the players' lives and careers that I can continue doing this in the long-term."

By the time Nolan had finished answering my question, very little color had returned to Adam's face. He looked lost and panicked when he realized it was his turn to answer.

Before it became too obvious that Adam was struggling, I jumped to his rescue, determined not to let this interview go off the rails. A good reporter not only had to find a story to tell, but they had to make sure the story was delivered properly.

"Adam, you have been such a steady presence in the sports world. Between your mentorship of young athletes and your celebration of sport. Have you considered settling into a job that realigns you with the community?"

The color returned to Adam's face quickly as he discreetly let out a breath between his lips. "Are you asking me if I should take your job, Harper?"

A surprised laugh burst out of me, and I rushed to cover my mouth with the back of my hand. A mischievous gleam was the only sign that Adam knew what kind of a comment he'd just delivered.

"Maybe not *my* job," I joked back. "But I do believe the sports industry could use your analysis of the game. I think the industry is better off with both of you still in it to some capacity."

The deep appreciation on Adam's face would go down as one of my favorite moments in an interview to date. The rest of the conversation continued off without a hitch. Both men shared their favorite moments within their careers while discussing tips for those coming up to retirement about how best to handle it. The amount of vulnerability they displayed was touching and by the time I called for the interview to wrap, I felt the three of us had developed a bond that hadn't been there before.

"Derek wasn't kidding when he said you are talented," Nolan told me as the three of us stood up from our chairs in the living room and walked over to the kitchen where Nora had poured everyone a glass of wine.

"That's very kind of you," I told him as I accepted my glass from Nora.

"Don't let her fool you," Jamil jumped in. "She's too modest for her own good. If there's one thing she's excellent at, it's hunting for a good story."

Jamil stood across the kitchen, looking at everyone but me. I flashed him a confused look, hoping to catch his eye, but he turned to ask Nolan a question about the upcoming training camp instead. My heart clenched from the rollercoaster of emotion that Jamil was sending me on. His words were a compliment wrapped in barbed wire. If I didn't figure out what had gotten into him soon, I feared that I would simply bleed out.

"What exactly is going on between the two of you?" I started at the question before realizing that Nora had sidled up next to me.

"What do you mean?" I asked her, my eyes still locked on the side of Jamil's face. I desperately wanted to grab his attention and see one of those smiles that he saved just for me.

"Jamil's attention seems to be centered around you lately." Nora spun the stem of her wineglass between her fingertips as she waited for my reply.

"I don't think much of anything will happen between us," I told her with my eyes still cast toward Jamil, sadness washing over me as I realized my words could very well be the truth. "There are things in both of our lives that we're preoccupied with."

"Are you talking about Jordan?" Nora asked me, her voice hushed.

My eyes snapped to hers. "You know about Jordan?"

Nora's eyes filled with sadness as she, too, looked over at Jamil who was deep in conversation with her husband and Nolan.

"It's been weighing quite heavily on Jamil lately. Between Jordan walking out of treatment what feels like every other month, as well as asking Jamil for more money to gamble with . . ." Nora trailed off with a sigh. "I'm not sure how he deals with it all."

Gambling.

The pieces started to fall together—treatment, his complicated relationship with his brother, his frustration, and his concern over his well-being. My heart broke for Jamil and his family. Addiction was a terrible beast that took hold of a loved one, its claws sometimes sinking so deep that it never let them go. Other times, people had to fight with everything they had to get out of its grip. The worst realization was when your loved one didn't even try to get better—broken promises and meaningless words.

My boss came to mind. This was exactly what he'd be looking for. The best player in the league dealing with an older brother who was in rehabilitation for a gambling problem.

I finally understood why Jamil had been trying so hard to stay out of the news. He didn't want reporters looking too closely, fearful that they'd take advantage of Jordan's situation for a few clicks or a moment of reporting triumph that would only wreak havoc in his family's life.

Are you willing to do that?

Are you willing to ruin whatever relationship you have with Jamil to climb a ladder for a company that would replace you without a second thought?

"I will say," Nora continued, oblivious that I was still reeling from what she'd told me. "I've never seen him happier than these past few months. Even right after spring training, I remember him coming back from Florida with an extra pep in his step and now it makes sense if that was where the two of you had met."

"I'm sure that was just a coincidence," I told her. "He had a great spring training and with the season starting, I'm sure he was just excited to get back at it."

Nora cocked an eyebrow at me. "Sure, we can go with that."

Before I caught sight of him, I could feel Jamil coming closer. My body somehow tuned to his, like it was an extension of my own. He'd stopped a few feet away and even that distance felt like an ocean. Whatever was going on inside his head was a mystery to me, but I was going to make it my mission to find out.

"Are you ready to go?" he asked me. Nobody else in the room caught the lack of warmth in his words. I held his gaze, wanting him to convey to me what was wrong. He tore his eyes from mine, his lips pressing together tightly.

"Yes, I am." I grabbed my bag from the counter and turned to thank Nolan and Adam. "You two were amazing. Thank you for agreeing to do this. The message the two of you had will resonate with so many people."

"You have a gift," Nolan told me. "I think your future is quite bright."

I walked over to give him a hug first before turning to Adam. "I was serious when I said I think the industry could use you. I left some people for you to contact with Nora. If that's what you want."

Adam reached out to pull me into a hug. The tension I'd witnessed in him during the interview nowhere to be seen. "I really appreciate that. I think I've sat around at home long enough. By the end of the month, I think I'll run out of home improvement projects to do around the house, and I need to get out of Nora's hair."

"Thank you both again. I'm sure I'll see you soon."

"We're planning on making it to a game in the near feature," Nolan told me as he cuffed Adam on the shoulder. "We want to watch Jamil in action this season. Especially since he's somehow managing to top his performance from last season."

Jamil ducked his head and pulled his keys out of his pocket. "I think that's our cue to leave before Adam starts listing off statistics around my performance again."

I followed behind him as we left the Steels' home. When Jamil walked around to the driver's side and didn't bother with opening my door, I knew I hadn't been imagining it all.

Chapter 28

Jamil

"Okay, what is going on with you?" Harper asked me the second she got into the passenger seat.

I didn't answer right away as I turned around in the Steels' driveway and headed back toward the road.

"It's been less than twenty-four hours since the game ended last night. What happened since then? I thought we were fine!"

My emotions were still warring inside of me. Throughout the entire interview, I cycled between feeling so proud of Harper and feeling betrayal if she really was going to write a story on me after I'd told her I was trying my best to avoid as much press as I could. It felt wrong to think that she was no different than the other sharks that circled until they smelled blood in the water, attacking with no sign of remorse.

"Are you writing a story on me?" My voice was barely above a whisper, but it still seemed to echo inside the quiet of the car.

"I'm sorry?"

"My mother mentioned that she met your boss yesterday at the game and he told her that you were covering a feature story on me this season." Harper closed her eyes and let out a long breath before she leaned back in her seat.

I thought she wasn't going to respond as the silence continued to stretch on between us. "Can we have this conversation not in the car?"

"I was going to cook you dinner tonight to celebrate another successful interview," I told her, even though celebrating was the last thing I felt like doing right now.

"I would just like to have this conversation when you're not behind the wheel of a car."

My mind was already taking off at the speed of light with questions.

Did that mean she thought I was going to get angry enough to put us in danger?

Was it worse than I thought?

Did I really start falling for someone that was only using me this entire time?

Was any of it real?

"That's probably best," I told her as I lightened the death grip I had on my steering wheel.

Harper looked like she wanted to say something else, desperation in her eyes. I hated that all I wanted to do was reach over for her hand to reassure her. I hated that seeing her upset affected me the way that it did, despite the lingering unknown of her intentions. It felt like whiplash with how quickly my mind went from the woman I was getting to know, how sweet and kind she was, to the person who could do something like this.

The only sense of rationality I had left whispered, *you don't know the whole situation, nor do you know the topic of the story.*

"Jamil," Harper started as I pulled into the driveway, completely lost in my thoughts.

"Let's wait until we get inside," I told her as I hit the garage door opener.

"No, Jamil. Look!" Harper was pointing toward my front door, which was sitting slightly ajar.

"What the hell?" I threw the car in park, not even bothering with pulling it into the garage before I undid my seatbelt and took off. Our conversation forgotten.

"Where's your mom?" Harper's voice was full of panic as she thought about the worst-case scenario.

"She was going to an off-Broadway show tonight, I think." My brain felt like it was moving through molasses as I barreled toward my front door, every thought unclear.

"Wait!" Harper called after me.

I whirled around, my foot on the first step up to my front porch, to see her shutting her door and racing after me. "No," I told her. "You stay out here. We don't know if anyone's still inside."

"We should call 911. You shouldn't go in either!" Her eyes were wide and wild-looking as she glanced between me and the door.

"It'll be okay. Call 911 and tell them my house has been broken into."

Harper reached out for me, but I took another step up onto my front porch. "We could be sitting ducks out here. I'm just going to look."

Before I could even push the door open, Harper was pulling me backward. "You could be a sitting duck walking inside there. 911 is going to tell us to wait in the car until police show up. You don't need to go in there and be a hero. Let them canvas it first."

Her grip tightened when I glanced back to the door, her hand shaking with fear that I would barrel inside anyways.

"Fine. Call them." The previous disappointment and anger that had been building up all day seemed less important. The only thing on my mind was making sure that we were safe as I wrapped an arm around Harper's waist and escorted her back to the car.

I could hear the 911 operator telling her that we'd done the right thing by waiting on the police before heading inside. The closest unit was five minutes out and those minutes we waited felt like the longest of my life.

As soon as Harper hung up the phone, she turned to look at me, still too hesitant to come closer than a few feet. The fear on her face mirrored the emotion racking my body. None of the previous animosity I had in the car was left as soon as her hand slipped into mine and she let me pull her into my arms.

You can forgive her, my brain whispered to me as we sank into each other for support. *You can forgive her if it means you get to keep her. Nothing worth having is ever easy.*

In my heart, I knew that whatever Harper was doing, she meant well.

The sirens could be heard a few blocks away, growing louder the closer they got until the lights were visible on top of the cop car as it came racing down the street. Neither of us had said a word since Harper had hung up the 911 call, our eyes locked on the front door still sitting ajar.

"I hope they didn't take anything of importance," I heard Harper say quietly as we watched two more cop cars arrive as backup.

"I don't care about anything in the house," I told her, squeezing her in tighter to my body. I was thankful that neither of us had been here. That my mother hadn't been here.

"You should call your mom and tell her not to come home yet," Harper suggested as the cops approached us.

"Have you searched the home yet?" one of the officers asked us. I shook my head.

"Can you give us a quick overview of the layout of your home before we go in?" one of the officers asked me.

I walked him through the floor plan, including areas of interest—like the safe I had set behind a photo in my bedroom or my upstairs office where my files were kept.

The cops left me standing on my front lawn—helpless and only able to watch them enter through the front door. I sent a text to my mother letting her know what had happened and to avoid coming home for a bit.

"It'll be okay." Harper appeared next to me, her hand resting gently on my forearm.

"I'm just trying to figure out why. We don't get break-ins in this neighborhood. And why only my house?"

Had my fame grown too much? Had all this attention brought this upon me? Should I have listened to Nico when all of this started happening at the end of last season and considered security?

Harper stayed quiet, only moving so her back pressed into me and provided me something solid to focus on as we waited for the officers to come back out.

"All clear!" the first officer shouted out to us as they walked back out the front door.

I reached down to slip Harper's hand into mine as we went to meet them on the front porch.

"Before you go inside, we want to ask that you don't touch anything to avoid tampering with potential evidence, unless you clear it with us first."

"Evidence?" Harper asked, trying to catch a glimpse of the living room.

One of the officers turned to address me. "This is going to be treated as a crime scene. If you could go through the home and look for anything you think is missing before letting us know for our reports, we'd appreciate it. We'll have some questions for you afterward to see if you have any idea of who could have done this."

My eyes settled on the open door as I prepared myself to go in. Harper squeezed my hand to grab my attention, "Do you want me to go in with you?"

"Please," I replied. "Maybe you'll see something I don't."

The officers stepped aside to let us enter.

It was strange crossing the threshold into my own home, the one place I considered a sanctuary from the rest of life, only to see it devolved into chaos. The entry table had been overturned, every drawer in the kitchen had been yanked open. The living room entertainment center was ransacked. There wasn't a cabinet or drawer that had been missed as Harper and I worked our way through the house. Each room making my heart drop even further.

I wasn't even sure where to start on a list of things that could have been taken based on the state of the place. At first glance, all the larger valuables had been passed over. The television still hung on the wall in the living room, the more expensive appliances were on the counter in the kitchen, and the art that I had imported was still there.

"This feels like they were looking for something very specific," Harper told me, noticing much of the same as we walked toward my bedroom. "This wasn't a smash and grab. They left too many things of high value."

The bedroom looked like the rest of the house. Both nightstands had been left open, the contents thrown all over the bed. All my clothes in my closet had been tossed in a pile in the middle, every shoe box overturned, and every drawer emptied.

I felt numb as I looked at the place I loved coming home to, torn apart like a war zone. The only thing keeping me grounded was Harper's hand in mine. It wasn't until I saw the painting next to my dresser that covered my safe that I had an inkling of what had happened.

The painting was on hinges and had been thrown open, along with the safe it was hiding. I normally kept a few thousand dollars of cash in there for emergencies, along with some of my more expensive watches. Now I was staring at an empty safe with nothing inside of it.

My stomach curdled. The world came to a sudden halt. I'd never experienced shock before, but the way my blood roared through my ears was jarring.

"What's wrong?" Harper asked me. She stepped in front of my frozen body, trying to draw my focus away from the mess around us. "Tell me what's going through your mind right now. You stopped dead in your tracks the second you saw the safe had been emptied."

"This feels like a cover-up job," I told her. She nodded in agreement, taking in the hurried way the person had ransacked every drawer. "Almost methodical. As if someone knew exactly what they were looking for. A random break-in wouldn't have found the safe. If they hadn't bothered with any of the other art out in the living room, why would they in here? The only thing I can think about is that they knew that the safe existed and the only people that know about the safe are myself . . ."

"And who?" Harper reached out to squeeze my hand for encouragement. "Who else knew?"

I stared into that empty safe a few moments longer because once I spoke the words out loud, it would make the betrayal that much more real. "My brother. He is in some trouble with a debt he couldn't pay. He asked me to pay it for him, but I refused. I guess he took matters into his own hands."

Harper's lips parted slowly. My mother had given her a few details about Jordan, but she was still largely in the dark when it came to the extent of my brother's problems. She was trying her best to be there for me, but without the full story, she was left in the dark.

"Let's go talk to the officers outside and then I think you and I have a lot to discuss."

To no one's surprise, Harper didn't press me for details immediately. Instead, she slipped her arm through mine—always there to provide me silent support as we walked back out of my trashed home. A home that had been wrecked by my very own family.

"Do you mind if I go pack a few things for him while he talks to you?" Harper asked the officers as soon as we walked back out the front door. "I'll avoid all the areas that Jamil thinks will be important for you. I just want to grab him some clothes and toiletries."

"That's fine," an officer told her.

My head felt full of cotton when it came to her, but my heart clenched as I watched her walk back into my home, sparing me from having to do it myself.

"I know who did this," I told the officers once Harper had disappeared inside of my house. I recalled the empty safe sitting ajar in my room and the only other person who knew of its existence. The pieces started to fall into place. Jordan wanting to visit me at my home. His disappearance right when we arrived. The pressure he felt to pay off his previous debts.

One of the officers looked at me expectantly, his pen hovering over his notepad.

"It was my brother." Only the smallest raise of an eyebrow was any indication that the officers were surprised by the news. I walked them through the past few years, fighting the struggle to detail my brother's life since moving to Chicago.

When I told them about Jordan's recent visit to my home, the officers' interest piqued. "When he was here, did you notice anything strange from him?"

I'd been through plenty of moments where stress levels ran high, but nothing compared to this moment with my heart pumping loud enough that my ears began ringing. The only memory my brain could cling to was the stretch of time when we'd first arrived at my house and Jordan was nowhere to be found. Part of me wished I could disprove my own instincts, but my gut told me I wasn't wrong.

The disappointment racked through my body as the officers finished their notes. I barely registered one of them asking me if I had a place to stay for the next few days at least while they continued their investigation and for my own safety.

"He'll stay with me." Harper emerged back out of the house with a bag slung over her shoulder, saving me from gaping at the officers who were looking at me like they should call an ambulance to the scene before I passed out.

Her arm slipped around my waist and the pressure was the only thing keeping me from toppling over as she guided me back toward my car.

"Do you have the keys?" she asked me as she gently patted down my front pockets before locating them. "Let's get you to my place so you can lie down."

The wariness in her eyes was the same as in the officers' as she helped me into the passenger seat and reached across my body to buckle me in. I'd had a couple of panic attacks in my life—after being cornered in the grocery store by two fans who wouldn't let me go or the time I'd gone out for drinks with Tommy right after the World Series win and the bar we rented to celebrate in downtown Chicago ended up getting swarmed with fans. But this felt completely different.

My thoughts were detached from my body, floating around me as Harper put the car into drive and we pulled away from the house. The lights from the cop cars flashed against the front façade of my home rhythmically. I knew that this would be plastered all over the news tomorrow, but the despair I felt for my brother's betrayal was taking too much of my energy for me to care.

I heard Harper on the phone with my mother, filling her in on what had happened.

"How's Jamil?" Harper glanced over at me warily as she navigated back into the city toward her apartment.

"I'm not sure," she told my mother. "He hasn't said much since we left."

"Let him know I'll call him tomorrow. I managed to get a flight home tonight. I board in thirty minutes. My husband thought it would be best if we reconvened on what to do about Jordan. We've let Jamil carry too much of this on his own."

I ended up in a guest bedroom with grey walls and a white comforter that I sunk into immediately. Harper set a glass of water down on the nightstand and unpacked the things she had grabbed for me before we left my house. She cracked the door, leaving me to fend off the beast inside my head that was roaring at me, taunting me, telling me that nothing I did would ever bring my brother back to me.

You're a fool for continuing to believe in him when time and time again he proves you wrong.

Chapter 29

Harper

Before going to bed last night, I'd called Tommy to let him know what had happened. He offered to meet us at my apartment, but I told him that Jamil wanted to go to bed, leaving out that he hadn't spoken a word from the moment we left his house to the second I helped him into the guest room bed. Tommy told me that he'd call their manager to fill him in and I woke up to a text this morning indicating that Jamil was to stay home from the game today. He'd already reached out to Derek to see if he was available to help keep Jamil company while I was away at work.

This was what having people that truly cared about you was like.

It was already nine in the morning and the guest bedroom remained dark. I sipped on my morning coffee while I stared at the blank document in front of me. There was still not a single word that I'd written on Jamil's story, but I was up against a clock that was quickly running out of time. The dry-erase board had been wiped clean and discarded back to its box to avoid Jamil seeing his name in black ink on my wall.

I listed out what I did know—his stats for the season so far, his charitable contributions, the care he put into his friendships, and then I hesitated when it came to writing down his family troubles.

Terry Wilson would be happy to receive a story detailing everything going on with Jamil's brother like some gossip column with no morals. If I delivered a piece like that, I knew that Terry would personally hand me the promotion I'd been working so hard for. But that wasn't the kind of story I wanted to put out into the world.

Not only would I be betraying Jamil's trust, but I would also be doing him a disservice.

The world chalked Jamil Edman up to his accolades and statistics, but they had no idea the kind of person he truly was. They didn't see the selflessness he had when it came to his family or how he would do anything for his friends to celebrate and uplift them the same way the world continued to do to him.

I knew that Jamil hated the attention he got, and he wished the public would look elsewhere—at his teammates, at other players, at *anybody* but him.

My fingers began to fly across my keyboard. Jamil may hate the focus that was put on him because of how charming he was and how successful he was, but everything was surface level. So why not give them what they wanted?

"Hey," a voice croaked, startling me out of my writing stupor.

Jamil stood in the doorway of the guest room, still in the rumpled clothes from yesterday. Dark circles were forming under his eyes despite the heavy sleep he'd fallen into the second I'd pushed him back onto the guest bed last night.

"Good morning." The tension in the room was palpable.

"Where's your shower?" he asked me, still trying to rub the sleep out of his eyes.

"The door just to your right. There are towels in the closet and I put everything I grabbed from your shower last night in there already."

He turned to walk into the bathroom before pausing. "Thank you for doing all of that yesterday."

There was so much still unspoken, between our conversation in the car on the way back to his house and the break-in.

"Of course," I told him, because I meant it. No matter what it was that Jamil was upset about yesterday, the least I could do was be there for him through this.

When I heard the shower turn on in the bathroom, I glanced back at my Word document, now one page long. Jamil tried so hard to keep as much as he could from the public, but what if he didn't? What if he told them *exactly* what it was like to be him?

Steam billowed out of the bathroom as the door opened. Followed by Jamil with a towel slung low on his hips. It took everything in me not to stare at the hard planes of his body, especially amid everything that had happened.

"Tommy messaged me this morning. Your coaches want you to stay home today." Jamil walked back out of the guest room, pulling a t-shirt down over his head. His abs flexed before disappearing underneath the fabric.

"They texted me this morning." His voice was hoarse, like he'd spent all day yelling, despite the fact that he'd barely spoken a single word last night.

"Your mother also flew back to Florida last night," I added, not sure if he had caught my conversation in the car with his mother. I watched him cautiously as he slid onto one of the open barstools next to me.

"She texted me, too."

There was no sign of the chipper version of him that I was used to. Instead of being painted in multicolor, he was one shade of grey—all the life sucked out from him.

"Do you want breakfast?" I asked, trying anything to catch a glimpse of his smile.

"Have you had anything?"

"My coffee."

Jamil rolled his eyes, the barest smirk playing on his lips. My heart fluttered at the sight, relieving some of my worry. "Coffee isn't a meal, Harper. I'll cook us something."

I stared at his back as he investigated my fridge, trying to figure out what he could use for a meal. I couldn't remember the last time I got groceries with all the traveling, so I was sure the options were limited.

"Maybe we should order something to be delivered?" he suggested, the same cheeky smirk still on his face.

"Good idea," I agreed, before falling silent again. There was so much I wanted to ask him, but I'd only risk sending him back into his own head just as he was starting to reemerge.

"What are you working on?" he asked as he ordered breakfast for us.

"A feature story," I started before hesitating to tell him that he was the subject of it. Even if I thought I had a good reason for it. "About you."

Jamil blew out a long breath, like he was releasing all the air in his body. That barest hint of a smile was no longer there.

"My mother was right," Jamil replied as he set his phone down. "You're writing something on me?"

I wanted to shut down or disappear under the weight of his gaze. Maybe it was because of my relationship with my mother, but I avoided conflict at all costs. When there was no way of avoiding it, my body went into fight or flight and I never knew which one I'd end up choosing. Right now, everything in me screamed to diffuse, deflect, do anything to bring a smile back to Jamil's face.

I'd never experienced true disappointment before I saw Jamil's aversion for this conversation. Even the disappointment I felt for the lack of movement in my career paled in comparison to the sinking feeling in my stomach right now.

"Jamil, listen—"

Jamil turned to look at me and I was stunned into silence at the anger I saw there. In the few months I'd known him, I'd never seen him angry. Not when the fans demanded too much and not even when it came to his brother. "I thought we had an agreement. I thought you understood *why* we had an agreement."

"It's for my promotion!" I jumped to interrupt him before he shredded my heart any further. I needed him to know that I wasn't doing this to hurt him. "My boss asked me to write a story on you after the first game I covered and has been leveraging it against me for the promotion."

My stomach clenched as my brain screamed at me for how selfish I was for not pushing back against Terry. Even after getting to know Jamil further and realizing I had grown feelings for him.

What did that say about me?

Jamil stared at me for a few seconds before he spoke again. "Have you been collecting information behind my back? This entire time? I told you I wanted to date you and now I guess it makes sense why you never said anything back. To save whatever morals you have left?"

Each accusation felt like a dagger sinking into me, piercing my most vulnerable thoughts. "Jamil, that's not what happened. That's not what I was doing."

"Are you going to write about this? About my brother?" Jamil continued.

"No!" I exclaimed. The cursor on my screen blinked at me, taunting me as it watched this moment crumble around me. "I wouldn't do that to you, to Jordan, or your family. Please, just let me explain."

"I'm not sure there is anything you can say that will make any of this better."

Maybe he's right. He deserves someone better.

"I get why you're so against having more coverage than necessary in the media. Journalism nowadays loves to have clickable titles that draw readers in despite the damage it does to the subject of the material. But that's not what I'm wanting to do." Desperation crawled up my throat, raking it raw, as tears threatened to build in the corners of my eyes. "I want to write a feature that showcases exactly what it's like to be you this year—the good, the bad, the ugly. I wasn't going to write about Jordan. That's not my story to tell. I want people to realize everything you do for the community and what you have to endure to play a sport you love."

Jamil sighed and any hope I had at him seeing some reason in my explanation evaporated. "I don't need them to have more pieces of me than they already have."

The thought of Jamil walking out the door of my apartment flashed through my mind and the fear of only ever seeing him at games gripped my entire body. Was my job so important that I would risk losing one of the first real connections I'd had with anyone in my life?

"I can scrap the story. I'll figure out something else to do to get the promotion. The interview with Adam and Nolan is set to come out in the next couple of days. Maybe that will be enough."

The sound of a notification on his phone filled the silence between us.

I wanted to reach out to touch him, but I shoved my hands under my thighs instead. "I don't want you to focus on this when you have everything with Jordan going on."

"I'm not sure there's anything left to worry about." Jamil had yet to look at me since I first delved into my long-winded explanation for the feature story. His eyes remained firmly on his hands as he interlaced and unlaced his fingers.

"What do you mean?" I asked him. We were still waiting for an update from the cops on the investigation or even word from the facility that Jordan was supposed to be checked into.

"I'm not sure I have any care left in me when it comes to my brother. I told myself I wouldn't give up on him. But this feels like the last straw. If I give him another chance without him proving to me that he deserves it, I'm just enabling him. He thinks that there will always be a safety net for him on every fall he has. I can't be that safety net anymore."

My heart broke for the man sitting across from me. I saw a glimpse of the little boy that grew up following his older brother, wanting to do as he did and be what he was. Now he was coming to the stark realization that his hero was just a troubled man who was as lost in this world as he was.

"You've done everything you can for him. Now it's his choice." I laid my hand on top of his and gave it a squeeze. "Are we okay?"

Jamil took a moment to respond, and my breathing slowed with each second that passed. "Yeah, we're fine."

His response felt forced, tentative, with no real meaning behind it. He was telling me what I wanted to hear. The silence that followed his words wanted to swallow me whole. We'd taken three steps forward only to take five back with this single conversation. All the progress we'd made had crumbled to the ground. Despite his reassurance, the feeling that nothing between us would ever be the same echoed in my mind.

Chapter 30

Jamil

"He broke into your home and cleaned your safe out?" Derek asked as he came back from his kitchen with three beers. He passed one to Tommy and then the other to me.

"That's what it seems like," I told him. The facility had called me earlier to confirm that Jordan was once again no longer there.

"Why would he do that?" Tommy asked me as he took a sip from his beer.

As soon as Harper left for the game, I texted Derek and asked if I could come over. I needed some time in a neutral space where I wasn't reminded of Harper and her feature story or my brother. Tommy came as soon as the game was over. They'd managed to scrape out a win to keep us in the lead for our league, but worrying about our standings was the farthest thing from my mind.

"He texted me about a month ago that he was in some trouble with a bookie. I don't know if they came to collect or what. But he asked me for money, and I'd told him no. I think he took matters into his own hands this time."

Derek blew a breath out between his lips.

"And he knew where your safe was?" Tommy asked.

I nodded my head, a sweeping wave of disappointment washing over me.

"He helped me move in when we first came to Chicago and lived with me for a few months. When he came over to visit with me last week, I think he was scoping out if it was still there and if it still had anything in it. I'm just surprised he remembered the code."

It was difficult to say why Jordan was doing this. His back was against a wall, and he'd lashed out, hoping to solve his problems without having to face himself in the mirror.

"You're less distraught over this than I thought you would be," Derek noted, his eyes tracking every time I brought the bottle of beer up to my lips.

"I've already spent too long worrying about him or trying to help him without getting any gratitude in return. I can't do it any longer."

Tommy and Derek exchanged a look, clearly worried over my aloof point of view on all of this.

"If that's how you feel about your brother, then what else is bothering you?" Tommy studied me with the eyes of someone who knew me like the back of his own hand.

"You think that I'm upset about something other than my brother?" Tommy and Derek continued to stare at me with the kind of worry that made me want to crawl out of my skin. When the silence began to stretch on past the point of uncomfortable, I let out a sigh. For the first time, I hated having friends that knew me so well. "It's Harper."

"What could possibly be wrong between the two of you?" Tommy asked. "You seemed closer than ever at the gala last Tuesday."

"I thought the two of you were moving toward something more serious," Derek added. "You work so well together. I could see it at my interview with her. The support you gave her and how she fed off that was like watching a couple that had been together for years."

If the sharp sting of betrayal wasn't still present, I would have even agreed with him. From the first moment I met Harper, we had an instant connection. Conversation had always been easy between us and spending time with her felt like spending time with someone I'd known forever. I had thought after the gala that Harper needed to build more trust between the two of us when she'd hesitated to confirm if she wanted to pursue a relationship with me. But now I was beginning to wonder if her hesitation was born from something else entirely.

"I found out that she's writing a feature story on me," I told them as I downed the rest of my beer.

My phone vibrated on the arm of my chair. The screen lighting up with a text message.

Harper: *Just got back from the game. Wanted to check in to see if you were staying here again tonight. Would love to talk with you before we have to take off for the next bout of away series games in a few days.*

"And that's a bad thing?" Derek asked me.

My eyes were locked on the message, and I had to force myself to turn the phone over before replying. "You know how I feel about all the extra media attention I've gotten after last year. I thought she understood that, and we were under a mutual understanding that she wouldn't cover me. She was going to cover other people to give me some time out of the tabloids."

"But Harper's interviews aren't like typical tabloid fodder." Tommy's response was cautious, like he was trying to avoid poking a bear. "She has always ended up positively highlighting everyone she's interviewed between Derek, Nolan, and Adam. Even the average sports fans have come to enjoy her pre- and postgame interviews because of the light she frames those she's interviewing in. How can that be bad for you? Maybe it'll be a good thing for a change?"

"Why does everyone think I need to respond to the media attention with *more* media attention? That's bullshit."

Derek offered me a small smile. Especially after the way the attention from the Bobcats' fanbase swung from Nolan to him. "Because for the first time the world would get to see you the way we see you."

"Harper didn't tell you she was going to do a feature story?" Tommy asked. He was the most sensible between the three of us, always trying to make sense of something that seemed nonsensical.

"She didn't. I found out because of my mother. Her boss showed up at the last home game I played in and mentioned the feature story that Harper is to write on me to my mother. I had meant to talk to her about it after the interview yesterday with Nolan and Adam, but then we rolled up on my ransacked home and any thoughts about talking through it went out the window. This morning, I walked out to her typing up a document and when I asked her about it, she fully admitted it was a feature story on me that she was working on."

"But she admitted it directly when you asked her?" Derek pressed.

Since when did he become the reasonable one?

"She did, but it doesn't make me feel any better about it right now." I could still see the desperation in Harper's eyes from this morning every time I closed my eyes.

"Harper doesn't have bad intentions, J," Derek continued. "All of us have seen the way she treats you and the way you treat her. We've seen a completely new Jamil these past couple months. You're happier and you're coming around to hang out more. You're willing to go out. You and I both know the reason for all of that. Maybe this is all a misunderstanding that you just need to listen to her more clearly on. You don't walk away from a good woman like that, even if the path to happily ever after is riddled with detours."

Tommy and I both stared at Derek slack jawed. Where was this sage advice coming from? And why was it coming from Derek Allen of all people? He was the happy-go-lucky one out of all of us and now he sounded like he was hung up over someone. Someone that Tommy and I both could guess.

"You sound like you're speaking from experience," I noted casually, thankful for the attention to be taken off me, even for just a moment.

Derek narrowed his eyes. As Tommy sat forward with interest, Derek knew he wasn't going to dodge this one.

"I'm just saying that when you find a woman who cares about you, understands you, and excites you all at once, you find a way to keep her."

Tommy chuckled under his breath as he stood up to dispose of our beer bottles.

"And you've found someone like that?" I pressed, enjoying watching Derek roll his eyes at me.

Everyone knew that Derek had developed a crush on Olivia Thompson. But even though Derek was clearly smitten with her, Olivia seemed to be oblivious of Derek's feelings.

He'd been, for lack of a better term, friend zoned.

"He's found someone, but she doesn't know it yet!" Tommy called from Derek's kitchen. Derek turned a deep shade of red.

"This isn't about me, J." This time I let Derek deflect the attention back to me. I'd poked enough fun at him for the day. "What are you going to do about Harper?"

Despite the hurt that I felt, part of me knew the emptiness I'd feel with Harper no longer in my life would be so much worse.

"I think I will figure out a way to get over it eventually, but I need some space. Tomorrow is a new day."

Tommy came back from the kitchen with a bowl of chips that he poached from Derek's pantry. "Have you asked her to be something more? The two of you have been dancing around each other for a couple months now."

"I did at the gala, actually," I told him as I swiped some chips from the bowl. "I told her what I wanted and she . . . didn't really say anything."

Derek raised an eyebrow in surprise. "Do you think it's because of the story?"

I rubbed at my chest, thinking that it would make the pain there go away. "I'm not sure. But I could be jumping to conclusions. I know her and I have more to talk about after what we already covered this morning, but I just need to give myself some space tonight."

Because the thought of lying on the other side of a wall from her again after everything that had happened would only cloud my judgment. When it came to Harper, just the mere thought of her had me second-guessing everything.

"You're going to crash on my couch then?" Derek joked.

I gave him a smirk and watched his face pale. "It's not getting used for much else, is it?"

Tommy nearly choked on a handful of chips.

"You're such an ass," Derek mumbled as he picked up a chip and threw it at me. I dodged it just in time before it smacked me in the middle of my forehead.

When our laughter died down, Tommy gave me one of his sincerest looks. "There's a reason Harper was brought into your life this year, J. I know that it wasn't to add more chaos onto a year where you're already dealing with so much."

"And you aren't really upset at Harper. What Harper is doing isn't really anything out of the ordinary," Derek added. "You're misplacing your anger. Your relationship with the media has changed because of someone else in your life. Maybe you should consider that."

Long after Tommy left and Derek had gone to sleep, I lay awake on the couch thinking about our conversation. Between dealing with the newfound attention and my brother's worsening condition, I had thought Harper was a breath of fresh air. She was the one person I could be with where everything finally slowed down. But reality never stayed away for long.

Chapter 31

Harper

My phone lay on the kitchen island, still silent, with no texts or calls from Jamil. I'd come home from the game a few nights back to an empty apartment, with a text letting me know that he would be staying at Derek's. I'd spent the better part of our games fighting between trying to get his attention and desperately avoiding making eye contact out of fear of what I'd do once I had it. I couldn't blame him for wanting to stay somewhere else to clear his head and get some space from everything happening in his life all at once. But that didn't stop the ache that was growing in my chest with every minute I spent without him.

"Shit!" I exclaimed as the coffee I'd been pouring overflowed down the sides of my mug and onto the counter.

I swiped a kitchen towel over the spill, my eyes flitting back to my phone with no new notifications. Last night, I'd lain awake long into the night going through almost every decision I'd made over the past four years and wondering how I'd gotten my identity so wrapped up in my career that I'd potentially thrown away the beginnings of something special. I'd done the one thing I promised myself I'd never do—become my mother.

"What did that coffee do to you?" I nearly jumped out of my skin at the sound of Jamil's voice.

He stood in the entry hallway, a backpack slung over his shoulder. The sight of him still nearly stole my breath away, despite the heavy anticipation of seeing each other again. I could have stared at the color of his eyes past the point of what was considered normal if it weren't for him waiting for me to reply.

"I just got distracted," I told him as I finished mopping up the spilled coffee.

Jamil walked further into my apartment and deposited his backpack on one of the empty barstools. "By what?"

His casual disposition was a stark contrast to the racing beat of my heart, as my anxiety grew over the possibility that this could be the point when he changed his mind. Even though he'd told me everything was fine between us, maybe he realized he needed to end whatever was happening between us with the few days of space we had.

But what if he doesn't? What if you were honest with him to a fault? Then you can't regret anything if he still chooses to leave.

"By you. I was distracted by you," I told him.

He walked around the island, keeping enough distance from me that I could still think, but close enough that I could make out the light smattering of freckles across his nose from the sun he was getting.

"I wasn't even here. How could I have been distracting you?" he asked.

Take courage, my heart.

I sucked in a deep breath, preparing myself to do one of the most vulnerable things I'd ever done with Jamil—be completely honest without holding back. "Because you distract me whether you're near me or not. I was waiting on a call or text from you because I was scared that you wouldn't come back."

Honestly, if the situation was reversed, I wasn't sure I would have come back either. Not after someone went behind my back, despite the person's best intentions.

Don't get your hopes up.

But it was already too late.

"Why wouldn't I come back?"

"Because you changed your mind and you realized you were actually upset with me and the feature story." I felt small under his gaze. "And you no longer want to be around me."

"Of course I'm upset, Harper."

I swore my heart stopped beating in my chest.

"That doesn't mean I'm tossing you to the side or I would just walk out without saying a word to you. I just needed a minute to myself to clear my head. A lot has happened lately, and I was overwhelmed. I've since had others much wiser than me, surprisingly, remind me that my anger is misplaced. I took the anger and fear that's been building up for years for my brother and directed that at you. That wasn't fair of me."

Jamil's mouth was tight as he watched me stand across from him trying to process our conversation. He was right that he misplaced some of his anger on me. However, he wasn't wrong for being upset with me. I'd allowed my work life to drive people away in my personal life. Yet here I was trying to pick up the pieces that I had a hand in splintering. If I looked in the mirror in my bathroom, would I see myself or would I see a young Maria Nelson, sacrificing her way to the top?

When I didn't say anything back right away, Jamil continued. "Can you tell me more about your idea for the feature story?"

"It doesn't matter anymore. I should never have agreed to do it. I could have told my boss to pick someone else."

"I want to hear your idea." Jamil stared at me with the same sincerity in his eyes that he did at every interview we'd worked together on this season. He still had respect for me and my craft and that gave me the courage to have this conversation, knowing that he'd listen.

"My boss wanted to cover a story on you." Jamil pressed his lips together into a thin line but didn't interrupt me. "Any journalist after finding out about your brother would have used that for their story. But I couldn't do that to either of you. Especially because, in my opinion, that's not the story worth telling."

I'd discarded my workbag on one of the barstools when I got home from the game last night and I pulled my laptop out so I could show him what I had been planning.

"When anyone covers something about Jamil Edman, they either focus on your statistical achievements, a single-game performance, or something without substance for clicks."

"Like a grocery store run?" Jamil mumbled under his breath, and I chuckled in agreement.

"But no one has covered *you*. They don't know what motivates you to keep playing, which is supporting those you love. They don't know about your origin story and where your love for the game started. They don't know how much you support the surrounding community of Chicago. They don't know how hard life has become for you over the last year because of your success. You've had to change your routines, basically your entire life here in the city to still have some semblance of normality. No one knows any of that unless they know you because you've never shown that part of yourself to the world."

"Because they don't deserve all of those pieces of me."

"Why not?" I pressed him. "You're selling yourself short, Jamil. At your core you want to help others. Think about what that could do on a global level or with the newfound pull that you have. You have this hatred for the media because of the pressure you feel it's brought, but why not embrace it? You can show them how this has affected you and set boundaries on *your* terms. The only reason they put out the ridiculous articles they do is because you've made yourself a prized commodity. You don't give interviews, and no one knows anything about you. A story about what kind of takeout you like to get on a Friday night will sell because you give them nothing else."

"Are you sure you want to be a journalist?" Jamil asked.

"Of course. Why would you ask that?" He, of all people, knew the hard work I'd dedicated to this career.

He knew that I loved getting to showcase people in a light that reflected their best to the world.

"Because a journalist would never pass up an opportunity to run a story like Jordan's, not even if it ruined my life."

Jamil was looking at me with hesitation, like he was waiting for me to say "sike" and run a story that he had worked so hard to keep others from knowing.

"I'm not that kind of journalist, J. That's not how I want to treat people. I want to be known as the reporter that athletes come to when they have a story *they* want to tell. Not someone they dread covering a story on them. I'm sorry I made you feel that I would do something like that to you."

He was quiet for a moment as he considered my words. "I meant it when I said we were okay. Of course I'm going to be upset you kept this from me. But I'm beginning to understand why you did it."

Maybe this is for the best.

"Can I ask you something that's been bothering me though?" Jamil asked. "Did you not respond to me when I told you I wanted to date you because you felt conflicted about your story?"

"It didn't feel right telling you that I wanted to date you, too. Not when I knew I had this story to write. I had been putting it off so far this season and at the time you asked me, I hadn't written anything yet. But it was still there in the back of my mind."

Jamil mulled over my words before he lifted his eyes to mine, the barest hint of his usual playful glint in them. "But you want to date me?"

I choked on a laugh as the tension that had been building inside me finally subsided. "Yes, Jamil. I do."

"This isn't me asking you. It's good to know that when I do, I won't be rejected."

"You're ridiculous."

"Maybe," he replied softly. He paused for a moment. "Can you promise me that next time something like this happens, you tell me from the beginning?"

"Yes." I took a tentative step toward him. "I think I was hoping that it would all disappear, and I'd never have to have the conversation with you, which was stupid of me as well."

Jamil closed the distance between us and wrapped me up in his arms. He held on to me like I was a buoy keeping him above the raging waters of his life, and I held on to him just as tightly to let him know that I was there.

"What about Jordan?" I asked after minutes had passed of us holding each other in the middle of my kitchen.

He untangled himself from my arms and turned to lean on the counter next to us. His shoulders were drawn up toward his ears as he let out a long sigh.

"I feel like I have no other choice but to release him. I've been holding on to the person that I used to know, and I fear that he's no longer that person. If I keep waiting for the time that he'll stop disappointing me and help himself for a moment, I think I'll be waiting forever."

If only I could take some of the weight this decision was putting on him onto my own shoulders. But instead, I wrapped an arm around his waist and allowed him to lean into me. For so long, I'd had to shoulder the challenges of my life on my own. Now I knew that it wasn't having someone that could fix your burdens and make your life easier. It was having someone that allowed you to face it on your own but would pick you up the second you fell.

There was nothing I could do to fix this situation for either Jamil or Jordan. But I could be the one to pick Jamil up and help him keep moving forward.

"You shouldn't look at this as a failure. You've done everything you can to give Jordan more opportunities and you've run out of runway to keep going. That's all. Now he has to fly on his own."

His eyes were glassy when he turned his head to look at me. "It feels like I'm mourning someone who's still alive."

"You haven't lost him," I told him. My hand rubbed an endless circle on his back. "You're just letting him stand on his own two feet."

Jamil nodded his head, trying to force himself to believe in what I was telling him.

"Do you mind if I stay here? After we get back from this round of away series while my house is fixed? They think it will be a couple more weeks before the police are done and the locksmith is finished, not to mention the contractors fixing the damage. I'm sure Derek will let me crash on his couch again if I need to. I wasn't sure if it was appropriate or if you'd want some space—"

I held up a hand to stop him. "I'm right down the road from the stadium and I have an extra room. It would be silly if you went anywhere else."

He stared at me intently. "Are you sure?"

"Positive. Now, you and I have flights to make."

"Are you ready to go back home?"

Home.

I hadn't stopped to consider that tomorrow I'd be back in Washington DC for the first of the next two away series on the Cougars' schedule. I'd lived there for all my adult life, but it had never felt like home, only the place where my parents lived.

"I don't think DC is home anymore," I told him. It had stopped feeling that way the moment I'd packed my life up and left for Chicago.

"Do you think your parents will want to see you?"

The last thing I wanted to think about was enduring another dinner with my parents, but the likelihood of that happening felt high.

"Let's hope not."

Chapter 32

Jamil

We landed in Washington DC a few hours before we were due to be at the stadium. Media was already waiting for us as we made our way to the locker room. My first instinct was to walk right past them like I'd done most of the season to avoid giving them a story I didn't want them to have. But no matter what, articles speculating about the women I signed autographs for or what gym I frequented in the off-season still showed up in the tabloids every day.

Maybe Harper was right and if I gave them *something* they'd stop wanting *everything*.

"Jamil!" One of the regular sports bloggers I recognized was desperately trying to wave me down. Most athletes didn't give him the time of day because he wasn't associated with a big network, even though his following was loyal due to his commitment to delivering unique stories.

"Billy, right?" I asked when I came to a stop in front of him.

Billy's eyebrows shot up when he realized I was talking to him. Tommy stopped a few feet away to talk to someone from a local news station about this series and how we were looking like we could be going deep into the post-season once again.

"Billy Kirk." Billy stuck his hand out for me to shake. "It's a pleasure to get to talk to you, Jamil. You are quite the difficult man to try to get an interview with."

My stomach clenched and I fought to keep a red flush of embarrassment from spreading across my cheeks. I fell in love with baseball as a young kid after going to a game with my older brother and my father, just like so many others before me. Everyone that worked around the sport had their own moment they fell in love with the game of baseball. The only thing that made me any different than anybody else was that I was now the one they were coming to watch. We all fell in love with the impossibility of someone hitting a pitch going so fast that the chances were every one-in-four attempt on average. Yet every game, the impossibility became possible. We all fell in love with the greats who played with their hearts on their sleeves and rejoiced with those in the stands who loved the game as much as them.

Not only had I been doing a disservice to the game by being closed off, but I'd also made it nearly impossible for the little kids in the stands who wanted to be in my shoes when they were older to view me as a role model.

That wasn't the kind of player or person I wanted to be known as.

"What would you like to know, Billy?" I asked and watched the man grow flustered as he realized that I was giving him the opportunity to ask whatever came to mind.

Once he collected himself, he turned on a voice recorder and poised his pen over his notepad, ready to write down what I shared with him. "After last year, it feels like there's not much else you can do to write your name in the record books of the history of baseball. What kinds of goals do you have for this season?"

Instead of forcing myself to give textbook media responses with very little substance, I cleared my throat and told Billy the truth.

"If you'd asked me that during spring training, I would have told you that I wanted to go back-to-back and give the city of Chicago another World Series like the Bobcats won back-to-back Super Bowls."

"But that's changed?" Billy asked, his pen hovering over his notepad.

"If that happens this season, that would be amazing. But it's not my focus. I've had a lot of noise going on outside of the game and I haven't done the best job at managing it all."

It wasn't a secret that I'd gone from just a professional baseball player to being on nearly every advertisement when you turned on the television or having my face on cereal boxes.

"Do you feel that's taken some of your focus away from the game?" Billy flipped to his notes, which I saw were filled with my stats from the previous games. "Besides the game that you did not appear for, I would argue that your performance this season has been arguably better than last season's."

"Baseball has always been my favorite outlet throughout my entire life. No matter what is going on, baseball has always been the best way for me to work through everything." I ignored every instinct in my body screaming at me to stop talking, to stop drawing so much attention to the fact that I was struggling. If people wanted to know why, they'd start to dig and if they dug hard enough . . .

"If your performance has been so spectacular, then why do you feel so unsatisfied?" Billy had been around the game for decades. He'd watched players, some great and some not, come and go. He'd covered stories on some of the best games in baseball history and his eagerness to do right by the game was evident.

"I think that's because I feel so disconnected from the fanbase and the city of Chicago, but it's of my own doing. I want to give the city as much kindness as they've given me."

"You have a record of donating to various charities for the city. For instance, you raised nearly a quarter of a million dollars for the Boys & Girls Club of Chicago, which your teammate Tommy Mikals is deeply involved with."

"I have really enjoyed involving myself with my friends' and teammates' organizations. But I don't feel as though I've done enough myself to showcase my appreciation for this city and I hope to remedy that."

Billy gave me a grateful look before he checked his notes again.

"Jamil, I know that you are tuned in to Chicago sports. What are your thoughts on Nate Rousch being traded to Texas after all the rumors coming out of that clubhouse?"

I didn't know Nate Rousch personally, but there wasn't an athlete or soul on the planet who hadn't heard about the mess that the Chicago Lynx locker room had devolved into at the beginning of the NHL season.

"I don't know Nate personally. I wish him the best in his new adventure down in Texas. I think a fresh start would be good for him and I wish the best for the Chicago Lynx going into post-season."

"Thanks, Jamil." Billy backed away, letting me continue toward the locker room. Tommy was nowhere to be found, having already wrapped up his conversations with the media.

My shoulders felt lighter as I pushed into the locker room to get ready for the game. The media had always felt like such a burden, but maybe Harper was on to something. If I approached them and gave them what *I* wanted to, maybe they weren't as bad as I originally thought.

It was time that I took control of my life again.

*

"Nico," I greeted my agent as soon as he picked up my call.

"Jamil! You should be getting ready for a game here shortly, right?"

"This shouldn't take long," I told him. "I wanted to talk about further business deals and before I tell you what I want to do, I want to make sure you understand that I've thought about this thoroughly and I'm sure."

"Okay," Nico replied hesitantly. Rightfully so since I was about to take his cash cow away.

"I want to start my own charity organization for those recovering from addiction. Is that something you can help me with?"

There was a pause on the other end of the line. I was certain Nico was trying to figure out where this was coming from. Where the connections were. "I can. I'll work on that for you today."

"Great. Also, moving forward, I only want to work for companies that are making an effort at change. Companies with a mission to make *something* better. After my current contracts run out, we can evaluate if I want to move forward with who I'm currently working with. I'm no longer going to take every deal that comes my way. I want to connect with the people that understand why I love this game so much. I want to give back to them."

After my long-winded speech, I was preparing for Nico to try and talk me out of my plan. To tell me that I'd be losing out on money, but I didn't care about the money. I didn't care about the fame or the attention.

"Okay, J." Nico must have heard the determined edge in my voice because he didn't fight it. By the time I hung up the phone, that always-present pressure on my chest had lessened and was almost gone entirely.

*

"Do you want to grab dinner?" Tommy asked me as we walked toward the busses that would bring us back to the hotel. Olivia and Maggie had already boarded and hadn't bothered to wait for us as we showered.

Tonight's game was a blowout, with the Capitols being last in our league and struggling to string together a series win all season.

"Maybe," I started to tell him before I caught sight of Harper standing in the parking lot, her phone pressed to her ear. "Hold on, let me see if Harper would want to come."

"The two of you are okay?" Tommy asked me, not bothering to hide his excitement.

"We're still working through some things, but we're okay." Tommy fist-pumped excitedly at the news as I walked toward Harper. "Hey!"

She turned around and pointed toward her phone to let me know she was speaking with someone. "I can meet the two of you there. You're already there? Why didn't you ask me sooner? No. Fine. Fine!"

I cocked an eyebrow at her as she angrily punched the button to end the call on her phone screen.

"Are you okay?" I asked her.

"No. My parents are at dinner, and they saw the game on the television, so they started calling me during the third inning and wouldn't stop until I picked up the phone just now. They want me to come meet them."

"Do you want company?"

Harper laughed, the sound coming out more like a choked sob. "You've already been subjected to one meal with Maria Nelson. There's no need for you to sit through another one."

"But I haven't met your father yet."

This time Harper rolled her eyes at me. I'd sit through the worst dinner I've ever had a million times over if it meant being the only person in the room that could make her smile like that.

"I couldn't ask you to do that." Harper shook her head, still trying to fight me even though both of us knew her efforts were useless.

"Let me call a car to come pick us up."

"You're going to regret this," Harper warned as I ordered us a taxi.

"There is nothing on this planet that could make me regret spending time with you, Moon."

She let out a long sigh before she closed her hand around mine. "Thank you."

"Anytime," I told her as I reached over to smooth a stray hair that had escaped from behind her ear.

"We'll see if you are still saying that by the end of the night."

Chapter 33

Harper

"Harper!" my mother exclaimed as we walked up to them, drawing the attention of more than one of the tables around us. "And you brought Jamil again! How wonderful. I enjoyed our conversation last time. You were better company than my own daughter."

"Mrs. Nelson, it's a pleasure to see you again. I find your daughter to be the best company, however." Jamil reached out to wrap my normally non-sentimental mother into a hug. Her body stiffened in Jamil's arms before she gave him an awkward pat on the shoulder in return.

Jamil turned to my father who was watching the interaction between his wife and the Chicago Cougars' centerfielder with amusement. "Mr. Nelson, it's wonderful to meet you."

"What a pleasant surprise that our Harper brought you tonight." My father reached out to shake Jamil's hand. "And please, call me Robert."

I didn't miss the curious look my mother was giving me as the four of us took our seats. Bringing Jamil to a family dinner once could be written off as friendly. Bringing him twice was sure to raise a few questions.

A waiter came to take mine and Jamil's drink orders before announcing that my parents had already ordered me a steak and asked Jamil what he would like. The interlude was only putting off the inevitable conversation that would take place. Once the waiter stepped away, my mother wasted no time.

"Happy early birthday." My father slid an envelope across the table toward me. His signature illegible doctor's scrawl was visible on the back. I slipped my thumb under the lip and ripped the top open. The card had a cheesy quote about the gift that daughters were and inside was more of my father's handwriting. He'd signed it from himself and my mother, but I had a feeling that she had no idea he'd gotten me a birthday card.

"Birthday?" Jamil asked, looking at me like I'd seriously offended him.

"It's not until the fifteenth of June."

Jamil narrowed his eyes at me as if that information did little to make up for the fact that I'd left out something so important.

"That's just under two weeks away."

I narrowed my eyes as I watched him send a text off on his phone before sliding it back in his pocket.

"So how is your pursuit for a promotion going?" My mother was trying to come across as nonchalant, but her goal for the conversation was clear.

"That interview you did with Derek Allen was quite something," my father chimed in. He gave me a soft smile that I returned. While my father was often the buffer between me and my mother, when the chips settled, he was always on my mother's side of the conversation rather than mine.

"I have another one coming out. I think the team said either tomorrow or the next day. I interviewed Adam Steel and Nolan Hill."

Jamil gave me an encouraging smile. However, I couldn't help but notice the absence of his hand on my leg or in mine. Even though he'd offered to come with me tonight to this dinner because he knew how hard it was for me to be around my parents, there was still a distance between us that was my own fault.

"And has your boss mentioned anything about these interviews you're doing? Are they helping you toward your goal or are you exhausting yourself and your team over a lost cause?"

No congratulations. No compliments over securing another interview with respected athletes. No encouragement at all.

I glanced over at Jamil. His eyes were intense as he tried to convey to me that *he* was there, and *he* believed in me. I'd watched him struggle to come to terms with having to cut ties with his brother, his own family. But after realizing there was nothing else he could do to help him and continuing to do so was only bringing more stress into his own life, his decision had become obvious.

Maybe the same applied to my own life.

What if I just got up and walked away right now?
Could I do it?
Would I regret it?

"Harper?" My mother looked at me expectantly after I'd hesitated to respond for too long.

"He and I haven't discussed the interview at length yet."

My eyes flicked toward Jamil. I didn't mention that all Terry was concerned about right now was the story he was expecting and now that I'd decided I wasn't going to do it out of respect for Jamil, I had no idea what was going to come of it. I could very well have kissed those four years of hard work goodbye.

"Maybe that's because he has no intention of giving you what you're wanting."

With every comment my mother made, my irritation toward her grew like a beast inside me. It filled my mind with anger. It took hold of my tongue, wanting to lash out. It poisoned everything it could, leaving me stewing in my seat.

"Maybe you're just rooting for my failure." The words sounded like they had been spoken by someone else. My mother's mouth dropped open, the only sign that she was taken aback. My father's eyes were wide as he glanced between us, probably trying to figure out how he'd put this growing fire out.

"Excuse me?" my mother asked, her voice almost deadly quiet.

"It's hard not to think that when all you do is talk negatively about my career since I first told you I wanted to be a sports reporter. You've never supported me. You've never bothered to congratulate me when I have a new achievement. Of course I feel like you're rooting for my failure."

"Harper," my father warned, but I was already past the point of no return.

"Don't you think it's a failure to stay stagnant in the same job for four years?" My jaw went slack at my mother's question she tried to pose as an innocent inquiry.

"How can you say something like that?"

"Because apparently I'm the only one who can see any sort of reason," my mother shot back at me. "You've been hanging on to this dream far longer than you should have. I told you that if you didn't get the promotion to a more stable position after this season, you'd be moving back to DC and you'd be working for me. That is still going to happen and more likely every day it seems."

It was obvious why my mother was known as being such a hard woman to negotiate with on Capitol Hill, but the other congressmen and women hadn't grown up around her like I had. My skin had grown thicker over time.

Out of the corner of my eye, I noticed Jamil open his mouth as if he were about to jump to my defense. But before he could, I caught his eye and shook my head.

"I've got this," I told him. I'd watched him work through his own family problems himself. I could do the same.

I turned my attention back to my mother, who was smiling at me like she'd already won.

"This *dream* is what I want to do with my life. If it doesn't happen with this company, I'll figure something else out. I've done nothing but support both of your careers my entire life. I thought that eventually the parent would support the child's dreams, but, apparently, I was mistaken to think such a thing. The last thing I want is to end up sitting at a table next to my spouse who I barely know anymore because I misplaced my priorities. I've already started to make that mistake and I won't continue to do so. If this career falls apart, fine. I'll pick myself up, without your help. Because I never had it in the first place." I stood up from the table. "Dad, thank you for the birthday card."

"Are you leaving?" my mother exclaimed. She glanced around at the other patrons dining in the restaurant to see if they were watching all of this go down.

I didn't bother to turn back around because there was nothing else that I wanted to say. It wasn't until I reached the restaurant door that I realized Jamil was not with me. When I turned around, I noticed him making his way through the restaurant tables, my parents looking whiter than ghosts still sitting at the table behind him.

"Did you say something to them?" I asked once he was close enough. Jamil slipped a hand to the small of my back to direct me the rest of the way out of the building. He looked tense as we turned the corner and started walking with no destination in mind. Jamil still hadn't answered my question as he clicked away on his phone, probably getting us a car back to the hotel.

"Jamil," I tried again, pulling the both of us to a stop. "Did you say something to them?"

He let out a frustrated puff of air before he finally looked at me. "I told them that I thought anyone who claimed to care about you wouldn't be anything but one hundred percent behind you. They wouldn't put down your career aspirations because of their own backward opinions. And they especially wouldn't make you feel less than because you are anything but. I told them that the only good thing they've done when it comes to you was bringing you into this world. The rest you've done yourself."

Silence had never been so loud. I felt like I'd had a bucket of ice water tossed over me. I had been surprised that Jamil managed to stay quiet through dinner, only attempting to jump in once it was obvious my mother was out for blood tonight. But he didn't blink an eye when I wanted to handle my parents myself.

"You said that to them?"

Jamil's eyes widened and he opened his mouth like he wanted to defend himself.

"I'm not mad," I hurried to add.

He visibly relaxed once he noticed I wasn't upset. "I couldn't help myself. Especially after you stood up for yourself like that, you didn't see your mother's face as you walked away from her. She was so angry, like she was plotting to get you back. Who does that?"

Sadness filled me as I realized I wanted to laugh at something that horrified Jamil. Even with battling her son's addiction and the disappointment she had to face all these years, Jamil's mother had never given up hope for Jordan. She'd never stopped loving him and she'd never stopped supporting him. All I asked of my parents was to support my career aspirations and they acted like I'd personally offended them in some way.

"That's my mother for you." I tried to sound light-hearted, but the crack in my voice at the end gave me away.

Jamil's eyes softened. His arms lifted like he wanted to hug me before he hesitated. I stepped forward and wrapped myself around him before the moment could pass. I wouldn't let my career destroy one more relationship in my life.

"What did your mother mean about working for her?" Jamil asked me as I was still in his arms.

I sighed because while my mother was right that I needed to figure something else out at the end of this season, I had no idea what that would look like, and I'd do everything in my power to avoid moving back to Washington DC and subjecting myself to the career my mother wanted for me. Besides, my parents weren't going to help support me any longer—especially after tonight's dinner.

"Being a field reporter doesn't pay a lot. It's a grind. Most of the benefits come from expenses being paid for while traveling, but my parents have been the ones to truly support me financially through this career. Before I came to Chicago, my mother told me that I had to move forward in my career somehow by the end of this season or they'd stop supporting me. Which would leave me with the only option they were giving me—work for my mother on her campaign trail."

Jamil pulled away from me, his eyes wide with concern. "That would be a death sentence for you."

"My thoughts exactly. Which is why I've been so desperate to get that host position. The only way to do that was to prove to my boss that I was a heavy hitter. You've already given me my best shot with these interviews you've helped me get."

"The success you've had is all your own. I have nothing to do with that," Jamil replied fiercely. His hands wrapped around my arms so he could hold me in place, forcing me to look him in the eyes. "You deserve that promotion. If your boss doesn't give it to you at the end of this season, surely another company would give you a shot."

I gave him a sad smile. "The problem with that is it would most likely take me away from Chicago and I'm starting to fear that will be my only option when it's all said and done."

Jamil turned his gaze to the city around us. His eyes searched the faces of the people passing by, looking for nothing until he finally resounded. "And you don't want to leave Chicago?"

"No, I don't."

"And the interview you were going to do of me was going to be your sure way to get the job you wanted?"

My mouth grew dry as I realized what Jamil was thinking about. "No." I shook my head vehemently. "No. I won't ask that of you. We've already had this conversation. I'll find another way and if that's not enough, then I'll find somewhere else to work."

"But finding somewhere else to work could take you away from Chicago."

If I didn't change the subject now, he would talk himself into doing something he didn't want to.

"Let's not worry about that now."

"Okay," Jamil agreed. "Let's worry about the fact that your birthday is coming up and you hadn't bothered to mention it to anyone."

I sighed as I realized I was jumping out of one frying pan and into another. "I didn't think I needed to because I'm so used to celebrating on my own every year. It wasn't intentional."

"Sure, it wasn't." The smirk that grew on Jamil's face told me I should be worried. "You may have given me and Tommy a tall task putting together a birthday party so last minute, but I promise it'll still be the best one you ever had."

"You and Tommy are doing *what*?"

"Derek requested that there be karaoke. He and I on the microphone are pure entertainment."

"You really don't have to do anything," I tried to argue, even though I knew it was no use.

"It falls on a day off and you think we won't do something?" Jamil prowled toward me until my back hit the wall of the building we were next to. "I told you I don't make a habit of ignoring the blessings life puts in my path, Moon."

Chapter 34

Harper

"The interview with Adam Steel and Nolan Hill was quite impressive," Terry Wilson told me over our video call. After the interview had gone live yesterday, it had generated more traffic for SC News than my interview with Derek had. Terry had emailed me yesterday evening after the last game of the series against the DC Capitols asking to meet, and I hadn't been able to think about anything else since I first read it.

"Thank you, sir."

"Views are skyrocketing every hour. People really appreciate the sincerity you helped deliver and I've heard from executives at different networks that some retired athletes found it quite inspiring." Terry cleared his throat. "I'm excited to see what you do with the story on Jamil Edman, if this is what you're covering on other athletes of your own accord."

My stomach soured as I fought to keep my face neutral. Irrationally, I'd hoped that Terry would have completely forgotten about the story he wanted on Jamil and I wouldn't have to have the ensuing conversation.

"About that story, Terry," I started, wringing my hands together under the table out of view of my computer camera.

"Did you run into a snag? Jamil does seem to be picture perfect, doesn't he?" Terry's pondering did nothing to quell my nerves.

Take courage, my heart.

Nothing worth it is ever easy.

"Actually, I was thinking I could do a story on a different athlete. Jamil is quite saturated in the media already, don't you think?" I wanted to celebrate the lack of quiver in my voice as I managed to get the words out.

However, judging by the unamused look on my boss's face, he didn't agree with me.

"Which is why I instructed you to find something that no one else has covered on him. Nearly all the coverage on Jamil Edman features his stats or a quick interview after a game. Before last year, he used to be much more fun for the media to cover. The most we've seen out of him this season have been the postgame interviews he's done with you."

My resolve was cracking with every word he said. I could practically feel the opportunity at a host seat slipping away from me.

"I understand that, sir. His life has changed drastically since last year. Anyone with all of that resting on their shoulders would grow quite somber, don't you think?"

"There's a story in that transformation, *don't you think*?" Terry cocked an eyebrow at me.

There is one, but not one that I'm willing to tell.

"I can find another story to highlight the Cougars." At this point, I wasn't sure if I was above begging. "There are some interesting developing stories. Especially since the Cougars are on track to be as successful or more so than last season."

"Largely due to Jamil Edman's performance."

Terry clearly wasn't budging.

"I'll get you a story," I told him, hoping he'd give me some leeway after the Nolan and Adam interview.

"I'm looking forward to it," Terry replied.

Then the screen went black.

"Fuck," I breathed as I leaned back in my chair.

It wasn't even nine in the morning, and I was already wishing for something stronger. We'd arrived in Tampa late last night after the last game of the series ended against the Capitols. It was a Friday in the first week of June and the Florida humidity was so thick outside that it deterred any thoughts of going for a run to try and work this pent-up energy out of me.

With a slam of my laptop, I grabbed my hotel room key and went in search of something to take my mind off what felt like a clock ticking down to my final moments with SC News if I couldn't deliver what Terry wanted.

The lobby was mostly empty when the elevator doors opened, and I made my way to the restaurant in hopes that a greasy breakfast would take my mind off things.

"We have a habit of running into each other in hotel lobbies it appears." Standing off by the barista with a cup of coffee in his hands looking far too chipper already was Jamil.

"What'd you get?" I asked, reaching out toward his coffee cup. Jamil only raised an eyebrow as I snatched the cup out of his hands and brought it to my lips.

"Man, does the network need to include coffee in your travel budget? You're drinking that like you've never experienced caffeine before."

I paused, the coffee cup mere inches from my lips. The last thing I wanted was to tell him how my conversation with Terry went because Jamil would only go against everything he wanted if it meant doing something that would help me.

"Rough morning," I told him, keeping it vague.

"Would a distraction help?" Jamil's cheeky smile was slowly melting away all the frustration that had made me grow bitter in the time it took me to ride the elevator down from my room.

"A distraction is exactly what I'm looking for."

Jamil offered me his elbow. "Lucky for you, our chariot awaits us outside."

With a quick skip, Jamil led me out the front doors of the hotel where an SUV was waiting with a woman in the front seat that looked familiar.

"It's about damn time!" The woman leaned over onto the console and tilted her sunglasses down the tip of her nose.

Recognition dawned on me. I'd seen her in the photos lining Jamil's walls. The similarity between the two could be seen in the easy smile on the woman's face, the dimple in her right cheek, and the smattering of freckles across her nose.

"I found a hitchhiker. Hopefully Mom won't mind." Jamil opened the passenger door and motioned for me to get in.

"Oh, I don't want to take your time away from visiting with your sister," I floundered, glancing between the open seat and Jamil.

"Babe, I've had twenty-five years of time with him. I would much rather spend time getting to know you."

"Jayden is the feistiest of all of us," Jamil leaned in close to whisper in my ear.

Jayden rolled her eyes at her older brother. "You've never been good at being secretive, J." She turned her eyes, the same color as Jamil's, to me. "Come on, I'll tell you about the time that Jamil got caught kissing his first girlfriend in high school goodnight and was chased down the driveway by her father."

I shot a look at the man in question over my shoulder before sliding into the passenger seat and letting Jamil close the door behind me.

"It's her favorite story to tell," Jamil mumbled as he climbed into the back.

"Because it never gets old," Jayden replied happily as she pulled the car away from the hotel.

*

Triple Play

Jamil's childhood home was exactly how I pictured it. Pictures on nearly every inch of free wall space. Memorabilia not only from his early baseball career, but from his siblings' lives too. The warmth in this house was like nothing I'd experienced in my own childhood.

My childhood house was kept in pristine order in case anyone stopped by. The pillows were always perfectly fluffed, the couch cushions didn't even remotely have a dent in them, and all the pictures on the wall were professionally taken to make us appear like the perfect nuclear family. It lacked the charm and love of the home I was standing in.

Voices filled the room as delicious aromas hit my nose the second we walked through the front door.

"Jamil?" I heard his mother call from the kitchen. Her back was turned as she stirred something on the stove. "Please tell me you didn't eat before you came here. You know better than that."

"I didn't, Ma. I know you would have strung me out with the laundry." Jamil crossed through the living room where Jamil's older sister sat with a small baby bouncing on her lap to kiss his mother on the cheek.

"J brought a guest!" Jayden announced cheerily, clearly enjoying putting her older brother back in the center of attention. She had to have been a handful when they were younger.

"A guest?" Denise turned around from the stove, an apron tied around her lower half and a spoon in her hand—nearly the spitting image from when she stayed with Jamil in Chicago. "Oh my goodness, Harper!"

"You knew about her?" Jayden asked, downright offended that she wasn't about to watch her brother be questioned over family breakfast.

"Of course, I knew about her." Denise crossed the kitchen to give me a hug. She placed a hand on my cheek. "It sure is nice to welcome you into my home this time."

"So you knew about her for weeks and didn't think to tell us?" Jayden pressed as she reached for a muffin that looked fresh out of the oven.

Denise leaned over and smacked her hand. "Not until we are all seated at the table. And a mother can keep her child's life to herself until they are ready for others to know. Don't act so surprised."

Jayden stared at her mother like she'd grown a second head. "But you told Janessa about the date I went on last weekend!"

"That's because that man didn't open your car door for you, nor did he even introduce himself to me. I absolutely told your sister about that idiot."

Jamil choked back a laugh as he glanced between his mother and his younger sister.

"James and I watched your latest interview," Denise told me. "We just couldn't believe how good it was. You really have an amazing gift."

"I second that," Jamil's older sister, Janessa added. "My husband, Kota, and I watched it. We loved every second of it." Her daughter shrieked on her lap.

"It sounds like baby Kyla agrees," Jamil cooed as he swooped in to take his niece from Janessa. "Is Dad at the lumber yard?"

"He is. He'll be at your game tonight. I'm sure he will hate that he missed getting to meet Harper." Denise gave me another warm smile.

"Will baby Kyla be there?" Jamil asked his niece as he leaned in to bury his face in her belly. Now I understood what baby fever felt like.

"In your jersey, as per usual. Kota and I thought we could spare a late bedtime to have your biggest fan there to cheer you on."

"Will Kota be here?" I asked, walking over to join Janessa in the living room.

She shook her head. "No. He's a surgeon. A few more hours left in his shift rotation. But he'll be there tonight. None of us would miss one of J's games in Florida."

"Alright, everyone grab a seat!" Denise called out as she pulled plates from a cabinet.

Everyone slid into seats that had been claimed years before. Jamil noticed me still standing awkwardly in the living room and gestured for me to take the open seat next to him.

"Do you want some casserole, sweetheart?" Denise asked me as Jamil handed her my plate.

"Sure." I knew better than to say no to anything that Denise Edman cooked.

As silverware scraped against plates and Kyla cooed in the background, I finally felt like I had a goal for something other than my career. Janessa poked fun at the date that Jayden was bringing to tonight's game while Jamil jumped in with his own line of protective questioning, and it dawned on me just how much I missed growing up at the expense of my parents' career-driven choices.

When it came down to it, companies would replace you in a heartbeat. But nothing could replace the love you feel while sitting around a table full of people that care about you unconditionally, people that show up for you, and people that only want to see you achieve *your* goals and not their own.

"Is this a proper distraction?" Jamil leaned over after Jayden had been thoroughly questioned.

"The best," I told him and meant it.

Chapter 35

Harper

"We would like to welcome Nick O'Connor to the lineup. We are so excited to have you at the desk with us!" I stared in disbelief at those blindingly white teeth that I'd come to hate as he was welcomed on to SC News's daytime show.

"You've got to be fucking kidding me," I cursed as I stared at Nick on the screen.

"Please don't spill coffee all over the counter!" Jamil called from his bedroom. "It's just an innocent bystander."

I glanced down at the coffee pot in my hand and gently put it down on the counter.

"What happened?" he asked as he emerged from his bedroom, looking freshly showered.

"Did you go for a run?" I asked.

"I needed it after this last series in Florida. I think my body is hitting that time in the season where I'm starting to feel it."

"And you didn't wake me up to go with you?"

Jamil pointed a finger at me. "Don't try to distract from whatever is happening." He walked up behind me and looked at the television. "Is that your coworker?"

"Yes, it is," I sighed, waiting for anger to consume me, but was left feeling rather numb.

Jamil studied me as he weighed his next words. "And he got a host job?"

"It appears that way."

"And you still haven't heard anything from your boss?" He looked at me like he was waiting for me to explode or go on a rant about how unfair it was for Nick to get this opportunity before me after all I've done for the company, but I suddenly no longer had it in me to make that argument. Why waste my breath when it's never done any good before?

"He and I talked while we were still in Florida about the content he's expecting from me the remainder of this season."

"But he hasn't mentioned anything about next year?"

Jamil's growing outrage was rather touching. At least one of us still cared about my aspirations. Seeing Nick's face on my television only confirmed for me that the goalposts were constantly moving, adjusting, and forcing me to do more—*be more*—before I could be rewarded. I was beginning to wonder if I wanted to unsubscribe from the entire game and go somewhere else where I could achieve my dreams.

"He hasn't."

Jamil hung his head, looking crushed enough for the both of us. "What are you going to do?"

The heaviness in his eyes told me he understood how my options were dwindling and soon I'd be forced to choose—stay stagnant and unfulfilled or take a chance on something greater.

"I have no idea. I hadn't even truly thought it would ever get to this point. I've delivered two great interviews for the network that have brought in viewership and revenue. Yet that still isn't enough." I hated how defeated I sounded. This job had sucked nearly all the life out of me. "I can't take another year of this."

Even the strongest of warriors lost faith after they'd been taken advantage of for too long.

"Maybe it's time you start to hedge your bets and figure out some backup plans." I buried myself into the scent of Jamil's body. The only thing I was sure of nowadays was how safe I felt right here—in his arms. When Jamil had first asked me if I wanted to officially date him at the Boys & Girls Club gala, I'd been too afraid to go for it because of my career. Now, I was beginning to wonder if it was too late, and I'd ruined any chance at something meaningful.

Would I take a job that would send me away from Chicago and officially destroy any last chance I had with him?

"I think I'm going to make some calls today and see if any of my industry connections know of any openings."

Jamil stepped back, the moment his arms dropped from around me, I wanted nothing more than to bury myself back in them and not leave them for the rest of our day off.

"I'm going to stop by the house to check on the progress before I swing over to Tommy's to plan your birthday. You'll have your apartment back while you do your research."

"Are you sure you don't want me to come with you to your house?" I asked him. With the away series coming right after the break-in, I'd had very little time to check in on him. Jamil welcomed the time away from Chicago as a distraction and a decompression. But now he had no other choice but to face the aftermath head on.

"I'll be okay." Jamil reached up to brush his thumb over the corner of my lips. "We both have our own battles to conquer. We can reconvene later to share our accomplishments."

My eyes scanned Jamil's face, trying to pick up on any sign that would tell me he wasn't okay. He'd learned to hide his struggles behind a smile or a joke. But I wanted him to know that he didn't have to keep that mask up with me.

"I'm fine," he stressed, his thumb still caressing my cheek. "If I need you, I'll let you know. I just want to check in with the progress. I'm more excited to plan your birthday so we can celebrate you."

I leaned into his touch as I rolled my eyes at him. "You really don't need to throw me a birthday party."

"Yes, I do!" Jamil looked at me as if I'd personally offended him. "You deserve to be celebrated for more than just blessing all of us with your presence on this planet. Birthdays are sacred, Moon. I'm sorry that the people in your life so far have made you feel like you don't deserve a single day to be surrounded by people that love you and want to show you how much they love you."

He'd effectively silenced any other argument I had left, leaving me with the stark reality that I'd been forced to make myself smaller my entire life. To fit my parents' perfect family picture. To fit the role a predominately male-dominated industry asked of me. To never bring attention to myself and always the person sitting or standing across from me during an interview. I'd grown so accustomed to letting others shine that I'd forgotten how to allow myself to step into the spotlight for my own moment.

"No comeback? No witty response? Did I short-circuit you?" Jamil turned me around and pretended to look for a panel on my back.

"Oh, stop. Get out of here before I finally figure out a decent response to all of that."

Jamil was grinning from ear to ear as he leaned in and placed a quick kiss to my cheek. "Call me if you need more time alone in your own apartment."

"Wait!" I called after him as he had one hand on the doorknob. "You know you're not a burden or an intrusion by being here, right?"

There was hesitation before he gave me a nod, exposing the limbo we found ourselves in. The laws of attraction constantly pulled us together, only for fear to push us apart again. I'd already given up the one thing that had held me back from him before.

What was holding me back now?

But as I saw the haunted look in his eyes, I told myself it wasn't the right time to tell him how I felt. He already had too much on his plate and throwing this on top would only complicate things further. Not to mention I was beginning to realize my life may very well be pulling me in a different direction—away from him.

Jamil was gone with a quick wave, closing my apartment door behind him.

With nothing left to postpone the inevitable, I pulled out my computer and began sorting through my contacts with the hopes of finding someone who could help me.

After hours of sending messages to different people in my contacts and coming back empty-handed, I stumbled across a job opening for a news network out in California.

It would be based out of Los Angeles and was a chair on a well-known show that was styled as a daytime talk show covering any sporting news we wanted to. It had a large following and was growing in popularity every day. This was exactly what I'd been hoping for within SC News, it would just require me to move halfway across the country again and away from people I was beginning to consider my friends. People I was starting to think of as more of a family than my own was to me.

My finger hesitated over the button that would send my resume off. I could hear my mother's voice in my head telling me not to make a decision on my career off of feelings I had for someone else, that I should put myself first always. But I'd witnessed how that same game plan had turned her own marriage into an amicable partnership with no traces of love.

How is choosing to stay in Chicago not putting yourself first?

My hands itched to call Jamil and get his opinion, but not only did I not want to bother him, I also knew what he would tell me. Jamil would tell me to apply for the job because I'd worked so hard for this, and I deserved it. He would believe in me and tell me I would get it with certainty that no one else had ever given me.

"It's not even a sure thing you'll get it," I told myself before I closed my eyes and hit send.

When the notification confirming my resume was sent went off, I hadn't expected my stomach to feel like a bottomless pit leaving me devoid of any excitement.

Before I could think much further on it, a knock at the door drew my attention.

"Did you forget your keys?" I called out as I crossed to open the door, thinking Jamil was back already.

"Surprise!"

Standing in front of me with their arms full of various shopping bags were Maggie, Olivia, and Lottie.

"What do you mean surprise?" I asked, still staring at them like I was being properly pranked. "What are you doing here?"

"We're having a girls' night!" Olivia looked at me like it was the most obvious answer in the world before she shouldered her way into my apartment.

"It's not even three o'clock in the afternoon," I told her as I turned to watch her empty her bag full of food across my kitchen island.

"Jamil said to give you a couple hours before coming over." Maggie gave me one of her signature sweet smiles as she emptied her bag of nail polish on the coffee table in the living room.

I was completely lost at this point. "Jamil said?"

"He called us and said that you were having a bad day." Olivia turned to look at me, taking in my open laptop and messy bun that I'd thrown on top of my head when I first started my job search. "To me, it sounded like the kind of situation where I would show up unannounced and take your mind off of whatever is going on."

"You're serious?" I asked as Lottie threw herself down on my couch and began flipping through the different streaming services I'd downloaded onto my television.

"That's what friends do for each other, Harper." Maggie shrugged her shoulders at me like it was the simplest answer in the world.

Even though I'd begun to think of these women as my friends, the idea that they thought the same of me still caught me off guard. I'd done nothing to earn their friendship, yet here they were because Jamil told them I could use cheering up.

"We were all sitting around at my place watching television," Olivia told me. "Why not bring the party over here? Now, do you like Cool Ranch Doritos or Nacho Cheese Doritos?"

Chapter 36

Jamil

"When do you think we can get it on the market?" I asked my realtor as we took in the contractors' work so far.

The locks that Jordan had broken were already repaired, furniture had been replaced, and the holes in the wall had been patched. The house looked exactly how it had before that night, except it also looked completely unrecognizable at the same time. It was more than the blank walls that were missing the pictures I'd hung—the essence of what made this place my home was no longer here. I used to walk into this place and feel instantly calm. Now there was an oppressing emptiness where there was once a sense of happiness.

"Well, the contractors are basically done with everything they needed to do. We can get this on the market as early as next week if that's what you want to do." My realtor was eyeing me with a look I'd been receiving a lot over the past week—concern. "Do you want to think about this for a few days? I know how much you liked this house when we first found it."

"I'll let you know by the end of the week," I told her. "But I'm probably not going to change my mind."

I turned to leave, feeling devoid of anything I once felt for this place as my realtor followed behind me. Rationally I should have harbored some kind of anger toward my brother for taking this place away from me. Maybe I would eventually. But as I turned my key in the lock on the front door, whatever anger I should have carried with me stayed on the other side of the door.

"Do you want me to start looking for new places for you?" my realtor asked me as we walked toward our cars.

"Not yet," I told her because even though I felt myself letting go of this place that I'd called home for the entirety of the time I'd lived in Chicago, I wasn't ready to replace it yet.

"I look forward to hearing your decision. Talk soon!" Then she disappeared into her car, probably off to a meeting with another client.

With one last glance at the house behind me, I slid into my car knowing I needed to make one more stop before I went to Tommy's. Part of me wanted to call Harper to tell her where I was going because I knew she'd meet me there at the drop of a hat to support me despite if she thought I should do it or not.

But I continued driving across town, leaving my phone in the seat next to me to avoid dialing her number. The last thing I wanted to do was pull her away from chasing her dreams while I was seeking answers of my own. I dialed another number instead.

"Jamil! What do you want? I'm currently self-tanning and I got self-tanner on my phone for this call. Maggie and Lottie are on their way over for a girls' day so we can rot away on my couch, so make sure this is good." Olivia's voice came across my car speakers.

Leave it to Olivia to always find a way to make me laugh, even unintentionally.

"I need a favor," I told her.

There was barely a pause on the other end of the line before she replied. "Sure, what do you need?"

"Any chance you guys can take girls' day from your place over to Harper's? I can send you her address. She's had a rough morning, and I think she could use a day surrounded by people that care about her rather than sitting with it all by herself."

Again, without hesitation, "Absolutely. The three of us can go ambush her. It's about time she realized she doesn't have to face life alone anymore."

"Give her another hour or so before you bombard her."

"If you say so. Send her address! We'll go rot on the couch over there."

"Thanks, Liv," I told her as I pulled up outside of Jordan's facility. "I've got to go. I'll see you guys probably tonight when I get back to Harper's apartment."

"Are you okay, J?" Olivia asked, her voice growing concerned.

"I'm good. Thanks again, Liv." I ended the call before Olivia could interrogate me any further because she always had a way of reading exactly what was going on with me, even if I didn't have a clue.

I sat in the silence of my car, staring at the entrance for a few minutes before I finally found the courage to go inside. The previous day's call from the facility, reporting

Jordan's reappearance and the subsequent notification of authorities, left me with a turbulent mix of relief—a weight lifted—and a chilling fear for his future. I'd decided to keep Jordan's initial return from Harper, needing the quiet to process this decision alone. This moment had been brewing since the night of the break-in. From the second I saw the front door of my house slightly ajar. Maybe even from the first time Jordan had shown up on my front step, tears streaming down his face as he told me that he was in trouble and wanted my help. I'd felt needed as I became the one to offer a helping hand instead of the one needing the support.

But as I walked down the hallway toward Jordan's room, I only felt used.

An officer was posted outside of his room, only letting me inside after I showed him my identification. The investigation was ongoing, but I'd already told the detectives that I didn't want to press charges against my brother. He may have continued to tear our relationship apart, but I wouldn't join in contributing to that decimation. Jordan didn't need to be reprimanded for his decision to steal from me.

Battling his own demons was punishment enough.

Jordan was sitting by the window in his room reading a book, only looking up when he realized whoever had entered wasn't speaking.

Shock registered on his face first before fear filled his eyes. "Jamil? What are you doing here?"

"I think it's time we talked," I told him as I crossed the room to sit down in the open seat across from him.

My brother slowly closed his book before setting it on the side table next to him, never taking his eyes off me. His hands trembled as he clasped them in his lap.

Now that I was sitting in front of him all the pent-up emotion that I'd had in me for years was banging against my mouth, demanding to be heard. But I had no idea where to even begin.

"I can't do this anymore, Jordan." I sucked one more deep breath in before I let the flood gates open. "Everything I've been doing up until this point has only been perpetuating your addiction and I refuse to keep up the charade that you have any intention of wanting to get better."

"J, I *do* want to get better," Jordan pleaded with me and I noticed tears welling in the corners of his eyes.

"The moment I checked you into this place I told you this would be the hardest battle of your life, but you aren't even putting up a fight!" I wasn't holding anything back anymore. "First you get yourself in trouble with a bookie, *again*, while you are still in rehab. Then you ask me to bail you out, *again*. And when I say no, you break into my house. I'm done standing by and doing nothing as you continue to tear your life apart. I've got nothing left to help you with. Especially after this. I'm done."

"What are you saying?" Jordan asked me, the wobbling of his chin matching his voice.

"I will pay for one more term. Three months. If you check yourself out again, if you throw this last opportunity in the trash, I won't be here to catch you."

His mouth dropped open as he realized what I was telling him.

"I just want my brother back," I told him, my voice breaking on the last word. Now I was the one fighting back tears. "I've given you too much, Jordan."

"I didn't—I didn't realize this was how you felt."

"How else did you think I would feel? I've watched my hero become only a ghost of himself over time and I can't even blame him for it. I've guarded you from the vultures who would tear you apart in the news. I've contorted myself around all the attention this past year to protect *you*. But you repay me by breaking into my home and stealing from me? My house was the last straw."

Jordan stayed silent as I stood up from my seat after I had nothing left to say. Part of me expected him to stop me before I left his room, but he let me go without another word. The weight I'd been carrying all these years lightened as I left my words behind me.

*

"We've got a karaoke machine. Are you sure that's something Harper wants or just something you and Derek want?" Tommy eyed me as he looked up from his pad of paper.

"Keep it on the list," I told him. "It'll be entertainment."

"It'll be something," Tommy mumbled as he added a karaoke machine to the list. "We still haven't talked about *where* this is going to take place . . ."

Tommy trailed off as he looked up at me from his notes. His hesitation highlighted my current living predicament. Normally I would have hosted this at my house, but that no longer felt like an option. It wasn't a secret what had happened with my brother and the break-in, even if no one approached me about it.

"What if we rented out the bar like we did after the World Series win last year?" Tommy offered as I sat there trying to come up with an option.

"I think that would be perfect," I agreed as I found the contact information for the bar and fired off another email.

"I think that's it." Tommy glanced down at his list to confirm before he eyed me again. "Now are you going to tell me why you showed up here looking like you'd just come from a therapy session?"

A laugh of disbelief and exhaustion burst out of me as I leaned back on Tommy's couch. Between him and Olivia, there wasn't much I could get past them nowadays. They eyed me with caution as I grew from always being the one with a smile on my face to watching that light slowly dim.

"I went to see Jordan today. He showed back up at the facility yesterday. Probably after he'd paid off his debts."

Tommy's eyebrows shot up as he sank back in the couch. He didn't ask me how it went. He gave me the time and space to tell him what I wanted to.

"I needed to let him go finally. All these years, I think you can chalk me up to a helicopter parent with him and that clearly hasn't worked thus far." Tommy chuckled in agreement. "I feel like I've been walking on eggshells this last year trying to keep eyes off me so no one would find out about Jordan. I wanted him to heal without any scrutiny. Now I've closed myself off to the world and created more hurdles for myself to jump through than necessary."

"I would add that I do miss my best friend and all of his antics."

I smoothed my hands down my pants, noticing how sweaty my palms had grown. "My brain keeps telling me to let the flood gates open, but I don't even know what that means."

Tommy cocked his head to the side. "Like a tell-all?"

"No," I told him, shaking my head. "I won't air out Jordan's problems. But I want to talk about my experience, without outing him."

"I think I know someone who can do exactly what you're wanting to do." Tommy leaned forward to squeeze my shoulder.

My eyes met his as I realized who he was referring to. A war of emotions erupted inside of me. While the last thing I wanted was to put myself out there for the public to dissect, she was potentially throwing her career away at SC News because she wouldn't give her boss the one thing he wanted—me.

Maybe we could find a way to achieve what we both needed without giving away everything. Maybe I could find a way to heal whatever hole had formed inside of me over this past year while figuring out a way to keep Harper here in Chicago.

Because the thought of her leaving this place felt worse than having my entire life splashed across headlines for people to dissect.

I'd rather face the hunger of others desperate to distract themselves from their own lives by judging someone else's if she was by my side.

Chapter 37

Harper

"Watch out for that step," Jamil whispered in my ear as he kept one hand firmly pressed over my eyes while using the other one to support me, so I didn't go sprawling across the ground.

He'd kept tight-lipped all day long about what he had planned for my birthday. Olivia, Lottie, and Maggie took me to brunch while Jamil and Tommy disappeared to prepare for whatever they had planned, and I only saw him well after lunchtime once it was time to get ready for the party.

"One more step." His voice brushed against my ear, his hand steadying me as I climbed the final step.

All morning I'd been fixating on what would happen tonight. The most I'd ever had someone celebrate my birthday before was my parents when I was still a kid. They'd invited all their coworkers and their kids. Another congressman's son had leaned over to blow my candles out before me and all anyone did was laugh. No one even noticed the tears welling in my eyes as I watched the boy laugh with glee as he suddenly became the center of attention. After that birthday, I'd never asked for anyone to celebrate me again solely because I couldn't handle the disappointment I'd felt that day.

But Jamil had been so insistent that I couldn't tell him I didn't like to celebrate my birthday. His excitement over planning with Tommy had become so intoxicating that I'd even found myself being a little excited for tonight.

"Ready?" Jamil asked me. I heard a heavy door being pulled open as it scraped against the sidewalk.

"As ready as I'll ever be," I told him.

"Tonight's for you to have fun. You're acting like you're walking to your death."

"You saw how coordinated I am at dancing. I'm sure to ruin the whole thing."

"Impossible. You could never ruin a single thing and I promise you'll be the life of this party."

Jamil removed his hand from my eyes and I had to adjust to the low lighting of the bar I found myself in. Hundreds of balloons decorated the ceiling with their tails dangling down right above our heads. The room had old leather booths around the walls with a worn dance floor in the middle that was already full of people moving to the music pulsing through the speakers. But none of the decorations really mattered to me. It was the people that filled the room that stole the breath straight from my lungs.

"Surprise!" Everyone in the room shouted as I realized that Jamil and I were not alone.

All our friends were there and even some other players from the Cougars. Everyone had party poppers in their hands and were setting them off, sending confetti flying.

"This wasn't a surprise party," I laughed as I noticed Tommy and Derek sporting party hats while attempting to set off as many party poppers as they could.

"We weren't sure what else to say," Derek told me with a shrug of his shoulders.

"What I am sure of is that you need a drink in your hand." Olivia appeared with two cocktails in her hands and passed me one of them. "Come on!"

Olivia pulled me toward the middle of the dance floor where Lottie and Maggie were waiting for us. I glanced back over my shoulder as my hand slipped from Jamil's.

"I'll catch you out there in a second. Someone has to make sure you don't trip over your two left feet."

Jamil grabbed Tommy and Derek and the three of them disappeared behind the bar, leaving me with the three girls I was beginning to think of as real friends as they danced around me. I drank down the cocktail from Olivia over the course of two songs, enjoying the tingle that began to run through my extremities as I swayed to the music.

Just as the second song ended and I decided I needed another drink, Tommy, Derek, and Jamil reemerged from behind the bar with microphones in their hands. The music cut out before the first few notes of a familiar ABBA song came over the speakers.

Derek jumped on the bar top, grabbing the entire room's attention. Jamil and Tommy stood down in front of him as they all pointed toward me.

As soon as they opened their mouths to attempt their own rendition of "Dancing Queen," I was nearly bent over in a fit of laughter. Derek's party hat was sitting cockeyed on his head as he attempted his best disco moves. Jamil had a feather boa wrapped around his neck and Tommy had a sparkly cowboy hat with diamond fringe around the sides. The three of them looked utterly ridiculous, but my heart squeezed as they serenaded me.

I heard Nolan and Adam catcall the three of them from a table in the back. Jamil twirled the feather boa around in his hand as he prowled closer to where I was standing in the middle of the dance floor. Once he reached me, he grabbed my hand to spin me in a circle. More cheering erupted around the room as he dipped me. With one more twirl, he sent me spinning back toward Olivia, Maggie, and Lottie who caught me in their arms.

The final notes of the song rang out and the three men lined up to take a bow to a smattering of applause.

It was cheesy.

It was ridiculous.

It was perfect.

Normally I would have been uncomfortable having this kind of attention on me, but tonight I only felt an immense amount of love as I got to experience an entire room cheering for me for the first time in my life.

"Happy birthday!" Derek shouted into his microphone, the rest of the room echoing the sentiment right after him.

Another drink was pressed into my hand by Olivia or Maggie or Lottie, I wasn't sure, as the room raised their glasses toward me one more time. My eyes locked on to Jamil as he raised his own.

"Thank you," I mouthed to him.

"Always," he mouthed back.

Suddenly I was desperate for us to be alone, instead of surrounded by all our friends. We'd been dancing around each other for too long and it was time we finally addressed wherever we wanted this to go.

*

"I can't believe you guys sang ABBA to me tonight," I told Jamil as we walked through my apartment door. The buzz from all the drinks I'd had tonight was nearly gone. The high left behind from being surrounded by so much love.

I also couldn't believe how I'd ever survived without the group of people I was beginning to love like a family. I'd never felt so full, and the thread that brought all of these people into my life was the man standing in my apartment.

"Let's see if you still think that here in a minute. I've got one more surprise up my sleeve."

Jamil crossed to the kitchen where he opened the fridge and pulled out a single cupcake with a candle already in the center of it. With a flick of a lighter, the candle ignited sending shadows around the room.

"Maggie and Olivia wanted to get you a big cake and have the whole room sing to you, but I wasn't sure if that would be pushing your comfort zone too much. I thought you could make a wish here, just the two of us."

"That was sweet of you to think of," I told him as I considered the flickering candle on the cupcake.

What could I possibly wish for?

Triple Play

In the past I would have wished for the promotion I had been working so hard for. My priorities had been so focused on something that I now realized was fleeting, instead of wishing for more adventure or love in my life. As if a simple job promotion could fulfill every need I'd ever have.

But tonight, all I wanted was this feeling to never be taken from me. I wanted to create more life memories—moments in time that I'd remember for the entirety of my life with people that made me feel important.

I blew the candle out with a quick puff of air.

"What did you wish for?" Jamil asked me as he pulled the candle out of the center of the cupcake.

"If I told you, then it wouldn't come true," I told him with a wink.

"I have another present for you." Jamil disappeared into the guest room only to return with a pink gift bag in his hands with sparkly tissue paper sticking out of the top. "Here."

"You didn't have to get me anything." I gingerly took the bag from him. "The party was already more than enough."

"Just open it, Moon." Jamil was eyeing the bag with anticipation. I pulled the tissue out first, revealing what was inside—a Cougars jersey.

"Is this?"

"Go ahead." Jamil nodded his head toward the jersey, urging me to take it out of the bag.

A familiar name appeared as the jersey unfurled in my hands. I glanced back at Jamil, who looked rather smug about his present. Fueled on the energy from the night, I reached up on my tiptoes, so my nose was almost touching Jamil's. My fingers danced up Jamil's chest, inching toward his neck and then into the short strands of the hair at his nape.

"I feel like since the conversation about the feature story happened, we have had this rock between us that neither of us knows how to move. Before, when you asked me if I wanted us to date and label whatever is happening between us, I'd hesitated, and I've regretted that ever since. I let fear for my own career get in the way of something that could be much more fulfilling and important. I could be way too late now, and I would understand if you've come to realize that we should just stay friends, but I need to know what you want. The not knowing is starting to kill me and I'm not sure how much more I can take."

Jamil stayed silent for so long, I was beginning to wonder if he really had decided we should be just friends. I knew it could be a possibility, but the reality of it felt like a knife to my chest.

"I understand now why you had been so hesitant to become anything serious out of respect for me and I appreciate that. In hindsight, putting someone's needs before your own wants is one of the kindest things a person can do. However, I've come to realize that my desire to stay out of the media was based in an irrational fear that I had somehow concocted. I've made these past few months harder for myself than they needed to be because of that." When Jamil paused, it sent my heart flying into my throat.

"I've thought a lot about what you said. How I could control the narrative and tell my story, what it's like to have lived through this drastic change with all these external factors while dealing with my own personal issues."

"What are you saying, J?" I asked him.

"I want to do an interview with you. I don't want to directly talk about what's been going on with Jordan, but I do want to address everything I've been having to juggle this last year. If I give everyone the full picture and be brutally honest with the boundaries I want to have with the media, maybe I'll finally feel at peace again with my career and my life."

"You don't have to do an interview with me, Jamil," I rushed to tell him.

"This isn't because I want to help you with your career," Jamil paused. "At least, not entirely. Is that something you can help me with?"

I wasn't sure if I should be happy about this turn of events. By doing the interview, I'd be fulfilling Terry's requirement of a feature story on Jamil and the opportunity for a desk seat would be mine for the taking. Even if Jamil had come around to the idea of a sit-down interview, would he regret this on the other side?

"Don't do that." Jamil reached up for my hands that still were resting on the nape of his neck and held them firmly in his. "Don't convince yourself that I made this decision for anyone other than myself, even if it benefits you in the long run as well."

"I just don't want to put you in a position you don't want to be in," I told him.

Jamil shook his head. "No, you'd be putting me in the *exact* position I need to be in and I can't say I wouldn't mind keeping you in Chicago."

"Are you saying you still want to date me?" I asked, the last word sounding more like a squeak from the nerves inside of me.

"Harper, I may not have realized it in Florida or even when I first saw you reporting at our home game, but I've been wanting to date you for months."

"So, Jamil Edman. I suppose there is only one question left to ask." He cocked an eyebrow at me as he waited. "Will you be my boyfriend?"

"You know it's nice not having to be the one to ask this time." Jamil's playful dig had my cheeks turning red. His hand gently pushed aside my hair to cup the back of my neck, his thumb smoothing back and forth over my pulse. There was a fire in his eyes that seemed to say, *finally*. "Harper Nelson, there is nothing in this world that I want more than to be yours."

The cupcake from Jamil was the only thing I could focus on to distract me from the jumble of emotions tumbling around in my head.

Take courage, my heart.

I dipped a finger into the frosting and only looked back up at Jamil as I smeared it on the side of my neck without bothering to say another word.

"Now *that's* not fair," Jamil groaned, his eyes turning impossibly dark. His hands squeezed mine before desire completely took over his actions as he lifted me into his arms, his tongue swiping out at the frosting. He only pulled away to look at me once a moan slipped from my lips. "Two can play that game."

Jamil watched me with desire in his eyes as I stripped off the outfit I'd worn for my birthday party before slipping his jersey on. I gave him a full spin, so he could see his name across my back. When I finished my turn, he was looking at me with eyes ablaze.

"Come on, Edman. Show me what you've got."

Chapter 38

Jamil

"How are you feeling?" Harper asked me as her crew double-checked the lighting around us. A woman was standing over me, powdering away any of the shine that would be caught on camera.

"I'm not sure there's a word I know that can describe the way my stomach is twisting itself in knots right now," I told her.

Harper had taken a week to prepare for today's interview, crafting her questions and working with me to make sure she wasn't going to ask anything that would expose too much or too little. She was meticulous in her work, formulating the perfect story that would execute everything I wanted this interview to be, while still being entertaining for an audience. Give it five years and I knew she'd be the one on *60 Minutes* delivering high-powered interviews on the most current hard-hitting topics.

She might not fully realize it yet, but I could see it. She was meant for more than even SC News. The world was just beginning to recognize the star that she'd always been.

"We go at your speed. When you want to stop, we stop." Harper glanced at her notes one more time before she handed them off to one of her team members and settled into her seat, ready for the interview to begin.

"It's time I stop shying away from all of this. Let's do it."

Harper's crew counted her down to the moment they started recording. Each second they said making my heart race faster and faster until I feared it would speed away.

Breathe.

"Jamil Edman, it's a pleasure." Harper's smile was a salve for my anxiety. I wasn't doing this alone. The two of us were facing it together as a team.

"Thank you for having me," I told her, trying to control the shake in my voice.

"This season has been a different experience than you had last year, even though you and the rest of the Cougars have been dominating at the top of the conference once again. There's been heightened media attention and business deals. How are you managing all of that?"

Here it was. I could either give Harper the rehearsed response that Nico had drilled into me all these years—the one he would still want me to give to lessen the blowback—or I could give the truth.

"It's a learning experience," I told her. "Every athlete that plays professionally knows this comes with the job. But it takes getting used to."

Harper's wheels were turning as she listened to my response, trying to follow my lead on how this interview would go.

"You've been noticeably distant from media and signings this season. Some have even come to comment that they miss the carefree player they're used to. Would you say that this frenzy of attention has a play in that?"

What would be the worst thing that could happen? You lose your career? It has already taken away so much from you. Or you stand up for yourself. You place boundaries. Just because you get paid to play a sport and have extra attention doesn't mean people have a right into your life.

"After last season, I wasn't expecting the kind of attention that came with the accolades I received or the records I broke. I'm just a regular guy that fell in love with the game of baseball as a young kid, like so many others out there. At first, the extra attention didn't bother me. Until I started seeing people trying to take photos of me outside of my own home or mobbing me when I was doing errands like any other normal person. To manage all of it, I pulled away from the fans and from the media as much as I could. I hoped that people would give up eventually and the attention would die down, but it only seemed to make the interest grow."

Harper had a way of making the lights and cameras directed at us fade away. The nerves I had at the start of the interview were dissipating and all that was left was me and her.

"From a fan perspective, I think it's natural to want to know more about the guy that chased down an unbreakable record and beat it with ease. Baseball is America's favorite pastime. It's one of the first sports nearly every young kid learns to play, but not every young kid grows up to break historical records like you have. Don't you feel like you owe it to the fans to interact with them?"

"Playing on a public platform in a league with such a large fandom, the scrutiny and interest is bound to come. But the upward trajectory I've been shot into this past year has taken me away from that normal level of scrutiny and interest that I'm used to and into a completely different stratosphere."

"Much like that of a celebrity," Harper supplied.

"Exactly," I agreed. "And that wasn't necessarily what I signed up for when I started this entire journey. I just want to play baseball and share that love with the fans. The rest of it, I can do without. I don't need people trying to take pictures of me while I'm at the supermarket. I don't need people driving by my house because the address was leaked online. I don't need people digging into my personal life. If I want to share those things because I think they're relevant for the fans and baseball community to know, then I will share those things."

Harper smiled at me. "Boundaries."

"My family didn't sign up for this. They're normal people with normal lives. They're not the ones signing up for commercials or brand gigs. I've had to use myself as a shield this season just to give them the kind of privacy that I wish I had."

"You've always displayed your passion on a different level. You're unfiltered and joyous. You exemplify exactly why people love the game of baseball. I think if what you're asking of the media and of fans is to take a step back, they'd be more than happy to do that if it meant continuing to watch the game of baseball through your eyes. It's poetry in motion when you play. It would be a shame to limit that kind of talent. When you look back on your career thus far, what are you most proud of?"

"I'm most proud of getting to play for a team like the Chicago Cougars in a city filled with such amazing, energetic sports fans. I may be biased, but Chicago has the best fans for nearly every professional sport. I'm also most proud of how I've played the sport—for myself, my family, and for my teammates. Baseball is the one place I've had the chance to be my most authentic self and Chicago has embraced me for that."

"Your love for this city is evident. From your charitable donations to your support of other professional teams, you find ways to support the people of Chicago."

I nodded my head. "And I'm not done yet. I've got a lot of different things up my sleeve coming for this city that I'm excited about. I recognize how blessed I am and I want to share those blessings with others."

Harper shuffled the papers in her lap. "I want to backtrack to last year. You haven't talked much on last season's performance, and as I mentioned before, you are on the track of either repeating or even beating it under much more difficult circumstances from the sounds of it. How do you get in the zone and stay in the zone to continue to achieve such success with the kinds of distractions being thrown at you this year?"

My eyes locked on hers. The truth was, I finally had something outside of the game that I was excited for. Something that felt more important. Something that provided itself as a distraction to the nonsense. That something was *her*. I held her gaze long enough her cheeks turned a light shade of red and I was confident that she knew what my real answer was. The one I wouldn't dare give in an interview.

Harper Nelson was an unexpected addition. She was the shining light guiding me through treacherous waters. The kind of serendipity that was beginning to feel like fate. If I had to live through this period of my life over again, I would do it if it meant meeting her once more for the first time.

"Being surrounded by good people that make the rest of the world fall away," I finally told her, watching her swallow hard. We were finally at the starting line together and I wanted to make sure she knew I was all in.

"What kind of legacy do you want to leave behind once you decide it's time to hang the glove up? I know that's years down the line, but you're constantly building your legacy every day. You're being compared to the greats, you're breaking records. What is it though that *you* want to be known for?"

"I want to be known for the kind of person I was first and foremost. But, of course, the history books and the records that people say I'm chasing are always in the back of my mind. It's going to be a lot of hard work to get there. But even if my name is cemented next to some of the greats, I want fans to comment on my character first before they ever bring up my statistics. I want people to see the love I have for the game, the love I have for the people in my life, and the desire I have to be a good role model for the next generation. If I can do that, I can walk away from this game happy."

Harper's eyes were shiny as she nodded her head at her cameraman, confirming that we got what we needed. The room was silent, no one daring to move.

"You did amazing," Harper breathed, reaching across the foot of open space between us to take my hand in hers. One tear slipped from the corner of her eye, and I reached up to brush it away with the pad of my thumb, leaving it there for a second longer than necessary.

"Thanks to you," I told her. "I don't think I ever would have been able to do this if it weren't for you."

Harper smiled. "It takes a team."

"It does and I'm glad you're on mine."

I offered her my hand as I stood up out of the chair. "Do you think your boss will be satisfied with this?"

She shrugged. For the first time, she looked indifferent about that conversation. "I don't care at this point. I'm just glad I got to use my platform to help you. If I don't get the promotion after this, then it's time I move on. I shouldn't stay somewhere that doesn't value my worth anyways."

"You have every right to fight for what you want," I told her.

"What do you mean?"

"You're a proven asset to the network. It's time you started making a few demands of your own." We helped her crew clean up the space we were using for the interview. "And I'm not just saying that because I selfishly want you in Chicago."

"I doubt Terry would even listen to me if I told him I deserved a job."

As I handed the last piece of equipment off to Harper's team, I turned to look at her. "Weren't you the one who encouraged me to do this interview when I thought there was nothing that I could possibly do to fix my own situation?"

Harper rolled her eyes at me, but a small smile was playing on her lips.

"You're Harper Nelson, start acting like it. Now I think it's time we head home, don't you?"

Harper's eyes widened and it only made me grin wider as I extended a hand toward her.

"Home?"

I lifted one shoulder in a playful shrug. "My home is wherever you are, Moon."

The smile she gave me was dazzling. "Okay, then let's go home."

Chapter 39

Harper

I'd been staring at my screen for more than ten minutes, attempting to hype myself up enough to press the button to call my boss. The interview had been out for over a week and nearly every news outlet in America had picked the story up. The original video had surpassed a million views, the quickest video in network history to do so.

Yet, I still hadn't heard from Terry.

This morning before he'd left for a hitting session with Tommy, Jamil had told me to take my destiny into my own hands. I'd delivered more for the network than even some of the hosts did and I was well within my rights to highlight all of that while negotiating for the reward I deserved.

Before I chickened out completely, I hit the call button and listened to the video call ring. After I counted the tenth ring, I was certain he wouldn't be picking up and I'd have to go through the whole process of building enough confidence to do this again.

"Harper!" Terry's face filled the screen.

"Hi, Terry. How are you?"

You are in control of your own destiny, I told myself with my corporate smile plastered across my face.

"I'm great. Real busy. I'm sorry I haven't reached out recently. The interview you did with Jamil. That was some great stuff."

My eye twitched at how casually he discussed the one thing he held over my head this season. I delivered what he wanted and even went beyond his expectations, and it felt like I was getting a pat on the head for a job well done.

"Thank you," I told him through gritted teeth. "Listen, I'm actually calling pertaining to that interview and all of the other interviews I've delivered."

Terry's eyebrow shot up.

"What would you like to talk about?" he asked. After four years of working for Terry, I knew when he was preparing himself for a negotiation or news that he wasn't anticipating.

"I want a spot on one of the network's shows."

My boss tilted his head to the side as he considered my proposition. "There are a few different shows in our New York studio that I think you would be a good fit for."

I shook my head. "I'm not leaving Chicago."

You proved that you deserve even the smallest of demands. Do not fold. You are the commodity.

Now that Terry realized I was a formidable negotiator, he sat back in his chair and laced his hands together over his stomach.

"New York is our biggest studio with the widest audience," Terry pointed out.

"I've brought the network new numbers over the past few months. I'll build my own audience here. But I'm not leaving Chicago. This place has become home."

Terry studied me through the screen and not even a week ago, I would have been squirming under his scrutinizing gaze. The silence stretched on as I waited for him to potentially crush my dreams permanently. Despite all my hard work, I could still be turned away right when I'd crested the summit.

"We do have a few new shows we are considering for the Chicago studio," Terry mused as he examined me through the screen. "One is to cover all sporting news in the area. The other is experimental—an idea, let's say. We want to do an all-day talk show platform but are looking at bringing a few Chicago professional athletes into the mix, maybe giving them permanent seats. I think you'd be perfect for both. Maybe even spearhead the talk show project to get it off the ground. We need a few other personalities to create good conversation, but we'd love you to take the lead on choosing who you'd like to have sitting next to you."

My mouth fell open.

"Wait, really?" Did I hear him wrong or was this actually happening?

"You're a huge asset to SC News and it would be one of the worst decisions of my career to let you walk away. If this is what you are wanting, I think that's a reasonable ask for me to fulfill."

I wanted to celebrate. I *should* be celebrating. This had been the one thing I'd spent the last four years of my life working toward. So why did I feel so incomplete?

"Terry, can I ask you something?"

My boss nodded. "Sure."

Before I could chicken out, I asked the one question I'd been wondering all year. "Over the past four years, why now? Did I need improvement?"

"You've been our best reporter over these past few years. We could always rely on your interviews for good content."

Disappointment sank through every inch of my body. Terry's response shouldn't have surprised me. It was the unfortunate truth that I'd known all along. But it was different hearing him confirm that I'd done nothing wrong—in fact, I'd exceeded in my job—yet others were promoted before me because they couldn't afford losing me. They would have rather kept me stagnant in my career for the sake of their own success rather than give me the flowers I deserved.

"I understand. Thank you for this opportunity, Terry."

He nodded. "Of course. I'll have someone draft up the contract and send it over to you in the next few days. We will have you start at the end of the current season with the Cougars. We wouldn't want to take you away from potentially covering a back-to-back World Series team."

"No, of course not."

We exchanged pleasantries before we finally ended the call. I stared at my blank computer screen for a few minutes longer before I finally got up from the table.

At least now I knew it wasn't me.

The world had a terrible habit of trying to put the strongest down. But they were the strongest for a reason. When they crawled out from under the fist that had tried to keep them down, the very people that turned them away would claim their success as their own.

But the only person that could relish in my successes was *me*. I had worked my ass off so far this season to prove my worth, all while challenging myself along the way. Despite the opposition I faced with my boss, with Nick O'Connor, I persevered. *I did that*.

My phone buzzed, flashing my father's name across the screen.

"Dad?" I answered. I hadn't heard from either of my parents since the dinner in Washington DC. I didn't expect to hear from them after Jamil and I had walked out of the restaurant. My mother would have only been upset that I made her look bad in a dining room full of her peers.

"Hi, honey. I was just calling to check in. It's been a while."

Maybe it was the confidence I'd just garnered from my conversation with Terry, but I found myself clutching my phone even tighter. "Whose fault would that be?"

The other side of the phone went silent.

"Your mother is sorry for what she said at dinner."

My eyes rolled hard enough that I feared they'd roll straight out of my head. "I'll only believe it when she tells me that herself."

My father cleared his throat, clearly uncomfortable with my animosity.

Good. They'd made me uncomfortable for most of my life. It was time I repaid them.

"Would you believe me if I told you that she called off her potential campaign for president?" my father asked me. "The week after our dinner together in Washington DC."

I was stunned into silence. My mother, who loved her career more than her own family, canceled an opportunity to win the highest achievement in the industry she'd given so much to.

"But she's been working toward that her entire career."

She wouldn't give that all up over me telling her that they'd prioritized their careers over me my entire life. Would she?

"Sometimes people realize there are more important things in life than a job." My father paused as I tried to reconcile the woman that I'd always associated with crisp suits and perfectly styled hair my entire life. "I think she and I have come to realize that there are more relationships that we've neglected than just the one with our child. We've realized we're practically strangers in each other's lives and if you've neglected two of the most important people in your life, what else do you have?"

This conversation felt like one bomb going off after another. "Are you saying the two of you are getting a divorce?"

My father laughed like that was the funniest thing he'd heard in a long time. "Oh no, honey. We're just going to take some time off to get to know each other again. I'm not sure either of us would survive without the other."

"That's great, Dad."

"We're also wanting to maybe get on the road some and come watch the games you are covering."

I checked the time and date to make sure I hadn't entered a different dimension after logging off my call with Terry. "Well, you'll only have the rest of this season because I got the promotion I've been working for."

"Really?" my father exclaimed. "Oh, that's great! Maria! Harper got the promotion."

There was some commotion on the other end of the line, the sound of a door opening and closing.

"Hold on, she's in the backyard gardening," my father told me, the sounds of birds chirping in the background.

"She's *what*?" I asked. We'd never had a garden before and the idea of my mother digging in dirt truly had me wondering if I was dreaming. The call with Terry and this call with my father all a figment of my imagination.

"She's been out there all morning trying to get the seeds she bought planted since she's a little late into the season. Maria, Harper got the promotion."

I was expecting a snide remark or a backward compliment. Instead, I heard my mother's voice clear as day as she said, "Congratulations, Harper. We know how long and hard you've been working for it. I hope it's everything you wanted."

That was it. No line of questioning. Not even trying to put herself in the spotlight and take over my moment. Just a simple congratulations and recognition of the sacrifices I'd been making over the years.

This was the moment I'd been waiting for my entire life. I'd expected it to feel like some grand moment—finally getting recognized by my parents. I thought their validation would be all I wanted. But the only person that I needed validation from was myself. Their words of encouragement felt good for only a moment, but the pride I had for myself would last a lifetime.

My apartment door opened just as I was beginning to collect myself. Jamil walked through, drenched in sweat from his workout.

"Thanks, Mom." Jamil's eyebrows shot up as he realized who I was talking to.

"Harper, I want you to know that I'm sorry I ever made you feel like you weren't important. You and your father are more important to me than anything else in this world. I just want you to know I'm proud of you."

I paused to relish in the words. "I'm proud of you, too."

The phone clicked off.

"That was your parents?" Jamil asked as he dropped his bag by his old bedroom. After my birthday, he'd stopped sleeping in his own bed. The only time we slept apart was during an away series. He came up behind me and placed a gentle kiss to the top of my head.

"My mother is gardening and she's not running for president anymore. They've both decided to take some time off work to reconnect with themselves and maybe come watch some games."

"Woah," Jamil breathed.

"My thoughts exactly." I closed my laptop, taking my time before telling him the rest of the news I had. "Terry gave me a seat on one of the network's new shows."

The smile that lit up Jamil's face sent butterflies soaring throughout my stomach. I didn't think I'd ever get over how attractive he looked with that much joy on his face.

"If he didn't, he would have been an idiot. He knows the kind of talent he has in you. There was no way he was going to let that go." Jamil pulled me out of my seat and enveloped me in a hug. "Congratulations. You are more than deserving of this."

"Looks like that interview is changing both of our lives."

The tone of the articles covering Jamil in the media had changed after the interview had dropped. They had listened to how they'd acted like vultures, vying for any piece of information they could glean off his life and realized how they had been contributing to the problem. A few tabloids and gossip columns had spun stories to paint Jamil as weak, but nobody was reading those stories. Instead, they were reading the ones being put out that covered Jamil's charitable actions or his business ventures with his partnerships and how he tried to work with organizations that made a difference in the world. He was slowly becoming less of this mythical legend as fans discovered the true story of Jamil Edman.

Business opportunities had been pouring in over the last week. Jamil had to make it clear to his agent about what kinds of business ventures he wanted to pursue now that he had the opportunity to be picky.

Gone was the man who dreaded walking by fans demanding his autograph or ambushing him on the way into stadiums for a sound bite. Jamil had garnered respect from his peers, his fans, and from the rest of the sports world in a short time.

"Looks like we both have good news to share today," Jamil said with his chin resting on top of my head. "Jordan is going through the program. I got a call from his therapist today. I'm still holding my breath, in case he bails again. But this time feels different."

I squeezed Jamil back as hard as I could. "I know for so long you've had to tear tiny pieces of your heart out as you've watched your brother destroy himself. But you never gave up faith that one day he'd come back. It's because of that undying faith that Jordan is trying to make a difference now in his life. It's because of *you*."

Jamil's body started to shake as the pent-up emotion he'd been holding onto for years released from his body.

We held on to each other, no longer alone in our own fights—stronger together than we'd ever been alone.

Epilogue

Jamil

"I'm sure you're wishing for a real Christmas tree," Jayden laughed as I sat down next to her. I tossed an arm around her shoulder and pulled her into my side.

"No, a palm tree strung with Christmas lights reminds me of my childhood."

My parents had wrapped every palm tree in their backyard in colored lights. They'd even gone as far as getting a few blow-up decorations. They said it was for Kyla, even though she'd be too young to remember any of this. My mother had just retired from her time working for the city library, with my father to follow in a few years from his job. She spent all her free time spoiling the baby of the family. But I couldn't blame her, because I'd sent a care package every month to my niece.

When I leaned over to place a kiss to the top of my little sister's head she squirmed out of my grasp. "What has gotten into you?"

"I just love you," I told her as Janessa walked out of our parents' house with Kyla, who was now walking and keeping everyone on their toes.

"Ness, do you know if J fell and bumped his head? He's being far too affectionate for his normal self."

"It's Christmas, Jayden. Maybe you could learn a few things from him." Janessa had her eyes locked on to Kyla as she stomped toward me with the biggest smile on her face. Kota was finishing up his shift at the hospital. He would be joining us a little late for dinner.

"Baby Kyla!" I exclaimed, reaching down with open arms for her to walk into.

She let out a giggle that twisted my heart into a pretzel as I lifted her onto my lap.

"That girl has you wrapped around her little finger," Janessa told me as she fell onto one of the open chairs on the lanai.

Harper walked out of the back door next balancing two pies that she'd spent all morning baking. The dress she was wearing billowed around her ankles and showed off her tanned shoulders she'd gotten from trading the snow of Chicago for the sunshine of Florida these past few weeks.

"She's not the only girl in this house that has J wrapped around their little fingers," Jayden joked. Kyla let out a scream that sounded like her way of agreeing with her aunt and the two fell into a fit of giggles as Jayden stole Kyla from me.

Harper gently set both pies down on the table before sliding into the open seat Jayden made for her in the middle of the couch.

"Hi," I whispered as I turned my back to the arm rest and pulled her into my chest.

"Merry Christmas," Harper replied as she leaned her head back so she could look up at me.

"Merry Christmas." I bent down to place a kiss on her forehead.

"Are you happy?" she whispered, just as Jordan walked out of the house, balancing the food he'd been helping our mother make for dinner.

"Yeah, I am."

"Are you going to turn the game on?" Jordan called over to me as he deposited the food next to Harper's pies. "Kickoff should be any minute."

I leaned forward to grab the remote off the coffee table and turned the television on to the Chicago Bobcats game. Nick O'Connor's face smiled back at us as he talked with the other desk analysts. But this time, Harper was barely fazed.

"Your guys' show has had a lot of success so far," Jordan told Harper as he took an empty seat with the rest of us.

He looked different from the last time I saw him. He'd leaned out, taking to heart his therapist's suggestion of putting his time into something other than sports until he could watch a game again without feeling like he had to bet on it. He only gave himself one game a month to watch and had been slowly allowing himself to watch a few more with every month that passed without him breaking his recovery progress.

He'd moved back to Florida like he told me all those months ago when he was still in the throes of it all and was helping our father with his company. Harper had been right when she told me that it was his turn to fly because once all of us had let him go, he finally understood what he needed to do. Without us in the way telling him what *we* thought he needed to do, he was finally able to get better.

"Derek and Olivia have brought most of the attention to the show with their . . . interesting dynamic, but me and Jamil hold our own, I think."

When Harper had been offered the show by her boss, she knew the best way to get Chicago sports fans to tune in was to fill some of the seats with athletes that they loved and cherished—so she extended the opportunity to both me and Derek, two athletes that had won titles for their city. With one spot left to fill, Harper had graciously given the opportunity to Olivia after she'd decided she needed a shakeup in her life.

I just don't think Olivia had expected that shakeup to be Derek Allen becoming a part of her weekly routine.

We exchanged a knowing look.

Our new show had instant success. The city of Chicago loved the cross-over with having me and Derek on the same show covering relevant news stories. But our local show had skyrocketed into national and then global levels as fans got a behind-the-scenes look at both the Chicago Cougars and the Chicago Bobcats, after both teams had historic seasons winning championships for the city. Just as I knew she would, Harper stunned the sports world with her wealth of knowledge within the entirety of the sports industry and made viewers fall in love with her, just as I had.

"They sure have," Harper agreed with Jordan as everyone watched the analysts discuss the statistics for both teams while the captains finished the coin toss.

"How does it feel being on the other side of the interview?" Jordan asked as he took Kyla from Jayden's arms, her little hands reaching for her other uncle next to her.

"Actually, a lot of fun," I admitted. "I like getting to highlight other players that are deserving and talk about sports with people that are like-minded. The show has become a highlight of my week."

"You hated interviews," Jordan noted. "I wasn't sure if this was going to end up being a good fit for you or not."

I glanced down at the woman in my arms. "Someone helped me look at it differently. Instead of feeling like it was an interrogation, I needed to frame it as a historian trying to gather as much information on someone for others to study or celebrate as the years pass. I could share as little as I wanted or as much as I wanted. The good interviewers are never trying to dig for something that the person isn't willing to give up."

Jordan swallowed hard. He understood now the lengths I went to protect him against media scrutiny—what I sacrificed for him. He'd repaid me by giving me my brother back. The boy that I grew up with and looked up to all those years was finally making an appearance again. I'd tried my best to give him space to slay the beast of addiction roaring inside of him. I'd shielded him and protected him from prying eyes.

"You still want to come on the show?" I asked him. After Jordan had watched me talk about how difficult

Triple Play

it was for me to be thrust into this media spotlight that athletes often weren't accustomed to, he'd approached me when Harper and I had first arrived in Florida with the idea of coming on our show to tell his own story.

"I'm positive." The conviction in Jordan's voice was enough to prove how serious he was. He'd done so much to improve his own quality of life. Harper and I both felt it would be an incredible conversation for our viewers to listen to.

"How have you been liking your new job?" Jayden asked Harper as the moment between Jordan and I passed. "Do you miss traveling as much?"

Harper snuggled further into me and I wrapped my arms tighter around her.

"I was ready to be done with traveling. I like Chicago and I've been happy with the opportunities that SC News has given to me. They've offered me an open invitation to cover any games I want, whether that be for the Bobcats or the Cougars. So maybe I'll cover a game for nostalgia's sake. But I'm happy with where I am right now. Hosting this talk show has been challenging. It's a different medium for me and delivering news on this format was a little bit of a learning curve, but I think I've hit my stride. It's been amazing getting to live this dream out."

Love was a strange thing. Suddenly a piece of your happiness was attached to someone else's and watching them achieve their dreams felt like you were achieving your own.

"Are you still in your apartment?" Janessa asked as she poured herself a cup of eggnog. I eyed the heavy-handed pour. "What? Kota is driving us home."

Harper laughed, her body vibrating against my chest. "I am still in the same apartment. I have a few more months on my lease. I don't know if I'll stay in it or if I'll move somewhere else. It's in a convenient spot for work, but it's far from Jamil."

I had ultimately moved back into my home once the repairs had been completed, putting my feelings aside after the break-in and not wanting to impose on Harper's space so early on in our relationship. While the distance apart had allowed us to continue exploring our relationship during its early days . . . I had a better solution for Harper's problem.

"I can fix that," I told her. I hadn't planned to give her my Christmas present yet, but this felt like a sign. I pulled the small box out of my pocket and presented it to her.

Her eyes widened as she took in the small box with the little bow on top. I realized what the size of it probably suggested to her.

"Just open it," I told her, forcing the box into her hands.

With shaky fingers, she managed to lift the lid off. I watched my family lean in closer, waiting to see what was inside. When Harper produced a key for everyone to see, I watched a mixture of confusion pass around the room.

"A key?" Harper asked, her voice soft but her eyes fierce.

"I was thinking about a fresh start, for both of us." Harper glanced back down at the key in her hands. "It's a house out in the country, by that bar I took you to. Lots of land with peace and quiet."

When Harper continued to stare at the key in her hands without saying anything, pure panic seized me.

"Now I'm wondering if maybe I should have just offered the idea of a house as a gift and let you pick it out with me. Maybe I can see if we can sell it and—"

"J, this is perfect." Harper reached over and placed a hand on my arm to stop me from rambling on any further. "Do you have pictures?"

"Yes, yeah. Hold on." I hurried to pull my phone out of my pocket and bring up the listing for her to look through, noticing the way my father wrapped his arm around my mother as the two of them watched us with immense love in their eyes.

"Are you sure this is what you want to do?" Harper asked quietly so only I could hear as she took my phone from me.

I wanted to tell her that there was nothing more in the world I wanted right now. I wanted to come home from traveling to her beautiful face. I wanted to fill this house with memories the two of us would make together. Because she had become my sanctuary, my peace, my moon guiding me home during the darkest of nights.

"This is just the start of what I want," I told her, wanting her to hear the promise in my voice.

"It's perfect," she told me as she flipped through the pictures.

"And it's ours in one month."

"Plenty of time to figure out how to make it a home," she told me as she stared down at the picture of the white two-story home set back on a picturesque piece of land that felt like it could be our slice of heaven.

"The moment we walk through the front door it'll be home."

Harper's eyes shone as she looked back up from my phone at me. "Thank you."

When she leaned over to give me a kiss, I heard a sniffle in the background.

"What?" I heard Janessa exclaim. "I've just got something in my eye, that's all."

"Harper," my mother interrupted once the family had stopped laughing at my sister. "How are your parents this holiday? Are they by themselves?"

"They're on a cruise," Harper replied. "It's the first time they've taken time to relax or even do something just the two of them. Hopefully they both come off the ship alive when they return to port. So far, I've gotten a few pictures of the two of them wearing rather festive Hawaiian shirts drinking too many cocktails, so I think it's going well."

After nearly losing their daughter because of their own ambitions, Maria and Robert Nelson finally realized that it was time to start prioritizing more than their careers—starting with their own marriage. Harper and I weren't sure if a cruise was the best answer to that when they first called with their idea, but they set off anyways with limited space to escape each other. It seemed to be working out for the best so far. Maria had even uttered the word "retirement" on a call that nearly sent Harper into a stupor.

"It's nice having the entire family under one roof. It's been far too long since the last time this has happened." Denise emerged from the house with the remainder of the food, my father and Kota in his scrubs right behind her. "Let's take a picture before we eat."

Groans erupted from nearly everyone as we all shuffled in close together, so we'd all be in the frame.

"Harper, get in here. You're family, too!" my mother exclaimed as my father extended his arm for a group photo.

Harper stood off to the side, clearly unsure where she belonged. I already knew the answer.

"Come on, Moon," I told her as I extended her my hand. "You're with me."

Acknowledgements

Thank you to every single reader that has supported this series. I have had the honor of a lifetime getting to write stories that others find joy in. Book people are the best kind of people. I love getting to be a part of the community and contribute to the minutiae of it all.

This series will always hold a special place in my heart. It has shaped me into a completely new person—one I like even more than the person I was before it all began. Someone who has a whole lot less fear about what others think of her. Someone who dares to put herself out there.

Thank you to my agent, Saskia Leach for continuing to champion this book and this series. There isn't anyone else I'd rather have as a trusted advisor, partner, and friend through this process. I'm honored every day to call you my agent and to be a part of the Kate Nash Literary Agency family.

To the teams at 8th Note Press and Embla Books, I am always blown away by your relentless hard work on this series. There have been so many people that have worked tirelessly on editing, copywriting, the cover, the audiobook, and without all of you, none of this would have happened. So thank you from the bottom of my heart.

Thank you to my family and friends for supporting me endlessly. When times get rough, you are always there to remind me that the light at the end of the tunnel is coming.

And to my husband, Dawson, thank you for everything you do for me. From listening to my crazy ideas, to celebrating every win, or picking up the pieces with every loss. You are a truly exceptional partner and the most amazing husband.

About the Author

Ally Wiegand currently resides in Texas. *Triple Play* is her third novel in the Chicago Heartbreakers series. She loves her family, fall, and writing love stories that make your heart squeeze. Ally has dreamed of being a writer since she was a girl. She is a coffee addict, a classic car lover, and a cat mom to two furballs. Her dream is to make readers happy, make them sad – but, most importantly, to feel something.

To keep up with Ally and learn more about the Chicago Heartbreakers series, visit her online at www.allywiegand.com

About Embla Books

Embla Books is a digital-first publisher of standout commercial adult fiction. Passionate about storytelling, the team at Embla believe our lives are built on stories – and publish books that will make you 'laugh, love, look over your shoulder and lose sleep'. Launched by Bonnier Books UK in 2021, the imprint is named after the first woman from the creation myth in Norse mythology. Embla was carved by the gods from a tree trunk found on the seashore; an image of the kind of creative work and crafting that writers do, and a symbol of how stories shape our lives.

Find out about some of our other books and stay in touch:

X, Facebook, Instagram: @emblabooks
Newsletter: https://bit.ly/emblanewsletter